THE MAN WHO MEANT WELL – A BRILLIANT
EUROPEAN NOVEL IN THE GREAT TRADITION
OF THOMAS HARDY AND D. H. LAWRENCE

Gerard Walschap's brilliantly compassionate and evocative
novel of rustic life in Flanders during the early years of this
century is a deeply moving testament to the basic nobility
of the human spirit even under extreme stress and anguish.
In the central character, Thys Glorieus, the author has
created one of European literature's most memorable
figures, a man whose unswerving belief in and dedication to
an idealistic vision of human existence sustains him through
a heartbreaking series of misfortunes until he eventually
wins through to the calm after the storm.

This edition of *The Man Who Meant Well* marks the first
appearance of this modern classic of European literature in
English.

Gerard Walschap

The Man Who
Meant Well

Translated by Adrienne Dixon

Panther

Granada Publishing Limited
First published in Great Britain in 1975 by
Panther Books Ltd
Frogmore, St Albans, Herts AL2 2NF

Copyright © Uitgeverij Ontwikkeling s.v., Antwerp.
This translation copyright © 1975 by the Foundation
for the Promotion of Dutch Literary Works in
Translation, Singel 450, Amsterdam C, Netherlands.
Published by arrangement with Em. Querido's Uitgeverij
B.V., Singel 262, postbus 3879, Amsterdam C,
Netherlands.
Made and printed in Great Britain by
Cox & Wyman Ltd, London, Reading and Fakenham
Set in Linotype Times

The Man Who Meant Well

The Man Who Meant Well

ONE

At the age of eight Thys took up the fight. Against a cat. One day in early summer he was sitting in the shade of an elder tree with his back against the stone coping of the well, cutting whistles. The sky was cornflower-blue, the roof red, the wall white, with green door and shutters, the ground in front of the house black cinders; everything clean, quiet, peaceful, and Thys thought: I am happy. For more than an hour the cat had been peering, half asleep, from the edge of the low roof; a few feet below her, father had fixed the canary cage to the wall. Suddenly she came crashing down together with the cage. The canary fluttered frantically to and fro. Thys saw the cat pulling the tiny yellow creature through the bars by the head. She disappeared with it.

His blood stood still, he was struck to the heart, the stone coping chilled into a wall of ice against his back. He got up with leaden legs, panting as if the air around him was suddenly no longer sufficient. Nor could he bear to stand still. He walked away, not knowing where. Unthinkingly he chose the direction of the water-meadow where his father was cutting osiers. But he couldn't get to the other side of the ditch across which he had jumped hundreds of times. He followed it to where it joined the brook. There he sat down, weary, burdened, and he thought: I have a pain.

That evening mother boils buttermilk and fries potatoes with onions in sweet manna-grass. Thys ate but said nothing, although the others were talking about the canary. He even tried to chew the buttermilk. Opposite him, the cat lay blinking by the stove. After supper his brother and sister went out to play for a while, father squatted in the doorway, whistling, while mother cleared the table and washed the dishes. But Thys went to father's workshed, selected the biggest hammer he could find, and kneeling behind the cat, made a mighty swoop with both arms. Her head went crack. She darted away to die under the elder tree and then at last poor little Thys was able to cry, the heaviness in his heart dissolved, justice had been done. From outside father called, who's killed the cat? From the kitchen mother called back, that was our Thys. She laughed, father went on whistling, but a little faster than before.

Mother always laughed. The cottage was well-kept and clean. Wicker chairs, bird cages, a cover for the ham hanging from the ceiling, a flower stand with three potted plants, everything woven by the man from different coloured osiers, made it look friendly and cosy. Her husband was a strong, good, quiet man; her children were healthy and handsome, two boys and a girl.

Father never laughed but he made his wife laugh with dry humour. For the rest he whistled, softly and contentedly. The children were neither beaten nor scolded. There was no harm in them. The worst their mother ever did to them was to fall silent, to stop laughing and then father would go on whistling as if he hadn't noticed anything. Life looked after itself. What was too hot they didn't touch, what was too heavy they left alone, what belonged to someone else they respected as they themselves watched over what was theirs; no one should dare lay claim to it.

Such was the home, surrounded by fields, a home in which people grew quiet, wise and resigned, where Thys acquired the sense of justice which was to make him suffer. He suffered for the canary.

If a cat isn't allowed to catch birds, said mother, birds shouldn't eat flies or caterpillars either, it's all the same. Big 'uns eat little 'uns, that's life. Thys looked at her, unable to answer; what she said was true but it didn't convince him. Father said casually: now I shall have to bash his brains in, because he's done it to the cat. Mother laughed, but suddenly shuddered as if she felt cold; she pulled Thys protectively to her breast and soothingly rubbed his hard round head as if the blows were already hurting him. As if her hands had released the words in him, Thys shouted, with a savage look on his pale face: I can't bear injustice! Father said he must have heard that from Uncle Dolf. Now why did mother suddenly walk out of the room?

Father Do and mother Dina sent their children to school every morning. Thys's brother made it to the classroom on cold or wet days, but usually he stopped on the way and played till the others came back. But Thys went every day. He liked hearing about Joseph, sold by his brothers, and he hated the Romans who conquered Belgium which wasn't theirs to take. The schoolmaster described the savage battles in the forests; the Belgians were so brave that they fought till there were hardly fifty out of a thousand left. Thys put his hand up and asked, what about those fifty, what did they do? What could they have done except take to their heels, the battle was lost, the Romans were master. Thys snorted contemptuously at those fifty out of a thousand and had to swallow the bitter truth that injustice had prevailed. No matter how he argued that, after all, there had still been fifty of them, the schoolmaster shook his head with a smile and said, just like mother: that's life. He made a gesture to show that there was nothing he could do about it. But the boy felt burdened by it. If life is like that for others, it isn't so for him. In every game: strict honesty. If anyone stealthily pushed a marble closer to another, so as to flick them both at once with finger and thumb, and win, he was banned from the game without mercy and if he tried his luck elsewhere, Thys would pursue him. Don't play with him!

There was another weakness to which he fell prey: generosity. He was unable to walk off with his winnings. When his pockets were full of honestly won marbles, conkers or hazelnuts, the joy at having won would soon give way to a strange unease. The boys who had lost, with what sadness of heart did they go home? Thys couldn't leave them and gave back more than he had won. With a grave, mortified expression on his face, looking nowhere in particular, he said that he was merely giving away his surplus: I've got plenty more at home. Well yes, they did have two hazeltrees at home, but as to conkers and marbles, it wasn't quite the truth. Generosity taught him to lie and he who could be so uncompromising, couldn't stop himself. He loved emptying his pockets, sharing out bits of string, buttons and so on, and then looking at the happy faces. There was a warmth in his heart then and he would walk home whistling like his father.

People living away from the village are always thought to be less civilized. The schoolmasters aren't taken in when, from an outlying cottage in the Leas or the woods, a boy turns up, particularly bright and sensible, his eyes beaming with courage and candour. Sooner or later he's bound to show his barbarous, vicious nature; he'll start lying or stealing. That's how it went with Thys when a big bully-boy snatched a pocket-knife from the pale, puny son of the parish clerk. Perhaps it was only teasing, but Thys didn't go along with that kind of teasing. The little boy retaliated with a smart kick on the bully-boy's shin, for which he was rewarded with a fist, full in the face. At once Thys felt that pain, that sense of shrinking under the blow of injustice. He sprang at its throat with a shout, overpowered it and as three masters dragged him away the big boy was left lying on the ground. So here we have that promising little son of Do Glorieus, from out at the Leas. But sir, panted Thys furiously, tremblingly, it's because I can't bear injustice. Injustice, injustice, we'll teach you to use big words, injustice will be punished by us, do you hear, we'll injustice you!

Thys took his punishment with equanimity, as if he was receiving the beating and humiliation on behalf of the little chap who wouldn't have been strong enough to bear it, and he lost no time in telling the little chap so. He told him he had had such a drubbing that the little one would have fainted under it at least six times, he might even have died, who knows. Perhaps, said Thys in a wave of grandeur, you would have been buried today, if they'd beaten you only half as much as they did me, but to me it doesn't make any difference. I get beaten plenty of times at home, said Thys, immediately aware that he was lying, but it was so wonderful to see this little chap leaning against him and hear him saying that not even the biggest bully could frighten him as long as Thys was there. Thys put his powerful hand on the little boy's shoulder and said: you don't need to be frightened.

The girls come out of school five minutes earlier than the boys, but when they dawdle and the boys hurry, they are harassed and chased. They get clods of earth thrown at them, their hair ribbons are pulled off. But Thys, all on his own, turns on the whole gang; he walks behind the girls like a guard, keeping the boys at a distance. When he is hit on the head with a pebble he says, while the pain brings tears to his eyes, that the girls may think themselves lucky. If that pebble had hit them it might have got stuck half an inch deep in their head, but to him it's nothing, I was hit by a brick once. He is pleased when that six-year-old shrimp from Ridge Farm is tired or when her clog gets stuck in the muddy track. She looks helpless. Thys carries her.

Girls know how to be grateful. To start with, they always speak politely to him: please Thys, yes Thys, no Thys. They show him their needlework and Thys doesn't say at random which is the best work, but chooses that of a poor, timid little mite with a runny nose who hardly dares show her crumpled, grubby sampler.

'But look how dirty it is, Thys.'

'I know it's dirty, but it's still the best one.'

'And the cotton is bad.'

'It doesn't matter if it's not beautiful,' says Thys. 'I only look at the work itself. This one is the best.'

'Yes, Thys.'

One after the other they bring him something, a biscuit, two nuts, a pear. They know he won't accept anything openly, but they can put it in his pocket while he deliberately looks the other way. With these gifts he can act the bountiful benefactor at school, bestowing kindness on the smallest, poorest, palest creatures. Take it, I've got plenty more at home. Pounds and pounds!

But of course this causes jealousy, envy. The first time they shouted at him: flirt! he didn't know what they meant, but turned red and felt ashamed. The girls, startled and blushing, giggled behind their hands. Thys daren't look round to shake his fist.

The worst was still to come. After school the master told him, eye to eye, that it seemed to him that Thys was always following the girls, that he was a bit of a flirt. Thys didn't know where to look. It was as if he had done something wrong and that he was the only one to be unaware of it. He wanted to explain to the master how wonderful he felt when he saw the girls safely home, through all kinds of danger. If it wasn't for him, some of them might have had an eye ripped out by now. In his imagination he saw them going to school without him, one-eyed, limping, with pebbles in their heads which couldn't be dislodged. But the schoolmaster's stern face made him realize that this was a serious business, that all his good intentions had been stupid mistakes and that he had been carrying on like a flirt, time and time again, the most cowardly thing imaginable. The schoolmaster had more sense than to explain what was meant by a flirt, those kids from the Leas are precocious enough. He saw Thys blushing deeper and deeper, so he had understood what it meant all right. Yes, Glorieus, you've been running around like a flirt, you have.

The word began to prey on Thys. At first he thought it meant being a coward, a cissy, a cry-baby, someone who is afraid of the dark; then, someone walking around with a dummy in his mouth, or still drinking mother's milk. His stomach turned. But there was worse to come: it dawned on him he had behaved like someone who wets his bed at night, like all girls do. So that was why the girls had giggled with such embarrassment! It shattered him, he cried out that it wasn't true. The schoolmaster didn't mellow. Glorieus had better not try to deny it, things were bad enough as they were without adding lies. It makes one wonder what is going to become of a flirt like him. The schoolmaster intends to keep an eye on Glorieus to see if he mends his ways, and now Glorieus has permission to leave. Deeply wounded, Glorieus leaves.

He becomes quieter, he broods. For instance, when he stands with his legs astride and asks four boys to hang on his shoulders and a fifth to jump on his back; when he holds someone round the waist, lifts him and asks: how far shall I throw you; when he pushes his sleeve up and lets the others feel the hard bulge of his biceps, it isn't just for fun. You show me the flirt who can do all this!

When the nickname had caused him so much pain that he could bear it no longer, he flung it aside, boldly, resolutely, in the performance of a great deed. No one who heard of it will ever forget it.

After much practice in the yard at home, Thys walked into the school one bright morning, more than a quarter of an hour late. His face was proud and solemn. He stood in the porch leading to the classroom and listened how far they had got with the Scripture lesson, which he didn't want to interrupt. But at the usual signal to take out slates and pencils for the arithmetic lesson, Thys swung the door open and with a big leap landed on his hands; he kicked his heels together in military fashion, high up in the air, and walked calmly and with dignity, in deathly silence, all the way through the classroom to the lectern; steadily and swiftly he climbed the two steps of the podium and right in front of the flabbergasted schoolmaster Thys jumped elegantly to his feet, stood to attention, then, as in a painting, stretched out his arm like a commander reviewing his regiment and called out: How about this then? If you think I'm a flirt, you try to do this!

We shall never forget it, we were beside ourselves, out of all control, we jumped on the desks, we cheered Thys, in total disorder.

The two other masters came hurrying in, but even

between the three of them they couldn't get us quiet. We don't know what happened to Thys after that. He was handed over to the headmaster who dragged him to the empty coalshed. In the village there may have been a dozen men all told old and young, who have ever been alone in the coalshed with that man.

They never talk about it, just as an ex-convict never mentions the fact that he has been inside. But their howls were always heard and all who heard them shivered in the marrow of their bones. We listened breathlessly, waiting for Thys Glorieus to start howling. Naar Vranck, Noo van Hemelens, Rie Snackaert, big hefty boys, they were in our class, and our hope was set on them. We saw Naar sitting as straight as a candle, his head high, listening. We hoped he would not restrain himself, we hoped he would jump up from his seat with clenched fists and shout: Enough! We looked at our inkwells, we slipped our feet out of our clogs, so as to have these ready. When anyone was asked a question he would stand up mechanically, but he'd say three times Beg-pardon sir, not having heard the question; our minds were too preoccupied. We heard nothing. Our fear grew. In our imagination we saw Thys lying dead on the coal. Naar Vranck became restless. He looked round, pale. What was there to say? We looked at him, our eyes filled with fear and hatred. The silence in the classrooms on either side reached our ears. The hour was long, long.

At last it was break, but we didn't play. We whispered in little groups. When the headmaster appeared in the playground all eyes turned to him. Deep in our hearts we wished him a sudden but cruel death. Naar Vranck was walking all by himself. Whenever he caught the headmaster's eye he gave him such a withering look that the brute didn't know how to pretend not to notice.

The last lesson went on for ever. When finally we lined up to be sent home, Thys Glorieus suddenly appeared. Again a deathly silence fell. He held his head straight, his teeth were clenched. Naar Vranck left the line and went up to him.

Ignoring the master who ordered him to get back in the line, he took Thys's hand and said, come along Thys. As we were but ordinary boys, Thys was so overwhelmed by this little token of kindness that his strength failed him for one short moment. His mouth opened slightly, he bent his head, and gasped a few times. To Naar Vranck's immense pride Thys let his hand lean briefly on Naar's shoulder.

To our dying day the memory of that morning will send a chill through our bones, whenever we remember how Thys Glorieus endured the torture in the coalshed without uttering a sound.

Later, Thys Glorieus was to be alone with life in a dark shed many a time, enduring it without uttering a sound and returning among people with a smile.

TWO

That afternoon Pol Glorieus unexpectedly tripped his brother Thys up. Thys fell, jumped up to run after him, but Pol turned round and held him by the arms. Thys screamed with pain. Nothing more happened until evening, when mother asked him to try on a pullover she had knitted for him. His body hurt all over, but he daren't admit it. Careful mother, careful. Do watched them. When they had finished with the pullover, Do wanted to know what had been going on. Dina undressed the boy and this time she did not laugh. Thys tried to keep at least his trousers on but she pushed them down to his feet, and cried: Do, look at that! And wept loudly, caressing Thys's red, ravaged back with her cheeks and kissing it with her lips.

Do Glorieus's mouth was no longer pursed for whistling. It became wide and flat, the lips went thin. He kept turning away uneasily but he couldn't stop his eyes from wandering back and looking, again and again, at the red and blue bruises and the swollen buttocks. Dina's crying agitated him. He asked who had done this. The headmaster. Why? Because Thys had walked through the classroom on his hands. Why had he walked through the classroom on his hands, what kind of behaviour is that? Because the master had called him a flirt. At this they all laughed, Dina through her tears, Pol loudly in a leaping voice, but Do with a wry mouth. Why had the master called him a flirt? Because Thys can't bear it when the boys chase the girls after school, pulling their hair ribbons off and throwing clods of earth at them. That is why Thys walks home with the girls, keeping the boys at a distance.

And is that why you have to walk on your hands, exclaims Do. For God's sake, whatever next! Thys says: Now I've proved to them that it isn't true.

Only mothers understand such wonderful things of a child. Dina is still sitting on her knees behind Thys. She pulls him naked into her arms. He is still her little boy, she kisses him wildly, weepingly on the mouth, again and again. What the hell is going on here this evening, all this wailing and kissing! The men keep calm; they each leave by a different door, Do by the front door. But he doesn't lean against the wall, nor does he sit down on the doorstep to whistle a tune. He walks away and goes on walking for a long time. He follows the dirt track, across the little bridge, along the alder-bank, not in a rage at all, nor lost in thought, because he notices the hare that darts across his path; he kicks at it with his feet, you have to be quick for that. He walks past the black wall of the brewer's yard, then between the village houses.

Naar Vranck's father, the cobbler, is taking the air outside his house. He recognizes Do and asks when they'll go out sniggling again. Do stops for a while, to fix a day, and then says he's got to be off. He has to see the headmaster.

He rings. He asks the headmaster's wife if her husband is in, but spying him through the net curtains in the glass door he doesn't wait for an answer. The headmaster gets up from his wicker chair, because he has got a front room and doesn't receive in the kitchen. But with one blow of Do's fist he is back in his chair. He reaches for the poker which hangs by the stove but a second blow makes this superfluous. He jumps aside, only to land in the arms of Do Glorieus who flings him first against the cupboard, then against the table, and a third time on to the floor where he falls flat on his stomach. Do Glorieus sits down on top of him.

His wife first tries to pull Do away by the hair and then scratches his face till it bleeds, for she too is a teacher of the old guard and knows all about retaliation. Do repays the headmaster for Thys's bruised back until the man lies motionless. The wife then wants to pitch into Do as he gets up, but he grabs her by the wrists and squeezes them hard, or she might decide to kick him on the shins. Ma'am, says Do, now you must rub his back with butter, that's what we did at home to our Thys. You see, ma'am, says Do, I can teach lessons too, not even headmasters know all there is to be learnt.

Then Do goes home. Dina washes him in the tub. Thys has gone to sleep and she can laugh again, defiantly. She kisses Do on the mouth, there's no end to the kissing today. She has regained that sense of invulnerability which always makes her laugh and live recklessly, free in the free air of the Leas. It had escaped her when she discovered that it was possible for her child to walk out of the house and come back beaten up. But even from so far away, even against a headmaster, they were able to defend their proud immunity. With more than her usual vigour she lifts the boiler full of washing on to the stove.

'He won't try it a second time, Do.'

'The hell he won't,' says Do.

But as soon as the headmaster's wife had put her husband to bed she hurried across the street as fast as she could, to one of the other masters, and told him to call the police. Two policemen arrived and having established that this was a prima facie case of assault causing interior bruising, they decided to proceed at once to arrest the culprit.

On the way they started frightening each other. The older of the two suggested they should call in a third policeman, the younger one disagreed. According to the older one it was dangerous out in the Leas after dark. He had once been involved in arresting a bricklayer who had shot a game-keeper. The man had been standing on a scaffold, they'd called to him to come down. I'm working, he answered, if you want to talk to me you can come up here. One of the policeman's mates had climbed the ladder in order to handcuff the man, but he had hardly put his foot on the scaffolding when he received a blow on the head with a heavy mallet.

Perhaps it wasn't the blow that killed him, but as it made him topple over he fell to his death anyway, breaking his spine into the bargain on the edge of a hod. I called out to the chap above that he had the choice, either come down of his own accord or be shot down. I'm coming, he shouted back, and he leapt at my throat from a height of twelve feet, but I was too quick for him, I jumped at him from behind, wrested his hands behind his back and handcuffed him.

'And that was in broad daylight, was it?'

'Yes, but at night they shoot. They lie in ambush some-where in a furrow and you've had it. I've heard the bullets whistling about my ears at least a dozen times. You don't know them yet.'

'You don't think he'd shoot through the door when we knock, do you?'

'They often leave the door on the latch. With a bit of luck we can catch him in his bed.' Then they talked of the woman who'd be in the bed beside him, of Dina.

Dina heard them knocking and went to the door, who's there? In the name of the law, open up. She doesn't care in whose name she opens the door, as long as it isn't that one, and in great alarm she wakes up all her family. They come in their nightshirts, Do, Pol and Thys. Lieneke, the girl, is afraid to get up. When poachers are arrested in this fashion they usually hurry out by the back door and disappear into the fields, but Do doesn't want to do that. He's a quiet man, he's never been in trouble with the police before. He tells Dina to light the lamp while he opens the door.

The policemen leap in, revolvers at the ready, hands up everybody, because they are terrified. No one puts his hands up, why should they, are they doing anything wrong with their hands? The older policeman shouts that they must put their hands up or he'll shoot. Now watch it, says Do Glorieus earnestly, I won't have any shooting here, we're not doing any harm, what kind of behaviour is this? His voice sounds a bit higher when he asks with rare self-possession what they have come for. To arrest him, in the name of the law, and in order to show him that they mean business they put their hands on his shoulders. Do isn't used to people laying their hands on him. If he wants to be held by anyone he's got his Dina to do it and he will hold her: other people had better keep their hands off. It's hard to decide whether or not to go with them, now that they have taken this attitude; he looks at them wonderingly. They ask him whether by any chance he hasn't understood what they said. He looks thoughtfully at Dina and at the two boys. Thys, inflamed by his look and scenting injustice, Thys steps forward, barefooted and in his nightshirt and sternly demands to know what his father has done wrong. He knows nothing.

Shut up, you snot-nosed brat, says the younger policeman, but this is no answer to satisfy a worried mind. And Dina, who could have enlightened him, is unable to speak.

Listen boys, says Do. Do your duty if you must, but without any fuss, you understand, that will be better for all of us. All right? As long as you get my point, it's all right. Just let me get ready, there's no need to use force. We'll go to the police station, all three of us together, we won't make things difficult for each other. Dina, my suit.

He dresses quietly, the policemen feel relieved, not a word

is said. When he is ready something clinks in the hands of the younger one: handcuffs, but this time it is Do who puts his hands on their shoulders and says there's no need for bits of iron, he'll be pleased to go with them of his own accord. They would have been rougher if they hadn't been so frightened at first and then so relieved; they are prepared to accept his word of honour. There's nothing left for Do to do but to say good-bye, which doesn't take long; good-bye everybody. Thys sees his mother sink into a chair, leaning her head on the metal rail of the stove.

Cowards, shouts Thys, cowards, cowards. They start threatening him. Does he want to be sent to jail too? But they don't know Thys yet. You think you're so brave with your guns, says Thys, but I know you. You with the black moustache, you're Fatty and you're Big Per, you wait till we get you, cowards, dirty cowards. Let go of my father.

They are at a loss what to do. If they're going to box his ears they'll first have to handcuff Do. The mother is standing behind Thys, ready to jump, and shooting, even into the ceiling, is only a last resort. There is a glint of feverish preparedness in their eyes. The older one warns Dina that Thys may be no more than a child but that this is a dangerous game all the same; the police aren't going to let themselves be insulted in the exercise of their duty, you have been warned. But Thys can't bear the injustice of it.

Cowards, shouts Thys. Let my father go or you'll pay for it. All he can do is rage and scream, in a high-pitched voice, anguished and outraged.

This was how things stood when it happened: Big Per was already outside, Do in the doorway, the fat man still inside with his hand on the door-knob.

Thys screamed as one possessed, so piercingly and harrowingly that the fat man, suddenly losing his temper, rushed at him to box his ears, but at once Dina, Pol and Thys sprang upon him and coweringly he pushed the door shut with his back. Outside in the dark Do grabbed Big Per's armed hand, twisting it like a child's, and took the revolver.

It was all done in less than a minute. Hands up, ordered Do. He shoved them back into the kitchen. Four of them in a cluster were struggling breathlessly by the stove. The nest which would tolerate neither force nor bondage was defending itself. Dina clutched at the arm which held the revolver. Pol twisted the other arm behind the man's back, forcing him to bend over.

Thys tugged at his legs, trying to trip him up. Their teeth were clenched in pain, for the policeman was crushing their toes with his hobnail boots.

Do's usually quiet voice was unrecognizable as he shouted to the fat man to let go of his revolver and hands up, double quick. He had stopped caring what it would cost him. Bloody hell! Somehow these last words had an immediate effect. Dina took the revolver from a limp hand, gave it to Do.

Then at last she spoke. Holding the front of her buttonless nightshirt together she asked why they couldn't be left alone. They're honest folk, earning their bread decently, they don't want anything from anyone and they make no trouble for anyone. But they don't want anyone to make trouble for them either. Come to me, Thys. She throws his nightshirt over his head and shows them his blue and purple back. That is how their child has been treated. And they won't allow it, not on their life, you'd better get that straight. Leave them in peace and they will leave everyone else in peace. Just because they live out at the Leas that doesn't mean they're worse than other people. They've never had the police at the door before, not once. And now these two come bursting in here, treating them like criminals. Her Do is no criminal but that brute who beat up her child, he's a criminal and have they arrested him yet, or handcuffed him?

And now, says Do, they'll be off to the police station, he'll follow three paces behind them. And off they go. But first one more thing.

Once they get there, they might be tempted to have

another go at him. He'll tell them once and for all: they must do as they see fit, but don't forget, if they go for him it will be his turn again one day.

And so Do Glorieus walked in freedom to his imprisonment with two policemen under his orders. At the entrance he gave them their revolvers back and when they locked him up they told him they'd be back to pick a bone with him, but they must have thought better of it later, because they picked it on their own, without Do's help.

So everyone picks his bones on his own, Dina in bitterness, Pol in precocious cynicism, Lieneke in fear and Thys in a growing passion to see justice done. When Pol says that it's no use, that you never stand a chance against the bosses anyway, the best you can do is to keep out of their clutches, Thys's whole soul rebels. There might be justice. Dina no longer laughs. The free nest over which she ruled, where she was loved and cherished, has been violated. At mealtimes she bursts out crying, her mouth full of bread. Nothing could hit Thys as hard. It makes him flee the house, leaving his food uneaten. He goes straight to school.

We had no idea what was wrong with Thys. He had always had something untouchable about him which was the mark of his nest and a certain swaying jauntiness of the hips. Now there was something stiff in the way he held his neck and he no longer had that carefree look in his eyes. We cheered him up by being kind but we were unable to remove that invisible something between him and us. When he played with us it was as if he was doing it merely to please us. After the game he would share out his gains and now we realized that they were of no value to him. If we called him from another part of the playground to help us deal with a cheat he would come stalking up, straight and fearless, no matter how big and tough the opponent, sometimes confronting a whole gang on his own. When they saw him coming there was no need to fight; a word from him was enough. And we looked at him, a question in our eyes. He was lonely amongst us. Only one of us ever asked him bluntly where his father was.

Thys turned round, looked the questioner in the eye till he ran off not knowing where to turn, unable to free himself from that look.

We watched him as he took a message from our teacher to the headmaster. He stopped at a respectful distance and took off his cap, he was not lacking in courtesy, but so cold, so correct and measured was his politeness that the headmaster for all his efforts to appear unembarrassed was the inferior. Although Thys was our superior in class he was never allowed to be first. We told him that the teacher was deliberately hard on him so that his pets wouldn't be outshone by someone like him, but Thys smiled loftily and shrugged his shoulders. The others were welcome to his prizes.

How pleased we were when after a few months he suddenly seemed to be his old self again. He had brought us some medlars and when he had shared them out he suddenly gave away his pocketknife as well. I've got two more at home. Tomorrow, said Thys, my father is coming home. Tomorrow you won't see me.

But we did see his father. Do Glorieus came straight from the station to the school, he was still carrying his bundle of clothes. He saw the headmaster strolling in the playground and strode up to him. The headmaster hastily stepped through the little green door leading from the playground to the yard at the back of his house. Do Glorieus followed him and carefully closed the door behind him. Then he must have flung himself at the headmaster's throat. At least, we heard the poor man calling for help and a moment later his wife was calling too, but by that time Do had already conpleted his mission. We heard him say they could run for the police again for all he cared. He'd be waiting for them at home, he'd got his bundle ready. But he'd be back at the first opportunity, he promised them. Thereupon he calmly left by the green gate, greeted the other masters and asked them if Thys was there by any chance? No, Thys wasn't there, and Do Glorieus went home in peace like a man who has nothing to fear.

His house is half-way between the school and the station, its side turned towards the wide dirt track. Thys and Lieneke have gone out to meet father, Pol is weaving baskets in the open shed and keeps an eye on the path to the station. Dina, steadfast at her post by the front door, knits, her eyes on the horizon where Do must soon appear for the one o'clock train has long since arrived, long since left. This is why no one sees Do coming.

Cautiously he enters by the back door, soundlessly, and clasps Dina round the waist from behind. How she screams, but how brief is her joy for he has already been in a fight again and she fears he will be taken away a second time. There are shrieks of laughter and sudden silences that evening, no sleep the first night, but fits and starts at the ordinary sounds in the dark. Days go by before the anxiety gives way to a proud triumphant joy at having had the last word.

THREE

Do has been back for more than a month, everything seems forgotten and Dina laughs again, when suddenly the memories rise in his throat like a goitre. He walks to the village and gets drunk. It started in the same way, not long before Thys was born, when Dina had thought for weeks that all would remain well between them; he would suddenly disappear and come home drunk late at night, delivering speeches till the morning and then sleeping through the day. It stopped as abruptly as it had begun soon after Lieneke was born. And now again, Do comes home in the middle of the night, stands at the foot of the bed with his left hand in his pocket, wildly gesticulating with the other. The point, Dina, the point of the matter is, the real point, in short the point, for what other point could there be except the real point of the matter. It's as clear as crystal. A headmaster can understand it. And just in case he's a bit slow on the uptake, we're now talking about headmasters of course, a child can understand that, considering we're talking about the real point of the matter, but putting it briefly in a few clear, simple words, we'll come to the point: we're talking about the time. Five months. Who knows how long five months are?

There we are. It's a simple question that can be solved with one single hand, considering that after all a hand has got five fingers on it, therefore five months. And yet no one knows, even though the whole matter is as clear as crystal, how long time lasts. Are we alone? Is anyone listening?

All is quiet outside. Well now, the time we were talking about, the real time we're concerned with, that's a secret. No one is allowed to know but since everybody does know it's a reason to feel ashamed. Is that clear or isn't it? An honest man feels ashamed, it nags him inside. Vinus Glorieus, Do Glorieus's grandfather, on his father's side naturally, once lifted a big table with his teeth. He was fifty-six years old and his back went crack. He was broken. Finished he was, Vinus Glorieus.

Do Glorieus, his grandson, also on his father's side, not yet fifty, the point is not whether Do Glorieus is broken too, who would break Do Glorieus, that really is the point. No, Do Glorieus is unhappy. That's it.

Why should we waste any more words on it, did Christ waste any words when he was on the cross? I am thirsty, is what he said, just that, no more. Why all those words? Do they help? Why all this turning the matter over? Do Glorieus is unhappy. That's it. That is the whole point of the matter. One person is thirsty, another gets five months, a woman gets nine months, ha ha, and Do Glorieus is unhappy. That's it. The world was created good. Unhappiness, says Do, there's got to be unhappiness in the world, there must be something of everything, I don't want people to lack in anything, everybody should be allowed to live and let live because freedom is everything. I've always had everything but I've never been unhappy before and now I am. Very, very, very unhappy, more than very unhappy, to put it simply and plainly, because it's a grave matter, said the judge. No, not him, we won't mention him, I beg your pardon. I forbid it. We won't talk about the big boss, the one with the little white bands under his beard, for if there is a big boss there's always an even bigger boss. And that's why I say: big boss or bigger boss, boss as much as you like, I'm my own boss.

Bloody hell! All right, Do will hold his head up. Like this. Boss Dominicus Glorieus. Have a good look at him. Is he looking at the ground? Is he stealthily peering out of the corner of his eye? Can you tell from the way he looks that he feels ashamed? Bloody hell, all right then, we'll come to the point. The point is that Glorieus is a jailbird. Nothing can alter that fact. A jailbird he is and always will be. Hush, don't contradict, dear, it's far too grave a matter. I'll tell you once again, because it is important we should understand each other well, otherwise there will be arguments later on. Dina might try to wriggle out of it or Do might try to wriggle out of it or the children might say: we don't want to be the children of a jailbird. Out of the question. We have gathered together here to settle the matter and I will tell you once again so as to avoid all possible misunderstanding: Do Glorieus is boss, but don't forget, he's a jailbird as well. And what is Do Glorieus's answer?

His answer is: it can't be denied, a jailbird, that's what I am. Five months. You see? I can see that woman lying there sobbing and what kind of a woman is she? The best woman in the whole world. She was. And is! She's sobbing. All right. She thinks I don't see. All right. But I do.

A man who is unhappy sees everything, he thinks of everything. There she lies, sobbing, but what about him, is he sobbing too? Not him, he's thinking of his children. You see?

Stay here, calls Dina, but Do has already opened the door and there stands Thys, listening.

Hello my son. Shake hands with your father; mind you, your father is unhappy. Thank you, it is very good of you and very comforting to shake hands with your father. Honour thy father and thy mother so that thou shalt not be led into temptation. Your father calls you son, you shake hands with your father. Thank you, thank you very much. Mind you, I *call* you son. All right. You see, now he starts sobbing too. What for? No, not a word. Father is unhappy, let father be. Bloody hell. Quiet, I say, don't press on father's unhappiness. I will give you my blessing, my well-beloved son.

He slaps Thys so hard on the cheek that the boy is flung against the wall.

You're not my son!

Dina leaps out of bed, screaming. She takes Thys back to the little room where Pol goes on snoring. When she returns Do is sitting on a chair, his elbows on his knees, his head resting in his hands, whispering frantically.

Thys is unable to go back to sleep. His father's grief weighs on him, he feels responsible for it. The headmaster was only doing his duty, he himself should never have walked on his hands, that was how it all began.

Father has good reason to say that Thys is not his son. No one at home had ever before raised a hand against him, or to Pol or Lieneke. The unexpected blow has thrown him into an abyss. He feels unworthy of sleeping in a bed that belongs to his father, of living in his father's house, of eating the bread which his father has to earn for him. Tomorrow he will ask forgiveness, he will promise to make his clothes last longer, to eat no more than is absolutely necessary to stay alive, to go out to work as soon as he can leave school and then to pay back everything they have spent on him, from the very first day. That is his duty.

But in the morning the intentions of the night look different. Do avoided Thys with embarrassment and Thys asked or promised nothing. He was merely quieter than usual and touchingly helpful. It surprised him that mother was especially friendly to him as if she was trying to make amends for something. So much love weighed heavily on him. He wanted to tell her not to worry about him, explain to her that he understood quite well that he was to blame for everything that had happened to father and that he would much prefer just to be tolerated rather than be comforted with motherly love which only deepened his guilt.

His portion of rice pudding he shared out between Pol and Lieneke. He didn't want to eat sweet things any more. Bad for the teeth. But the true reason was that he thought he had no right to the superfluous; he merely borrowed temporarily the necessities of life which he would later repay with interest. Of the cakes which Dina always brought home from the weekly market he accepted the share that was given to him, but like father he put it on the mantelpiece and didn't look at it again. By the evening it had always disappeared of its own accord. At noon he carried the plates and laid the table, he weeded the garden, he forestalled the others in moving the goats' pegs and Do no longer needed to carry the cut and bundled osiers home; Thys did it while father was still cutting and bundling.

How much does a child cost? asked Thys. Dina burst out laughing. Did he want to buy one perhaps? No, it wasn't that, but the Podevyns have a fosterchild, a boy from Brussels, and they're being paid from Brussels, how much would that be per day? For how much per day would mother wish to bring up a child from the slums until it was fifteen? Because by that time Thys hopes to earn his own living and start with the repayments. When he knows the cost per day he will multiply it by 365 and then the total by 15, for he's good at sums. But he won't fret about the odd few centimes, on the contrary. Let him first get the amount right, then he'll round it off upwards to a handsome sum.

Father and Mother, he will write from Brussels, I know it is too much but to take an example, father was out of work for five months through my fault and wasn't able to earn anything. This is how I have worked it out and then there is always so much more to pay when you've got children, isn't there, so please accept it, you have a right to it.

But mother says she wouldn't take a strange child in the house for anything in the world and anyway, what one does for a child can't be measured in money. Well now, this fits in beautifully with the way Thys thought of ending his letter: 'because, dear father and mother, what you have done for me cannot be measured in money and when I think that I have brought you no joy but only trouble because of this weakness of mine, not being able to bear injustice or keep my mouth shut for the life of me whenever I see wrong being done and considering that I have been a worthless child to you, then I know that I shall never be able to repay you enough and shall always remain your indebted son Thys Glorieus.'

Fate smiled on Thys when Lieneke came home one day with a message for him from Ridge Farm. Would he please see Lett home after four o'clock. The days are beginning to draw in so early and the last ten minutes of the way back from the farm she is always on her own. They don't like it in the dark, not in daylight either for that matter, because Lett is such an odd creature, her sister sometimes says to her: it's as if you've got a tile loose. Some afternoons she takes more than two hours over those last ten minutes, says the maid. Yes, they've been sending the maid out to meet her, but she hasn't always got the time and in the dark, says she, she is frightened herself. So would Thys see her home, please.

If you want to make Thys happy, than ask him a service. Yet to him with his wide experience of life things are not as simple as they are to Lieneke. He folds his arms, stares thoughtfully at the steaming stew on the table and says he will give his answer at four o'clock. Mother smiles behind his back; he can talk so solemnly, like a grown-up, how sweet. The schoolmaster understands him no better. This boy who approaches him with exemplary politeness but without the slightest hint of fear and without timidly turning his eyes away, exasperates him. He imagines that the latest beating, which has remained unpunished, has made the boy saucy.

Sir, the owner of Ridge Farm has come to ask in person if Thys will please see his daughter Lett home after school, from the crossroads to the farm.

Yes, and what else? Thys: nothing else.

Is it not enough perhaps that this same Thys, who can do nothing right in the teachers' eyes and who is an unworthy son to his parents has been chosen by the master of Ridge Farm out of eleven other boys who could equally well see the child home? And is it still not good enough if Thys consults the schoolmaster about something he doesn't really have to ask permission for?

Nothing else, Glorieus, well then, do you come to tell me this? Is it any business of the schoolmaster's what the owner of Ridge Farm asks you? Do you think the schoolmaster is interested in you, Glorieus? All right, all right, it's big news, we'll make sure it gets into the paper.

Thys answers that he doesn't want people to talk ill of it later, if you please, sir.

Oh my goodness me, is that the reason? So we're not even allowed to criticize his lordship any more. All right, his lordship only needs to give his orders. When we write our article for the paper tonight we'll put that in too: it is to be well understood that no criticisms are to be levelled, or else.

Sir, says Thys, turning pale, I only came to tell you because I wanted to ask you if I have your permission. Mother and father say it's all right with them.

Calm down my boy, calm down, don't get excited, the schoolmaster is frightened enough as it is and you know why. And if you've got your parents' permission, well then, what more can the schoolmaster say? Out at the Leas they don't need any schoolmasters to tell them what to do, they're quite capable of bringing up their children on their own. But remember the schoolmaster's words, Glorieus; we'll see what will become of him, we'll see each other again.

Thys inspects his charge. She is a pale, thin child, too small for her age and she looks stupid and scared, in short, she's everything he could wish for. The strap of one of her clogs is loose; the first thing he does for her is to knock it with his own clog so that it is tight again. There's a button missing from her apron, he remarks on it. It must be mended by tomorrow, and he will stay at her house till she has asked for it to be sewn on. You don't have to be dressed smartly, says Thys, just like the schoolmaster, you don't have to wear new clothes, I don't ask that. But you must be neat, nothing untidy, I don't want to see anything untidy.

It's a bad, muddy track, rutted by carts and with a dip like a morass. She causes Thys some happy moments: the feeling of being needed, because without him she can't get across. She tells him that she always walks round this place, through the field.

Really, through the field! Treading on the young corn! That won't do from now on. Sit on my back. He carries her right through the mud. And you're not to walk through the field tomorrow morning. On his way back he will put a row of stones here, for her to walk across in future.

He walks into the farmyard with her through the wide, open gate. To the left are the cowsheds and the horses' stables, to the right the barns and the sheep pens, in front of them is the long low house.

There's a bustling of men and maids everywhere, a horse treads slowly in the threshing mill. And now the youngest daughter of this big wealthy farmer is under the protection of Thys Glorieus. Pull your hair straight, he says by the door.

The farmer's wife sits in a large, hooded wicker chair, as in the painting by Jordaens. She has been ill for years and moves about with a chair on which she constantly has to lean or sit down. Thys waits till Lett has told her that she wants a button sewn on her apron but when he is about to leave the farmer's wife asks him to tend the fire in the hearth. When he has tended the fire and has called in the maids to hang another kettle up, she asks him if he can churn. And when he has done some churning she wants to give him a few coins but this offends Thys deeply. If he can be of any help, ma'am, you only need to say so, but money, no, never. Thys, she doesn't think that's very clever of him, a workman is always worthy of his hire. Pass her the bread, please, and in that cupboard there is some butter and isn't there a piece of ham as well?

Thys reflects that at least this will save them a meal at home for which he won't later make a deduction. He and Lett eat, on either side of the wicker chair, behind them crackles the fire. From the chair a soft, slender hand is laid on his head: good boy. Thys flinches but manages to save himself in time from a sudden softness of heart by turning it into a joke.

Not everyone says he's a good boy. Why not? Because he can't bear injustice, ma'am, he always lashes out left, right and centre. Does he fight much then? Not really, only when it's necessary, but when he does he fights hard. If anyone were to bother Lett on the way, he'd probably beat him to a pulp. Laugh at him if you like, but you don't know him yet. And you don't need to be afraid of dogs either, or anything like that. He'd stand right in front of Lett, very close in front. She'd have to hold on tight to his coat and they'd walk on together. Even the most vicious dog wouldn't risk biting her. What did you say? Your young sheepdog? Let him come! Do you know what Thys will do? Thys will jump on him with his full weight and throttle him, like this. He's throttled one before, four even, but the other three were only little yappers, they don't count.

You'd better eat a lot, laughs the farmer's wife, you'll be even stronger.

Thys doesn't tell her all these things in order to boast, he says, but to reassure her. Lett will come to no harm.

How about a thick slice of farmbread now, with soft cheese and treacle?

Yes, says Thys earnestly, but I'll first have to loosen my belt. As he sits there eating with white and black beard and moustaches the thin hand is laid on his head again.

Our little Colette should have had such a boy for a brother. Thys's heart overflows, his face looks grave. He says, it doesn't make any difference to him that he's not her brother. He will look after her just the same as if she were his own sister. He doesn't even think about it, whether or not she's his sister. He's not like that, you see, she's in good hands with him, there's no need for you to be worried. Is there anything else she'd like him to do? If not, he'll just put some more wood on the fire and then he'll go home. Don't hesitate to call if you need him.

At home they've missed him, the firewood hasn't been chopped yet, but as he's already had his supper he can start right away. His life is filled with helping and caring. He falls asleep thinking how he will organize his work, so as to get it all done. They can never need him enough, he will put everything in order, all will go well and it will be his doing.

FOUR

But injustice exists everywhere, so why not at Ridge Farm too? The farmer didn't marry his second wife for the sake of that wicker chair and that slow-witted child. She's been chairbound for years now. For her sake he incurred the hostility of five grown children, and it was bearable as long as she, much younger than he, went about the house vivaciously, never resting, until the very last day, until the day her proudly swollen belly bore him a child. A second life for him; he talked of buying more land. She never regained her health and he read malicious glee in the eyes of the five older children: now the old rake has got what he deserves: a sickly wife. In the farmyard he grumbles and snarls, but more at himself than at others because his children snap back at him, and the servants, not slow to notice this, no longer show him respect either. Only his wife and child bear the full brunt of his temper. Coming into the house he'll kick the child's doll's cradle under the bench, doll and all, because it's supposedly in his way. His wife may stand before him doubled up with pain and with a mouth as if she is sucking a lemon, he doesn't notice. The child doesn't cry at the ill-treatment of her doll. She doesn't laugh readily either; she lives in dull complacency. Not so Thys. Thys picked up her doll and cradle and says sternly that the farmer ought to look out where he puts his feet. Of course the woman signals to him to be silent but later, when they are alone, he tells her bluntly that he doesn't like the way her husband behaves. It seems to me, says Thys, that you're not happily married; he looks at her worriedly, deliberating in his mind how he can put this matter right. She smiles at him kindly enough and talks earnestly: she doesn't think she is unhappily married. But she is ill and to be ill is always a misfortune, particularly on a farm. No, says Thys, it's true what I said: you're unhappily married. Hadn't she noticed, before it was too late, that he's got a big fat lump just under his cap, as big as a nut? Yes, sure, she laughs. And that big Adam's apple? That too, she laughs. Then I can't understand you at all, says Thys, didn't you know that all secret scoundrels have that? She sits back in her chair, limp with laughter, holding her loins as if the shaking hurt her. But Thys doesn't think there's anything to laugh about. He would never advise anyone to marry somebody with such a lump on his forehead and such an Adam's apple. He feels that he's come a bit too late here. The tragedy has already occurred.

One day he asks the little girl if she is often beaten at

home. She answers, yes, quite often. Who beats her? Father does. Why? She doesn't know, for all sorts of reasons. Thys then wants to know if she leads a miserable life at home and whether she would like to leave and live somewhere else, but this is too complicated a question and he can't get an answer out of her. She doesn't know herself what she wants; things happen to her simply because they have to happen, that's all.

One day, as he was sitting by the table with Lett and her mother, as usual, they failed to notice that the fire was nearly out, they were having such a pleasant time. The farmer entered unexpectedly and made such a fuss that the servants could hear it all over the farm. Was it asking too much of her, to watch the fire now and again? No, she must needs go and sit with her behind turned to it, so as not to have to look at it, no doubt. Why doesn't she stay in bed all day if she's too lazy to keep her eyes open?

It's my fault, says Thys, but finds no hearing; the bottled-up bitterness must be vented. Two tears trickle from the sick woman's eyelashes.

She has learnt to be silent but you can't be taught to feel no grief. Thys's heart breaks. It's my fault, he calls out, and you, have you no heart, how could it have been her fault, why do you torment the poor woman so, you should be ashamed of yourself. Yes, well, Thys is in for it now. Outside the door there are three, four maids, eavesdropping and winking at each other; they think it's wonderful that that little pup from the Leas is giving the old boy a piece of his mind. In the porch the two older sons are listening too. Funny little chap, that Thys! The farmer's wife, however, disapproves. She tells Thys to go home, in future they will ask someone else to see Colette home. The farmer grabs Thys by the scruff to throw him outside but he is rescued in the nick of time by the two sons. They want the boy to stay. He helps mother after school, doesn't he, she can't do without him. It's people who pick quarrels, people who kick up a row, pigheaded bullies that they can do without at Ridge Farm.

Can they now, have they forgotten who's boss at Ridge Farm?

They don't care who's boss but they're sick and tired of all this bickering and squabbling.

This is what happens wherever Thys goes; now they've found out what he's like at the Farm. He sits dejectedly by the fire and behind him sits the sick woman. Both are silent. The clock in its narrow, tall case ticks slowly and sadly. Now and then its chain rolls over with a rumble as if it is grumbling cantankerously. Please forgive me, says Thys, kneeling by the fire, to the silent woman behind him. She answers that it's all right now, but that he'd better go home.

He goes, it is dark. He feels a pain, he who always wants to do what is right and always sees it turning out wrong. He is lonely; he has a heart that wants to give itself to others and is not understood.

But look, in the midst of his desolation his mind hits on a great invention, a chair on wheels for the sick woman who wants nothing more to do with him. His spirits leap, he forgets his pain and absorbed in his plans he begins to whistle softly. He must have got it from his father.

The next day, at Ridge Farm, without a word, he takes his mother's tape measure from his pocket and measures the distance between the legs of the high-backed wicker-chair. He offers no explanations but quietly gets on with it. The farmer's wife is touched by the way he crawls around on his knees; he's like a faithful dog. Kicked around yesterday, disowned even by her, and yet today he has generously forgotten everything, he's busy caring and tending again. He can be so imperturbably serious. Come here, Thys, come and sit near me.

Yesterday he was very much in the wrong, he didn't behave correctly at all. The farmer is master here and if he's irritable at times that's his own affair, he has a right to be. And it isn't becoming for a little boy to stand up against someone so much older than himself.

I know my weakness, says Thys meekly.

She puts an arm round him, her hands tremble a little. Of the fondness which she, a woman, needs, he understands nothing. He lets himself be encircled, stiffly, holding his face turned away, for he doesn't care for such silliness. He talks like a man to her, tells her not to fret. It isn't good for her health to fret, she must remember that.

Suddenly she embraces him and weeps. And tells him he's a good boy. He must always remain a good boy but he must also learn to be silent, to grit his teeth, to see and yet not to see, otherwise he will see too much for his own good. And he must always keep coming to Ridge Farm.

As long as she lives. And always look after Colette, she's such a poor little mite.

A tremor goes through Thys. Agreed. His teeth are clenched, he could break a steel bar.

You're quite grown up already, and you're beginning to understand things, she says.

He presses her hand hard.

Two weeks later he comes along pushing his invention: a large high-backed wicker chair on four bicycle wheels. At the back a handle has been fixed to steer the towering colossus. The entire farm flocks out to see, except the farmer. They're all crowding round it and Thys is happy. They don't say what they think: that this thing has come a bit late and has been made rather too strongly for the short time it will be needed. Up till recently she was still able to move about fairly well by leaning on a kitchen chair. Now she can't do much more than sit, and for how long will she be able to do even that?

Perhaps the chair could have been more elegant, but it is solidly built with strong axles under the seat and iron hoops carefully woven in with cane, onto which the seat is mounted immovably. They ask Thys if this is really his own invention. Magnanimously disclaiming the sole credit he explains that they've worked on it together at home, father, Pol and himself. He beams with happiness when the farmer's wife hoists herself into the seat. Where do you want me to take you, just tell me.

She looks at him gratefully, affectionately: to the church. She hasn't been to church for years, her first outing must be to God's house. It's a good half hour's walk but luckily the road isn't too muddy and Thys sets off with her. He puts his left hand in his pocket in order to show them all at the farm that steering the chair is child's play.

He pushes her right up to the communion rail. She starts to weep, her face in her hands. A sparrow chirps inside the church. Thys sits patiently on a chair. She doesn't get tired. After praying and weeping for a long time she says she would like to do the stations of the cross.

But isn't that asking too much? Has he got time enough? Don't mind about him, please, just say what you want. He pushes her up one aisle, down the other, stopping in front of each of the fourteen stations.

It goes on for ever, but never too long for Thys, he's happy. When she has fortified herself with Christ's suffering she takes all her money out of her pocket, it isn't much, for the farmer gives her hardly anything. She distributes it among the different offertory boxes, a trifle more for St. Antony, a trifle less for St. Catherine. And then she wants to sit by the communion rail once again, but there has to be an end of it some time; the verger comes to lock up the church.

Through the dark he pushes her home and when they arrive at the gate of Ridge Farm she asks Thys to stop and come closer.

Thys, how much will this be?

Well, yes, that's a big question. That particular evening, two weeks ago, Thys had come home whistling: the mistress of Ridge Farm needs a wheelchair.

First he had tried to saw some wheels out of wood, but father and Pol had laughed derisively and when he had fetched four old bicycle wheels worrying how they were going to be paid for, they'd sent him off to the smithy with them, it would never work otherwise. Showing the smith exactly how he wanted it done was easy enough, but paying was not.

And then father and Pol had spent much time and energy weaving and plaiting. They'd never made anything like it, they wanted to show what they could do and after all, at Ridge Farm money would be no object. When Thys left the house with it, Dina told him: if they ask how much it costs you'd better tell them we don't know ourselves, because we haven't had the bills from the smith and the bicycle man yet. Now the farmer's wife wants to know how much her chair will cost and Thys can't even bring himself to give the answer his mother told him. After all, she never ordered the chair, it's a present from him and he's surely not going to make her pay for a gift. We won't talk of that, says Thys.

Oh yes, we will. But he mustn't tell them indoors how much it is. It's nobody's business. As she is figuring rapidly how long it will take her to save up her meagre pennies to pay the price, forgetting therefore to find out the exact sum, it is already clear to Thys that he's in a hopelessly tight spot. She says she'll pay off a little at a time. However much he objects that as she has never ordered anything there is no need to pay, she realizes that he's trying to please her and she will be grateful to him for the remainder of her life, but his father and brother can't be expected to work for nothing and anyway, they'll have to pay the smith as well.

For as long as she is still alive he gives her a ride to the church every day. At home she can move the chair around herself with a stick, the wheels roll so smoothly. There are no stairs to the bedroom; she can push herself up to the bed and sometimes one of the maids wheels her to the stables. She can still join in all the talk and a watchful eye is valuable on a big farm. And every evening before dark she is taken to the church.

The Lord does not therefore lengthen her days; he fortifies her soul, not her body. One morning she can't get out of bed and the oldest daughter takes her place in the big kitchen, the place which she reluctantly gave up many years ago. After school Thys sits by the bedside, grave and worried. Lett keeps wheeling the chair round the room; she has put her doll to sleep in it. The doll receives more attention than the mother. When Thys reflects aloud that they might make some alterations to the chair, spacing the wheels more widely and fixing a reclining seat on the frame, the woman smiles and says it's not worth the trouble any more. Reclining chairs no longer occupy her mind, her eyes follow with dull anxiety the child who wheels her doll round the room, for hours on end, lost in her play. The child has no inkling of what she is about to lose.

Sometimes the woman groans, although she is not in pain, but only Thys jumps up as if stung. The child merely glances at her, in surprise, and then calmly continues her play. For the last three years she has been in the same class at school and it's a constant cause of amazement to her sisters that she's even got that far.

There is no one at the farm to whom the mother can communicate her worries about the child. With her husband she has no chance to talk at all and the others only get annoyed. They say: you talk as if we don't treat the child well, so then she falls silent. Such crossness won't soften their feelings for the poor mite, that lives in its own hazy world, without apparent joy or sadness and alert to nothing. So the woman clings to this boy with his faithful dog's eyes who huddles on a chair just like his father at home, his back against the wall and his head between his knees, his feet on the seat; talking quietly, earnestly, like a grown-up person, as long as her eyes are open, and falling silent when they are shut. She asks him to fetch a little box from a drawer which she wants him to give to his mother, from her. And now she's going to ask him one more thing. Should our Lord call for her, will he keep coming to the farm as he has always done, at least as long as he's still at school and doesn't have to stay at home to work? But even later, even when he's got his own work to do, will he please come from time to time, to see how Colette is getting on? She doesn't mean to say that they're not good to her here, but all the same, it would be a reassurance. If she could feel that although the child is on her own Thys is still there.

Something tells Thys: this is the last time she will ask me anything. She must die in peace. He calls the child to come near the bed. Did she hear what her mother said just now? Yes. Thys holds out his left hand to her and raises his right hand: I swear it. When he gets home tonight and gives the little box to his mother he must tell her that it comes from the mistress of Ridge Farm, who has always envied her for having such a son. One must allow a sick woman to say such things; Thys doesn't turn a hair. He finds his share of happiness in her trust and his promise.

In the little box there are a big, round, solid brooch and two long golden earrings. At first Thys is eyed with suspicion. There is an atmosphere of perplexity; the box is put on the mantelpiece, no one speaks. An hour goes by and then suddenly Dina grabs the boy by the shoulders. She can't breathe, she says, it creeps up inside her, look in my eyes. Thys, *did* you steal them? Thys's candid eyes do not lie and he swears his second oath that day. Mother, he may drop dead if they weren't given to him as a present and he decides he might as well tell her the other thing too, at the same time; tell your mother, she said, that the mistress of Ridge Farm has always envied her for having such a son. Do Glorieus chuckles. If he had stabbed Thys slowly in the chest with a big knife, it would have hurt no more. Enraged by the pain, Thys holds up his hand again: I swear it. All right then, they won't talk about the wheelchair any more and tomorrow mother will go to the farm to thank the sick woman. Her fear turns to joy and later that evening she appears in the lamplight in her best dress and with the brooch and earrings. It touches something in Do. Shall we dance?

But early the next morning the church bells toll for the

mistress of Ridge Farm. If anyone should wish to speak to her now, where should he go?

FIVE

When the school year comes to a close, we are given our prizes. If it is our final year, we look round the playground for the last time and the daily accursed gate becomes the gate to freedom. In the half-century of the school's existence it has never occurred to any boy to say thank you to a teacher. He gave us knowledge in return for our freedom. On top of which we endured his cruelty. So the accounts were even. Thys Glorieus was the only one to feel this imponderability: gratitude-debt pressing on his heart, he who had the least reason to feel beholden. Thys Glorieus thanked the master for all he had done for him. Fortunately, the prize-givers, namely the priest and the councillors, were still standing close by, otherwise Thys would have received his last box on the ear for this mockery. As it was, the headmaster had to remain calm but he asked Thys who had told him to say thank you to the teacher. Naturally, he thought it must have been Do. Thys answered in surprise: no one. The headmaster changed his tune, he didn't address him as Glorieus any more but as Thys, and asked why Thys had done this, had nobody told him to, really and truly?

Thys saw in this show of friendliness his one and only chance to be understood at last: he denied forcefully. This appeared to move the headmaster very much, he took Thys's hand in his two hands. Giddy with happiness Thys doesn't even hear all the friendly words that are poured out over him. He gives the headmaster mother's and father's kind regards, generously takes the blame for the headmaster's past misjudgment and asks forgiveness. The head-master's eyes moisten.

When Thys tells them at Ridge Farm that he won't be going back to school after the holidays and therefore won't be able to see Lett home, they ask him what he's going to do now, is he going to learn how to make baskets like his father, couldn't they spare him at home, couldn't he come and work on the farm? This is just what he himself hadn't dared to ask.

Do gets enough assistance from Pol, and Dina is rather pleased that he has found employment so near home. Not until the third day did the farmer notice him and ask what that little whipper-snapper was doing here. A son and a daughter of his replied, with their backs towards him, that the boy was making himself useful. Nothing more, the old man had no further say in the matter. If he wanted to bark at anyone, he'd better look around for another wife, they weren't going to be barked at any more.

Thus Thys was able to carry out the dead woman's last request and keep his promise to her: watch over the child. He grew and so did she. He grew both in height and in width; he didn't sway from the hips like his father, but was straight and strong like Dina. He had her rosy cheeks but not her proud laugh. But the girl only grew in height, with a long, narrow face and a pursed, stupid mouth with thick lips. By the time she too left school she could just stand under his arm when he stretched it out.

She wasn't fit for any kind of work. They had to burn her dolls in the stove to teach her not to play all day. She looked at the flames with dull eyes; whether she was sad or angry no one could tell. She followed Thys about everywhere. That was all right, said Thys, it was time she started thinking of doing a proper day's work. She agreed with whatever he said. On Saturday he showed her the few measly francs he had earned and explained to her that you could only earn money by working.

She knew that with money you could buy buns and cakes

but for the rest she didn't understand much about it. He didn't buy her any buns, though, because the money was for his mother. At home, by his bed, he wrote down the exact amount he paid off each Saturday. Dina never understood why he made a point of telling her every week how much in all he had already given her. The cost of his clothes he deducted.

For several years Thys carried out his duties, remembering the oath at the deathbed. Everybody was fond of him, except the farmer who wasn't fond of anyone. No one dared ever be rough with Lett when he was around, because they had all seen his impetuousness, his passion for order and perfection, and they knew that he was happy when he was asked for advice, or a service, the more onerous the better. He had almost become one of the family and caring for Lett gave purpose to his life. He would sit musing, a frown on his face, worrying about her future.

One day Thys was sent to fetch a basket of potatoes from the cellar, with Rosa, the youngest of Lett's half-sisters. She stunned him by asking him why he was always running after Lett! He was so flabbergasted that he stood stock-still, with his hands on his hips, speechless.

She said she couldn't for the life of her understand what he saw in Lett. She had thought at first that they were simply good friends, from the time they'd been at school together, but surely now that he was older he had a bit more sense. Hadn't he ever noticed that Lett had a screw loose?

It was a long time before Thys could find words. When he did they were quite different from the ones he'd been meaning to say. He asked her why that schoolmaster from Lephem was always hovering about her, what do you want with him? Go on, Thys, him? She never even looks at him, that upstart. Did you think I wasn't free any more, Thys? Look how free I am, and she puts her arms round him, stretches her whole body, warm and soft, against him and kisses him long on the mouth. That's how free I am.

Luckily, at that moment a big rat fell with a thud from the

stacked straw on the potatoes. How else would Thys have got out of this! Grabbing hold of a weapon, they both started hitting and lashing out at the rat, running after it this way and that. Thys swept it off the ladder, it tried to get back on to the stack and in a corner he nearly caught it but it disappeared through a gap between the walls and the loam floor.

They knelt down by the hole, whispering about the rat, but their minds weren't on what they were saying. Her hair touched his cheek, now and then she gave him little kisses, quick ones, with a warm mouth, until, in a fluster, they stood up, leaning against each other, holding each other tightly. Then suddenly they started filling the basket as if nothing had happened.

Thys now looked at Lett with different eyes. He compared her with Rosa, much to Lett's disadvantage. Sitting on the haycart with unseeing eyes, lying in bed at home, unable to get to sleep, a warmth flowed through him, he longed to see Rosa. When he was near her he pretended to be indifferent, but she herself sought opportunities to be alone with him, although without her stratagems they would have found each other just as often, with a strange, unfailing instinct. On Saturdays, when the others were making plans to go out on Sunday, she was the only one who had no sweetheart and did not feel like going anywhere. Self-sacrificingly, she offered to stay at home to look after the house in the company of her old father who now shuffled along with a stick. She gave a rash laugh: her sweetheart Thys would come and help her!

There was nothing unusual about Thys coming to work on a Sunday. He was always willing to do extra work, without pay, out of hours, only too pleased that they needed him. And it didn't occur to anyone on the farm that Rosa could have taken a fancy to a Glorieus.

Thys took his duties seriously, sent Lett to Benediction, having made sure that she had got her rosary and her missal, that her mother's *in memoriam* card was still inside the missal, and watched her go, until she was lost from sight. With Lett gone, he knew that Rosa was waiting for him in the cowshed. It was his job to feed the cows while she did the milking; then he had to carry the milk to the cellar. Scrupulously he kept out of her way but somehow they always ended up close together.

Thys felt the blood rising to his head, he became a different person and he loved her. When the old man thumped his stick on the doorstep and called for them they quickly let go of each other and appeared in the farmyard from opposite directions.

He reminded her that her brothers were courting or had married rich girls and her sisters a vet and a brewer respectively, so why did she waste her time on him? But she pulled him back into the hay and between rapid, pecking kisses she whispered that she did what she wanted. This could mean anything, but he felt she was serious about him. Which was precisely what he didn't want her to be. Nor did he want it to be a game, and with this too he reproached her, and when he was alone, himself. What did he want then, she panted, passionately, don't talk such rubbish, you big dope of mine. She lay back, ready for him, with limp arms.

But he couldn't push the feeling aside that he was cheating the farmer and all his sons and daughters. Everything he had ever done for them out of the goodness of his heart, without thought of gain but simply for the pure pleasure of being generous, now seemed to have been a calculated trick, aimed at getting one of the daughters for himself.

He felt ashamed. In the months that followed he told her every time they met that this time was going to be the last, a few tears were enough to make him compensate her for his cruelty by giving her abundant happiness, for Thys could not bear tears. As soon as she lay comforted in his arms he began to suggest plans for a gradual, and therefore less painful separation. He argued that their love was sinful, taking all the blame on himself because he should have had more sense – sense not being something you could demand of a girl. If they were to get used to not being together without it hurting too much, they should see each other less often. But if he put their next date too far back she started crying again, yet as soon as he had reached the limit of compromise she changed tactics, reproaching him that he didn't love her enough and shaming him profoundly by saying that he only thought of himself. His face twitched as if in pain. Full of self-reproach he admitted she was right, yet professing his love and insisting on one thing only: that it was wrong for them to love each other.

But why, Thys? Why is it wrong, tell her that! Her older sister's husband, the vet, drinks and beats his wife. The husband of her other sister, the brewer, is never at home and she said the other day, what Albert gets up to when he's out, I hear all sorts of things, but I don't want to know. It's best to keep my mouth shut and pretend I know nothing.

Rosa concluded that happiness doesn't depend on money and social position, and Thys would always be nice to her, wouldn't he, great big dope?

It did not relieve Thys of the unbearable thoughts that plagued him, he avoided her more and more with the result that she sought him out more restlessly and with less caution. In order to keep her at arm's length he made sure of having Lett near him. He took her with him on the haycart, and to the meadows, and taught her to work as best he could. He was angry with himself for always comparing her with Rosa.

He noticed the first swelling of her small breasts and was ashamed because of her mother who saw him from heaven. But it's because I'm worried about her, honestly, and sitting on the cart he raised his eyes to the sky where she was. Lett is a woman now, but still as simple as a child. Suppose some good-for-nothing blackguard set his mind on her, what do you think would happen then? How would Thys then be able to face her mother, with his oath weighing heavily on his conscience? He thinks: I'm sure she'd let them do whatever they liked, she'd let them do anything. Gruffly he asks her whether she still plays with boys. She looks round innocently and smiles: I'm not allowed to any more. And Thys says gravely: No, and I won't let you either. When they have been working the whole afternoon Rosa brings them coffee and sandwiches in a basket, an errand she couldn't delegate to a maid.

She tries to get rid of Lett, telling her to fetch some deliberately forgotten pears, but Thys says he can't spare her that long or they'll never finish the job. So her plan to be alone with Thys, the only reason that drove her here, has failed and she departs sulkingly, jealous.

Thys and Lett sit on the bank of a dry ditch, eating their bread. Bluetits twitter in the old willow trees, there's no breeze, not a cloud in the sky, nothing but sun. Lett lets herself slide into the ditch, satisfied. While Thys is eating his last sandwich he looks down on her. Her eyes follow a flight of pigeons. He sits down beside her and smooths her black hair. Like a father. Gravely he says that she's a woman now. It makes her smile. He puts a hand on her breast and looks at her, to see if she is startled or jumps up. She only turns her head aside and picks at some bits of grass with two long nails. There is no excitement as with Rosalie. He unbuttons her dress, for a moment she looks with interest at his hand, then at him. Thys asks calmly if she has ever let anyone do this before. No. All right, that's good. Nor should she ever, I'm warning you. You see, he'd always thought she didn't know anything about that sort of thing. But she's no longer a child now, life is not a game. I'm warning you, that sort of thing is unchaste, a great sin.

As he carefully buttons up her dress, Rosa appears among the willow trees, with the pears. She has brought them herself after all, hoping that at last she might be alone with Thys. She approaches, deep red, with downcast eyes, but suddenly she hits Lett flat in the face, staring wildly at Thys as if she is about to throw herself at him. Then she flings the pears into his lap and runs, but by the last willow she falters, puts her arms round the tree and cries. This is more than Thys can bear, he melts inside. Educating Lett, comforting Rosa; he now goes to Rosa, but it is more difficult than he thought to convince her of his pedagogic intentions. Thys knows it is impossible to reason with women. He stands behind her and says softly, like a father, that she's behaving like a child and that if she knew what she was crying about she'd be laughing instead. Always the same childishness. If I was always to take notice of your crying, says Thys, I'd have my work cut out. He pushes a loose pin further into her hair and before he realizes what he is doing he has offered to meet her that evening. How many meetings has he tried to avoid, and now he suggests one himself! She abruptly stops crying and gives him a look that chills him. She says: what do you take me for? And she's gone.

All the same, he waits for her in the shed, and all the same she comes. But sullenly and with conditions. First of all, what is there between him and that dimwit? Secondly, whatever it is, it's got to stop. Thirdly, as far as the two of them are concerned, they've got to come to a decision, one way or another.

Thys opens his big heart. It is dark, a time when the heart thinks it can speak, when it deludes itself that it is not lonely. Between him and Lett there is nothing, Rosa. But at her mother's deathbed he swore a solemn oath that he would look after Lett. That is all, and he will continue to look after her as long as he lives or until he has found a husband for her and knows for certain that she is happy with him. Because you know, in this house Lett counts for nothing, without him she'd be beaten, she might even be sent to an institution.

Rosa's sister Karlien occasionally gave her a dress which could be altered for her, but what will happen now that Karlien is married? And why don't you ever give her any dresses, Rosa, why don't you give her that navy blue one? And another thing, she needs a pair of shoes, what size do you take? Seven. She could wear those then.

And that is all there is between him and Lett, nothing else.

She hasn't got any jewellery either, not even a single necklace, and Rosa has got at least six. How do you think she's ever going to get married if she always looks the way she looks now? Why don't you give her one of your necklaces? And now that he's said all this, she must also promise him to treat Lett more like a sister. A dimwit, she said just now.

Honestly, Thys had rather she kicked him on the shin than say such nasty things about Lett. And another thing: why don't you and Lett walk to church together, instead of always letting her go on her own as if she was an orphan? And the way the maids treat her, Rosa. Yesterday, it was 'stupid nit' here, 'silly clot' there. One day he'll take a swipe at those girls and knock them over, buckets and all. You shouldn't allow them to talk like that! You've got a right to tell them, after all, she is your half-sister. And that's all there is between him and Lett. If only he could find her a good husband, then she could leave the farm.

Now we'll have to talk about Rosa. She says they've got to come to a decision. How can they – he's still got to do his military service. And then he'll have to earn money, for his parents. But what does it matter if they have to wait a bit? He loves Rosa and he'll be faithful to her. But surely she doesn't think he'd want to marry a rich man's daughter in order to be boss on the farm in future? If she thinks that, she doesn't know him yet. He wants to get married, yes, but she mustn't have a penny of her own, she must be poor like him. Is it possible to demand such a thing of her? You see, that's why he is saying to her: Rosa, think hard about it. Marriage goes on for ever, and Thys is only Thys. Thys will work like a horse, Thys will work to make her rich, as sure as he's standing here, but if she asks him: Thys, what have you got to offer me *now*, *now*, he'll have to say to her: nothing. And what he may be one day, well, that's only guesswork.

Is it the darkness which carries him away or is it the contact with the girl's hand which gives him this sweet illusion that tempts to confidentiality? He can't stem the tide of his own words and begins to talk about Lett again. If he were married and hadn't found a husband for Lett, he would take the poor girl into his home because he hasn't sworn an oath for nothing.

And that, Rosa, is why he was sometimes wavering. That is why it can never come to anything between us. Sweet girl, she should forget him, he's saying this for her own good. It will hurt him more than it will hurt her, but . . .

Thys speaks softly. For I can't live without you any more. I lie awake half the night. I want to hold you and kiss you from head to toe, pinch you and bite you. When I see you I'm restless and when I don't see you I'm restless too.

And now he thinks he has really told her everything honestly. He waits. On the stacked straw something rustles, a cat or a rat. He looks towards the sound and as he looks Rosa slips away. He doesn't notice that she's going until a slit of late light falling through the door tickles his eyelashes. Finished, thinks Thys.

Not finished, but it had become too much for her, how could she have coped with it?

A man who is offered an opportunity will grab it. This boy doesn't grab precisely because it *is* an opportunity. It is the sort of thing you read of in books about chivalry, but out in the country people are at a loss to understand such things. All her feelings seemed inadequate and could not reach him. She daren't show jealousy at his concern for Lett and yet there remained a mistrust, that something so noble could be sincere. Following him in poverty she could not risk, nor dare she scoff at his pride. He became inaccessibly great and wonderful, all she knew was that she believed in him, as she lay awake in bed with her eyes open feeling how he had awakened in her a different desire than sensual passion, something that made her groan: Thys! If only he would allow her to lie in his arms, if only he was with her, that would be enough. More wasn't even allowed.

Her marriage plans became vaguer every day. She was so young, not yet a woman who could marry out of admiration, but only out of passion and with the sense of reality of her kind. Why should she have to become poor if she was not poor?

Naturally, the others soon noticed that she sought Thys out far more than before and without circumspection. It's easy enough to creep into a shed together and afterwards talk roughly to each other in order to mislead everyone, but what she now felt for Thys was a kind of tender adoration which she found hard to conceal. She could no longer bear to see others taking advantage of his kindness. She exclaimed that they were always ordering him about, Thys do this and Thys do that, the boy gets tired like anyone else, he's too kind-hearted. Everyone saw that she didn't mock him the way she used to, and as she no longer met him in secret she thought that this would not arouse suspicion.

She didn't know that Karlien and her two brothers had been discussing the matter seriously. Father was becoming senile, otherwise he would soon have put a stop to it, but she had better not imagine that the three of them would allow such a disgrace to befall their family. A Glorieus on Ridge Farm, wasn't it enough to give you a fit! They decided to bring up the question of the brooch and the earrings, as a start.

All those years they had never shown the slightest interest in those trinkets. When the oldest of the sisters, the one who was married to the vet, had first seen Dina wearing them at the fair, the possibility of theft hadn't even occurred to anyone. They had at once assumed it to have been a present from the dying mistress of the farm; she had been so fond of Thys and had been so grateful to him for taking her to church every day. When one of the boys suggested they should tease Thys that his mother had been showing off with those earrings at the fair, just to see Thys's face, as he said, the others had told him not to be silly.

Now they suddenly started talking about that jewellery and watched sharply for Rosa's reaction. One of them said indulgently that in his opinion those earrings probably *had* been given to Thys as a present, the other said that they'd never caught Thys taking anything since, but then, who would notice on a big farm like theirs if some trivial odds and ends disappeared from time to time. Dina probably hadn't needed to buy much butter over the years, but never mind, let it pass.

They see Rosa coming at them, sticking her neck out like a goat that is about to butt. You ought to be ashamed of yourselves!

Oh really, so they're the ones who ought to be ashamed, are they? Well, well, they hadn't realized. Don't fly off the handle, missy. Who was it that gave that red-haired Eulalie the sack, for no other reason than that she always went home with a bag full of stuff and what had she got in it? A few paltry turnips and carrots, dear me, and in the summer a bit of fruit. And now this selfsame Rosa is defending Thys. Who's saying anything against him, anyway? Who's begrudging him anything, have they ever made any objections? He can keep it for all they care; if he's got pilfering in his blood it won't be in their power to cure him.

But now Rosa will tell them a thing or two. She knows Thys, she knows what he's like and the whole lot of them, with their farm and all their money tied up in a bundle are nothing compared with Thys. 'You're a disgrace,' she shrieks, sobbing, but they roar with coarse, proud laughter and leave her alone in the kitchen.

Now they are convinced that they have let matters go too far and that Thys must go. He can take Lett with him, then they're rid of her too.

But it isn't as easy as they think. Thys, who usually needs no more than a hint or half a word, Thys who can always tell in advance what is expected of him and how he can please people, Thys turns a deaf ear to any subtle needling, whether he wants to remain a farmhand all his life, whether his father and Pol have a lot of work at home. Thys knows well enough that he is wasting his precious youth without learn-ing a trade that will one day make him rich, for he wants to get rich and share his wealth with others. He wants to grow a paunch on which to wear a fat gold watch chain, and with his thumbs in his waistcoat pockets he will look at his possessions and say to some poor devil: here, take this, you can have it. He wants to be able to take some precious object from his pocket, give it to Lett and then, in leaving, casually look round to see how pleased she is. Once a month he'll come home from Brussels, as a rich man, putting boxes on the table and sitting down by the stove and saying: go on, open them. He'll give Father and Pol an expensive cigar each and as he is talking to them, through clouds of smoke, he will pretend not to hear Dina and Lieneke exclaiming in delight. One day he will make them all so happy that they will be besides themselves with joy and kiss him. And how will he react? He will say, with indifference: if I'd known you'd be so pleased with it I would have brought it home sooner.

One day he will be married. To a beautiful lady, white of flesh and with plump breasts which she carries proud and high. One who knows the world, who can give dinner parties. But he himself will remain a simple man, he will invite half the village. And he himself will go round with the cream cake, twice, because village people wouldn't dare ask for a second piece. He will put another big slice on each of their plates. So what are they talking about at the farm? What do they want of him? To be a farmhand for ever? He has responsibilities here which he cannot explain, he doesn't understand their allusions, he's talking about something quite different.

Rosa, why are they fed up with me?

His question hurts her, angers her. That evening, prompted by a gruff remark which wasn't even meant unkindly, she starts a violent quarrel. The ground under Thys's feet is rent when suddenly he hears mention of the golden earrings. There it is, the injustice, the misunderstanding, the outrage, the pain. It would take him too long to edge his way carefully between table and bench, so he steps right across both bench and table and stands, white as a sheet, in the middle of the kitchen. The worst is that he doesn't know whom or what to lay into first. The old farmer regains his voice. A voice is all he has left. He now sits in the wicker chair, Thys's gift. He doesn't know what the quarrel is about, but a senile memory of his old dislike for the brat his wife was so fond of is enough. He points his stick at Thys, then at the door. Just this once the others agree with him. They too are pointing at the door. The older of the two brothers is still sitting by the table and with his mouth full of bread he shouts that Thys imagines he's already master at Ridge Farm, God Almighty, Rosa, a fine master you would have had there. Thys falters; with wide open eyes and mouth he looks at them all in bewilderment, and winces. The elder son roars with laughter. Thys takes his cap and leaves. On the bench sits Lett, in dull amazement.

At the gate Rosa catches up with him, pushes him against the wall, kisses him, sobbing. Thys, go to Brussels, learn a trade, start a business of your own and then we'll get married. Thys, forgive me, I love you more than ever. Thys, I'm coming with you. Her plans grow as she speaks. She can have two thousand francs at once. Father is sure to die before they're all gone. When he's dead she'll have her share. She'll go with Thys to Brussels, this evening, she'll stay the night with him, tomorrow you'll look for work. We'll manage somehow until I get my share and then we'll buy a shop. This is enough for Thys; her hot lips against his ear, her tears on his cheek, her body that wants to take possession of him. He gains control and becomes again the stronger one, taking her face in his hands and admonishing her to be sensible. And no more quarrelling at home on my account, he'll win through somehow, don't worry, why should he bother about her brothers. Come on now, or Thys will laugh at that crybaby that upsets herself about such trifles. Go inside now. He's got his plans ready, he won't tell her yet, wait and see. You'll soon be hearing from Thys. Don't cry any more, says Thys, 'I won't abandon you. Nor

Lett either.' Thys laughs manfully. And leaves, shedding a few tears.

When he arrives home, he's big Thys once again. He's handed in his notice at the farm and tomorrow he's going to Brussels to look for a job. They are baffled, no one speaks, but Thys goes on, raising his voice as if they'd attacked his most dearly held convictions. Surely they don't think, he exclaims, that he's going to remain a farmhand all his life! And mother, he'll soon be bringing home a different sort of wage. Dina looks at him with a motherly smile but for Thys any smile, even that of a stranger, would be enough, would make him give unstintingly whatever is his to give. Soberly, gravely, he announces that he wants to become rich. Father feels as if he is back in his own childhood and Thys is his brother Dolf. Dolf folded his arms on his chest and said, over father's head who was sitting on a low stool, smoking a clay pipe: you little twig-cutters, I'm going to get rich.

Now this Thys also folds his arms, his eyes have a distant look and he too wants to get rich. But he opens his arms wide in a vague, broad gesture; he adds: then you'll have a good life.

All well and good, but he hasn't said a word about Brussels yet and why should he have given up his job overnight? If Dina had gone to the farm the next day they would have told her plainly that Thys had gone off in a huff 'and there's an end of it, we won't talk about it any more and anyway, it's probably for the best, he'll be better off in Brussels.' However, quarrels at the farm never remain a secret, because there's always a lot of shouting and the maids overhear everything. Thus Dina learns that there was some argument about golden earrings and she goes straight to the farm to fling her jewels proudly on the table among the coffee cups. They aren't thieves. These were given to Thys as an honest present, but they don't need any presents, here, take them back, your precious earrings. Keep them. Keep your present, if you call it a present, without ever asking how much that chair cost, the one the old man is sitting in, but you can keep that as well, good-bye.

She would have preferred to keep Do out of it, but how can she hide from him that the jewellery has gone, how can she fail to tell him where it has gone and why? She tells him everything. For a week Do whistles a little less and thinks a little more; it will probably end up in a couple of days' hard drinking.

Thys travels to Brussels every morning, the city which advertises in the daily papers for workers, skilled and un-skilled, from the country. *Wanted by bakery, young lad, preferably from the country*, but when Thys applies they have already got someone, or the boy he would have had to replace has changed his mind and is staying after all. Or the boss gives him to understand that he will be taken on, calls his wife to discuss the details with him, and then Thys is sent away by the wife on the pretext that they will write to him at home by the end of the week. For these young lads start their careers at the age of fifteen or sixteen at half the wage, but by the time they reach Thys's age they have to be paid more. A very fat baker's wife, breathless from obesity, tells him blandly that he looks artless enough but that those are the first to get wise to the ways of the world when they get to the city. They soon start pleading their age and their size and keep pestering their boss for a wage rise. 'I'm nineteen, I'm big and strong enough, but they don't add how clumsy they are nor how little they know about the job.'

In the afternoon Thys sits on a seat on the pavement eating his sandwiches. Around him the city is hostile. It exasperates him; passers-by look at him disdainfully or not at all, he is vexed and thinks arrogantly: you'll see if I can't make a go of it here like everyone else. Then again the city becomes a huge, complacent, indifferent monster, all its treasures are spread out, ready for those who are bold enough to grab them. Towards evening the city becomes a dark force, a sea, churning and raging, totally without con-cern for the ships that sail on her. Thys, forlorn, is tossed about. And every evening he goes home feeling like a stranger in a world on which he would bestow his largesse but which snubs him and rejects him.

One day Dina asks him why he is so keen on working in the city. Neither she, nor Do, nor Pol can understand how anyone can spurn their free and easy nest for a city which is only good for visiting occasionally to feast the eye. But Thys has discovered at school, at home and at Ridge Farm that there is no room for boys like him here. Only in the city does he expect to find room.

Then comes the night which casts him loose. Do and Dina arrive home late and stumble into the wrong room by mistake. If I'm not mistaken, says Do, if my eyes aren't deceiving me, we're in the boys' room; we must talk quietly, Dina. Dina asks the boys if they are asleep. Pol is asleep, Thys says nothing. 'Just one more word,' says Do, 'about this business.'

But Dina doesn't want to hear any more words. All the same, Do must say just one last word about it. They giddily hold on to each other, trying not to reel about. Those earrings, were they really given to Thys or did he steal them, that, says Do, is the point. If he's stolen them, he's not my son, if they were given to him, he is. Do looks at Dina, man to woman: answer me this simple question, is Thys my son?

She says: You've always known it.

Thys's heart begins to thump audibly, but how could they hear his heart, those two boozers, as they blather on and on. Dina tries to get Do out of the room. Suddenly he declares loudly, with conviction: 'He's Dolf's.' They seem forever unable to get themselves out of the room. Do has got it into his head to give Thys a kiss and there he comes, surrounding Thys with the smell of beer and he kisses him. This kiss appears to soften Dina. She whispers into her husband's ear, hasn't she given him some fine children. They're getting merry and start chuckling as if they were telling each other jokes. He takes her in his arms and whispers in her ear that he's given her two and she's given him three. This startles her, she pulls him out of the room, but in the narrow corridor she's chuckling again. It sounds as if he's tickling her.

That night Thys packed his clothes. The brown paper crackled too much. He rolled everything in a pair of working day trousers, tied a string round the bundle and his clogs on the string and – Brussels, here comes Thys, for good.

SEVEN

Many years ago Dolf Glorieus had disappeared in the same way, but he vanished completely whereas Thys writes letters. What he doesn't write is that he's had to sleep three nights in the waiting room at North Station, half upright, his elbow leaning on his bundle, because you're not allowed to lie down on those seats; he only writes: dear parents, that he has been able to find work straight away, there is plenty of work in the city. Nor does he write that only by mere chance did he get a job, cycling with a bread cart, because one of the fifteen delivery boys, with whom they hadn't been very satisfied anyway, happened to be away one morning, but dear parents, he has chosen this job on purpose in order to get to know the city and now he is looking out for something more suitable. It is only the very first start, dearest Rosa, but it will keep him going until he goes into the army and as he is now finding out all about commerce and trade and city ways, he'll be able to get a good job as soon as he's finished his time. How is Lett? It's a pity he can't write to her directly, but as he doesn't think she'd be able to read it, would Rosa please be good enough to tell her that she must work hard and do as he has told her, then he will bring her a present from the city.

Jan, the foreman, lives in a little house at the back of the baker's yard. For years he has been studying the financial papers which have kindled a dream in him, of a country boy, arriving in the city young and poor, who will work hard, live sparingly, save much, and come to him, the foreman, with his savings for advice; under his guidance and with careful yet audacious speculation these savings will be multiplied and then, old but still youthful, he will retire to his native village, to a small country house, become an honorary member of the brass-band, an alderman, and take charge of the nest-eggs of the entire parish, as a disinterested adviser.

So now he lets his hand rest benevolently on Thys's shoulder, Thys, who on account of his youth, poverty and origins corresponds exactly to the early stages of his dream. He shows Thys the mottoes he has painted on the walls, after work: 'Work when young, rest when old'; 'Diligence will win'; 'Bake your loaf for later'.

It isn't long before he finds out that Thys washes by the tap every morning and without asking whether he spends the nights sleeping on a bench in the open or at the station, he offers him a little room in the flour loft. He used to sleep there himself when he was a young lad, for he is from the country too, you understand, from a village near Halle.

There are fifteen bread-carts. The worst one is for Thys, so is the most distant round. The first few days Thys makes nothing but futile journeys and the servant girls ask him whether that one with the ginger curls isn't coming any more, that nice one. Before shutting the door slowly in his face they look him up and down, him, the yokel. But winking has no effect on him, he hasn't come here to forget Rosa.

Once he knows his way around and returns to the bakery well before the others to take the extra deliveries, the other fourteen become his enemies.

Their leader is Jef, the oldest, a native of Brussels. He is at least thirty but remains a roundsman from choice, because he can be out and about all day. His wife has a cart too, but she has to push hers on foot. And she has to sell all her herrings, shrimps and snails, shouting herself hoarse, or risk the loss of unsold goods. He has his fixed addresses, no risk, nothing but friends everywhere. The whole town knows him, people start smiling from afar when they see him coming. He asks Thys whether he's hired a taxi by any chance, to pull him along. It won't do, you peasant, have you got that into your thick head?

If he wants to kill himself that's his affair but then let him go and sit in a park for an hour until the others are back, because they're not going to be penalized or ride themselves to death for his sake.

But Jan counts out Thys's first wages and Thys doesn't write that what he is sending home to Dina is his entire wage down to the last centime, nor how much he is having to do without, but he writes, dear parents, that he is sending them what he can spare, by living thriftily, for in the city everything is so expensive, even water. He hopes the money will be welcome, as a small repayment for everything they have done for him from early childhood, oh no, he will never forget it, father and mother. He doesn't write that he earns only a pittance and doesn't even get his board in the large Bakers and Confectioners of Cop & Co. Nor that he lives on leftovers, stale titbits, and now and then a sausage roll which Jan slips into his hand. Late orders coming in by 'phone, which usually aren't accepted, are now carried out by Thys and Jan has counted it all up, including tips. Dearest Rosa, the wages are only a first beginning, but the extra earnings increase every day.

For Jan is in earnest about him. But so is Jef. He slashes one of the tyres of Thys's cart with a knife. Thys chases him all round the kitchen past the ovens, loses him in the half-dark amongst the flour bags, gets a broom flung in his face from somewhere. The bakers roar with laughter but Thys pulls the man by the legs from a pile of firewood and gives him such a thrashing that the united bakers have to come to the rescue.

If it hadn't been for Jan, Thys would have got the sack for this, but now it is Jef who is told to go. Jan is the only one who never could abide that braggart from Brussels. Jef never managed to make him laugh; the crazier his jokes the stonier Jan looked: 'you'll go far with those jokes of yours'. But apart from Jan everyone in the bakery cursed the country bumpkin and in the ten months he has been working here he's had a bag full from that alone.

The foreman has promised him to take him on again after his military service and then he'll be promoted to baker.

One day the bakers send him, with a large box, very urgently, to a back alley somewhere in the Marolles. Thys wonders who could possibly have ordered patisserie here from Cop & Co, Bakers and Confectioners, and at the address he has been given there is only a dried fish hanging beside the door but no bell. The narrow shop window exhibits two crates of herrings, a bowl of mussels in vinegar, three lemons and two jars of salted herrings. Thys goes inside anyway and waits. At last the lamp hanging from the ceiling begins to jingle and sway, someone is coming down the stairs, and it turns out to be Jef. Jef doesn't say much; he opens the box full of goodies, a currant loaf, pastries, and he reads the note which says that here is a present from the bakers and they are sending him the bog-trotter into the bargain so that Jef can beat him up at leisure. Jef roars with laughter and bears no malice. Thys had better come upstairs and have a cup of coffee.

Upstairs it is even worse than in the shop. Beside the stove sits a very old woman with a cat in her lap. Jef calls out to her: gran, this is an old friend of his, he's the one that got him the sack. The old woman looks up at Thys with watery eyes and Thys's heart turns and turns and turns again. 'That is exactly why I have come,' says Thys. 'I'm very sorry it went the way it did; if only I had known.' He allows Jef to slap him cheerfully on the shoulder but he won't let himself be persuaded to change the subject because that would imply that all was forgiven and forgotten. 'It isn't forgiven and forgotten,' says Thys, 'I must make up for it and that's a fact,' and that's the reason why he has come.

Tall, upright, he stands between table and stove, talking about the excellent livelihood he had back at home. He only came to Brussels to learn a trade, but what can you learn at Cop & Co's if you've got to be out on the road all day? So he has been very disappointed but soon he'll be in the army anyway, so what does it matter to him if he sits around at home without a job for a while, he'll hand in his notice so that Jef can have his round back. He boasts that the foreman gives him his way in everything, he shouts into the old woman's ear that Jef will have his old job back, leave it to him, grandma, it's going to be all right. He refuses to eat any of the goodies, buys ten herrings in the shop downstairs which he shares out among the bakers with the compliments of Jef who sends them with many thanks for the pastries.

It's not his fault that Jan doesn't want that braggart from the Marolles back and Jef only has himself to blame for not bothering to come and ask about the job. He has a good reason to stay at home, since grandma can no longer get down the stairs to serve the customers and his wife is out hawking with all the more zeal now that she is the only breadwinner.

But Thys is still waiting for him and, dearest Rosa, he isn't quite sure whether he will go back to Cop & Co after his military service, for he has already learnt quite a lot more about the baker's trade than they think. He finds out about the price of flour and calculates the expenses and the profits. You lose a lot in overheads in a big business like this. If you could do most of the work and supervision yourself you would earn more in proportion. The foreman is almost like a father to him. And how is Lett? Be so kind as to tell her that she must work hard and do what he has told her and then he will bring her a present from the city. And he will bring one for you too, dearest Rosa. Sometimes despondency enters his heart; it is as if he hasn't seen her for years, but she mustn't think that he is unhappy. He works cheerfully day and night and quite understands that she doesn't get round to writing to him. Even though a letter from her would please him very much indeed, he thinks: no tidings, good tidings, and kisses her from afar. He startles at the word kiss, but there it is. Pondering uneasily he puts the letter into the envelope, takes it out again and inserts: hands. I kiss your hands from afar. That is permissible and it is also a sign of good manners.

He doesn't suspect that the schoolmaster has been kissing her at closer quarters.

And not only her hands either.

Yet this schoolmaster is of humble origins too, his father is only a cobbler with a nest full of children. In his own village he never gained the respect of the schoolchildren but now he has proudly given up his job and cycles every day to a village on the outskirts of Brussels. This gives him greater prestige, his father tells anyone who cares to listen that his son has already been appointed as headmaster and at his age too! It is but a small, new school with only two classrooms at present, but the area is growing. Our Karel, says the cobbler; the boy used to be called Charel.

Karel asks Rosa if she has been in love with someone else, because for a long time she didn't want to see him and then all of a sudden she made him so welcome. She asks who could she have been in love with, she has never been away from the farm, never been to a fair or a festival.

It would have had to be somebody at the farm then, that she had been in love with, old Heinke maybe? His wife died recently and he's already got eight kids so they wouldn't need to bother about that side of it.

'Perhaps', says the schoolmaster, 'it was that boy Thys who used to work here.' And she: oh yes, of course, Thys. But she can't laugh and when she tries to add that Thys now cycles around Brussels with a bread-cart it is as if something catches her by the throat, stopping her from mocking the man she is unworthy of, the man she is betraying.

'What's the matter, Rosa, what's wrong?'

'Nothing.'
'Have I said anything wrong?'
'No, not at all.'
What else would be the matter except his letters in which he is so kind and anxious, never mentioning the wrong that was done to him, never suspecting that she is less faithful than he, and he longs for a letter, he writes, but that is still no reason why she should write, I understand, dear Rosa.

She no longer enjoys Karel's kisses and as a result, nor does Karel. She wants him to leave before dark, because she's got work to do, as she says. He goes reluctantly, he finds her capricious; sometimes he is inexplicably weary of her. When he has gone she is cross with herself and irritable, for she knows that as far as Thys is concerned, nothing will ever come of it and yet she cannot teach her blood and every fibre in her body to stop yearning for Thys.

When Thys walks into the yard one fine day she puts a hand on her heart and changes colour several times. Not because he comes with such self-assurance to the farm from which he had been dismissed, nor because she has been unfaithful to him, and Karel might turn up at any moment, but because he appears in the gateway waving with an easy elegance she has never seen, because he is so smartly dressed, so tall. His walk is jauntier, more dashing, no longer the walk of a country boy. He is handsome, his voice has deepened. Hello Rosa, he says, inclining his right shoulder to shake hands with her. He asks, how are things, he goes indoors to say hello to everybody, but in the kitchen there are only Lett and her father. They are both asleep, the one with her head on the table, the other in Thys's old present. The farmer asks him who he is, and when he's been told, what he has come for, they have already got another farmhand. Lett looks at him with bleary eyes as if she doesn't know him. 'Who am I?' asks Thys. She: 'Thys.' He bends over her. Has she been beaten many times while he has been away? 'Yes.' 'Who by?' 'By everybody.' Hasn't she got a nicer dress than this one for Sundays? 'Yes.' 'Then go and put it on right away and wear it every Sunday from now on.' She has already got up from her chair.

The farmer shouts as loudly as is still in his power: we've already got someone else, go home.

Thys goes outside. He sees the schoolmaster jumping from his bike while still at the gate, and he is hardly a timid visitor. He walks straight up to Rosa and kisses her, before she has time to ward him off. Then he swiftly looks around, sensing something unusual, and perceives Thys in the doorway. Thys, not wishing to disturb them, goes back into the kitchen and the farmer shouts more angrily than before: we've already got someone else, I've told you, go home! There is nowhere for Thys to be, neither inside nor outside, not here, not at home, not in Brussels; he is being snarled at from his own wheelchair which has never been paid for, his present to the farmer's wife, not the farmer. He has no one left but Lett, the only one who does not reject his generosity. She lets him put the string of glass beads round her neck, sticks her hand through the imitation gold bracelet and he feels well rewarded when she shows all her teeth in a smile, for her teeth at least are beautiful.

He takes her for a walk, not in the fields, not looking for secret spots but in the spirit of her mother, to Benediction. He tells her the things her mother used to say to him when he was a boy. Ruefully he declares that life is a dismal business, honestly, you can believe him, he knows the world, in the city you find out so much. 'A human being,' says Thys, 'needs faith to comfort him.' He remembers these words, they were said to him by the farmer's wife, but the Glorieuses have never had much to say about faith. They'll have to die of something, like everyone else, but it certainly won't be of an excess of faith. Thys screws up his eyes trying to remember what else the woman told him on the subject. 'People must be kind to each other,' says Thys, 'and how can they be kind if they don't believe in anything, you understand that, don't you, Lett, so that just shows,' says Thys, 'how important it is to have faith. Does Rosa go out with that schoolmaster much?'

'Yes.'

'You see,' says Thys, without batting an eyelid, 'she's a nice respectable girl, so, naturally, respectable boys are interested in her. And that's how it will be with you if you go on being a nice, respectable girl. Your mother was always very anxious about you and she can see you from heaven, don't forget. Do they cuddle a lot, she and that schoolmaster, I mean, haven't you ever been out with boys yet?'

'No, Thys.'

'Good. You be careful, I'm telling you. With a respectable boy it would be different, I wouldn't mind them. Is there anyone, perhaps, that you're fond of?'

She smiles almost imperceptibly with soft full lips.

'You shouldn't mind telling me about it, you can tell me everything, you must tell me even, your mother wanted you to. I can see that you're fond of someone. Who is it?'

'You.'

'Me,' says Thys, startled, 'you are fond of me?'

'Yes.'

'Because we've always been together perhaps, from when we were children, but surely not like husband and wife, surely not to marry?'

'Yes.'

'What are we to do about you,' says Thys, 'is there never a word of sense to be got out of you? Don't you know it isn't decent what you're saying? Have you ever heard of a girl who takes the first step herself? How do you think you're ever going to get married if you behave like this? I'll be stuck with you.'

He carefully explains to her the ins and outs of these things. It's the boy who should first declare his love for her, and not just once but hundreds of times. And then she shouldn't be too quick to say yes. A respectable girl should be a bit shy, she blushes, she smiles a little and sweetly turns her head to one side. 'Like this,' says Thys, 'this is what they do.' He slants his good-natured face to one side, looks down at his nose and pulls his mouth in a timid pout. Boys understand that, they'll know that she doesn't mean to say no. But of course, you should never do that to someone you don't love, oh no, not just to anyone, you should never deceive anyone. And then, when he has asked many times, many many times, because if you love someone you should put him to the test, only then will a respectable girl put her arms round his neck, but she still doesn't bluntly say yes. It's much better to say nothing at all, but only to kiss him so lovingly that he feels: yes, she loves me. That's how it should be. And when you do say yes, you say it softly, a bit shyly. But really, Lett is a big girl now, why should he, a boy, have to teach her all this, is she going to remain a child forever?

Isn't there anyone else she is fond of, think hard about it, a bit of fondness is enough, the rest comes later, all of its own.

'No.'

'Well, anyway,' says Thys, 'I'm not going to take any notice of what you've been saying, that was child's talk, I don't even listen to it. A girl doesn't propose to a boy. As long as I haven't proposed to you, nothing has been proposed. So you're still free, remember, because one day there may be someone else.'

'I don't want anyone else.'

'That's silly talk,' says Thys. 'When is Rosa getting married?'

Lett doesn't know.

The days go too slowly for Thys. He doesn't want to visit the farm again, he wants to spare Rosa the embarrassment and it is better for Lett not to see him, she must forget him. At home, the food eaten in idleness has no taste. His parents, tolerating him, a stranger, burden him with a gratefulness that weighs too heavily upon him and when mother, unable to conceal that he is her favourite, shows him kindness, he glances uneasily at father to see if it vexes him,

When at last the time comes for him to leave, Dina prepares him a box of food, but he deliberately forgets it and has taken only half the money she gave him.

EIGHT

Officers know how to choose their batmen from the tall, quiet country boys who stand their ground, who are punctual and willing to serve. The captain who chooses Thys looks like a giant with powerful moustaches, but that is all. For the rest he is 'mon ami', that's what they call him. He always makes sure of having a batman from his own native region, but never from his own village because his brother is still gamekeeper there with the count who paid for his education.

It was at the castle of this count that he made the acquaintance of the beautiful daughter of a rich industrialist whose mother was somehow related to the aristocracy. She saw him, sighed, and fell in love with him. His appearance, voice and uniform had turned her head hopelessly and when he took pains to avoid her, reflecting that his brother always carried the hares shot by her father in the hunting season, she made up her mind that she must have him. The usual drama of family resistance precipitated the matter and before they had quite realized what was happening, they were married. Four years later they had four beautiful children. They were madly fond of them, and the captain, who had never been used to much social life would spend the whole evening playing on the floor with the toddlers, rolling across the carpet to his wife's chair, kissing her ankle, stroking her leg, and whispering: I want ten kiddies like this. She, however, missed her past life and suddenly resumed it. He was so used to letting her have her way in everything that they began to grow apart without him being aware of it. When he finally realized it, he attached himself even more to the children, playing with them, making hobby-horses, chairs, tables for them and cutting out harlequins. When it was too late, he occasionally let himself be dragged along by his wife to parties, but they bored him and he stopped going. When it was altogether too late they quarrelled and argued until they finally gave each other up for lost.

The quarrels had alienated the children from him because mother is always in the right. And besides, whenever presents arrived they were always from mother's family and it was with mother's family that they spent their holidays. On Sundays he could no longer take them to his brother who still lived in the gamekeeper's cottage, but from their way of never mentioning the village he knew what they thought of it. He retreated into his study, emerging only at meal-times, silent and absent-minded. The children saw this as pitiful boorishness, a rusticity he could not be cured of, proof of his inferiority.

He threw himself on books with the fresh eagerness of a tribe that has never been used to reading. He started with novels and read anything that came into his hands, haphazardly, without preference or discrimination, good ones and poor ones. He soon tired of them and looked for greater excitement; nothing would do but detective stories, but suddenly he tired of these too. Just as he had started on the one hundred and twentieth story he threw it aside, the first book he had thrown aside in his life, and felt bored for the rest of the evening. When his wife came home he wept, he complained, and then everything was going to be as it had been in the beginning. But even the next day he realized that it was no use, and again, he sat at home feeling bored. But the next day he went out and bought a different kind of book: *La femme dans l'art, La femme et l'amour, Le problème sexuel, Perversités antiques, Le nu.* These bored him even more quickly than the thrillers. One evening he began to write: *Mémoires d'un suicide.*

Mes chers enfants, why this book? Do I know it myself? Why do I ask myself this question? Read it and when you have read it, tell me whether or not I did right to write it.

I was born, mes chers enfants . . . He really did not know why he was writing it but it would have to become an autobiography and without thinking very much about it, it seemed inconceivable to him that his life could end in any other way but suicide. But when he had described how happy he had been in the little crooked cottage on the edge of the wood, when he had written in great detail about the games they used to play as children, making bonfires, going birds'-nesting, burning out wasps' nests, when he had explained how to recognize nightingales, blackbirds, finches, golden orioles by their wingbeat, how to make whistles, pop-guns, spinning tops, why to make a first-class bow you should leave the wood in the cesspit for a year, how his father and brother had kept watch by the body of an old witch who wore thirteen jackets teeming with lice and how they had peeled these garments off one by one with a pocket-knife, how he would never forget the summer mornings when the lark rose, singing, from the patch of corn in front of their house, and when after all this he had to start writing about his student years, he lost interest in it. He abandoned it and bought books on philosophy.

He searched and searched until Montaigne, Rousseau, Diderot, Voltaire finally gave him satisfaction.

'Venez, mon ami.' He introduced Thys to his wife and children. Madame. Monsieur Paul who is a student at the university. Monsieur Maurice, also a student at the university. Mademoiselle Irène, who studies at the conservatory and Mademoiselle Corinne who studies at the academy of art. Madame was so beautiful and proud that Thys immediately looked at the ground. They all stood up politely. They knew that papa demanded it, but no one spoke and they were cross. For the hundredth time they heard papa say that this was a young man from his province. At this point he always said a few sentences in broad Brabant dialect and then he would laugh heartily, for he loved talking dialect.

'Thys, quel nom est-ce donc, what kind of a name is that?' asks Madame, to cut him short, and appears somewhat relieved to hear from Maurice that it is the same name as the perfectly pronounceable Mathieu. 'We'll call him Mathieu then,' but the captain declares that he will go on calling him Thys.

And then there are the maids in the kitchen. Madame, they tell him, is a vixen, Monsieur is a good chap. So is Paul, but not Maurice. Corinne is crazy and Irène has a lovely voice. 'Can I do anything?' asks Thys. They give each other a quick glance, put the shoes of the entire family, including their own, in front of him and Thys starts polishing. They tell him that tomorrow he can turn the mangle, and expect him to curse, but he replies that he'll make sure to finish work in good time tomorrow, he doesn't think there will be any difficulty.

One by one they began to get the measure of Thys, the maids first of all. They were allowed to take Sundays off in turns, but they never stood in for each other, because they were never able to agree. But one of them, a girl from Brussels, knew how to handle men. She kept yawning, combing her hair and stretching herself in front of the mirror, out of boredom, hoping that Thys would be obliging, but Thys was absorbed in the newspaper. Then she went at it straight: she sat on his knee. Did he have to go out today? She did, you see. Would he be a very nice boy and stay at home, she promised to be back early. In less than a minute Thys had agreed, was rewarded with a kiss, and she hurried upstairs to change, even that didn't take long; 'see you soon, darling.'

When all is silent the captain comes out of his study, a quiet man with a curved pipe. 'We're the home guard, mon ami.'

Together they go out into the garden and look at the grass, with their hands in their pockets like all Brabant peasants. They talk about the quality of the soil, the fertilizers it needs. The captain's heart opens out. He solemnly forecasts rain and speaks with solicitude about the land which has had far too much rain already. And then Thys has to come and join him in the study. He is given a new pipe and through the clouds they speak dialect. It does him such a wealth of good, mon ami.

He laughs at some of the quaint words he had forgotten and talks of Anneke the witch. Two men from his village, people he knows very well indeed, people who don't lie, he'll swear to it, were keeping watch by her body. At midnight they heard a brass band playing in the attic, the coffin started dancing up and down and the door, which had been locked and barred, kept blowing open. But Thys doesn't believe in witchcraft, magic doesn't exist. The captain blows rings of smoke: 'nothing exists, mon ami.' Thys is startled; this was the sound of sorrow. He doesn't know why he thinks so and bursts out in loud laughter for he has never heard anything like it, sir. Nothing exists? Nothing, says the captain. He gets up, screws up his eyes, yawns, but not really, stretches himself, a splendid Hercules; 'nothing exists, mon ami. Fill another pipe and set your mind at rest.' Thys smokes, dumbfounded and dejected.

'Sir,' says Thys, 'you are unhappy.' This time the captain bursts out laughing. We won't start philosophizing. Has Thys got any egg shells at home? What does a golden oriole's egg look like? And a quail's egg? And a woodpecker's? 'When I was a little boy I once had a magpie, mon ami . . .'

The members of the household come home late. As soon as the first one rings the doorbell the captain says: 'See you next time.' He dismisses Thys, puts his chair against the wall and opens a book in front of him, like a schoolboy scared of being caught out.

On the first floor there is an annex of two interconnecting rooms. The first one was formerly the children's playroom, the second was used as a bedroom when one of the four was ill. The first one is now an untidy store room with baskets, chests and two dismantled cupboards, but Madame insists on the second room remaining untouched. She spent many a night on the couch which stands at right angles to a pretty little child's cot. The anxious hours of her life, when her husband and children still filled it, were spent in that room. There is a small writing desk with a wall cupboard above it which still serves as a medicine cabinet. She used to sit here writing letters to her husband, sometimes two a day, when he was away with his regiment and had no peace because of the sick child.

Thys has discovered this room to write letters to his parents and to Lett, because this requires peace and quiet. When all is silent, when he has finished all the work he has been able to find, he steals away to that little room to write his grave, ponderous letters. Three times all goes well but the fourth time the couch is occupied by Monsieur Paul and the servant girl from Brussels. Monsieur Paul asks him sternly what he is doing here. His tone leaves no doubt that not he, but Thys is at fault.

Everybody has discovered that little room. It is the most heavily used room in the whole house. Monsieur Maurice and the Flemish maid make frequent use of it. Mademoiselle Irène disappears to it with strangers from the musical world, Mademoiselle Corinne with merry companions from the noble world of art. When Madame feels depressed and needs a good cry, she retires to this little room where she has cried and sighed so often in the past. If one of the servant girls ever needs to hide her Jef from her Louis in a hurry, she ushers him in here. There are even times when the captain, listless and bored, shuffles around the house on hairy slippers in search of a hideout where he can feel even more secluded than in his study. Then he will end up in that little room; he cannot even go to the attic any longer since Corinne has turned it into a studio and it doesn't occur to him that the smell of his sweet cigars will hang around for two weeks. It is really quite amazing that anyone is ever safe in this room and that Thys has managed to write three letters in a row without being disturbed. But before long he surprises Monsieur Maurice with the youngest maid and Mademoiselle Corinne with a boy whose hair is as long as hers. None of them seem in the least embarrassed, but they give Thys a penetrating look as if the family's fortune was hidden somewhere between the medicine bottles and they suspect him of having designs on it. On his next visit he catches Monsieur Paul again, but this time with the other girl, Monsieur Maurice's girl. Why oh why don't they bother to answer when Thys modestly, prudently, knocks at the door, but no, they say nothing, but quickly sit up side by side, as respectably as two canons in the sanctuary, wait till Thys unsuspectingly opens the door and then ask him with that sharp look in their eyes: what have you come to steal? He, the righteous one!

If only he had written his letters elsewhere, anywhere, because in all other respects this is a house like any other. People eat well, in a convivial atmosphere. At table the chilly silence between husband and wife is no more unusual than in other families. The indifference of four grown-up children towards each other is not unusual either. The conversation is casual and easygoing. There is even a special kind of gaiety in this house, all the more spontaneous and carefree for being less constrained, less binding. It is only by having entered that little nursery room, quite gratuitously, that Thys is now seized by dismay, at living in a house of immorality, a house that creaks in all its joints and hinges. He wonders whether the captain is aware of all these goings on and whether he approves. And what about Madame! To the captain he daren't say anything because the poor man has enough troubles and in Madame he has no confidence. She is rarely at home and when she is, she busies herself with the maids, appearing imperiously in the kitchen and sowing fright wherever she looks or points her finger, but with her husband's batmen she will have nothing to do. She knows he takes a great deal of notice of them, too much, and she takes it out on them by stubborn surliness. To her, the girls have names: Alice do this, Marie do that; the batman hasn't. Orders without form of address are for him: go and fetch coal, post this letter at once. Thys doesn't even entertain the thought that he might unburden his heart to her.

And yet this is what she once did to him. She was alone at home with Mademoiselle Irène while Thys was quietly polishing the brass stair rods. In the drawing-room Irène shouted something very loudly, came running down the stairs and dashed out of the house. Madame appeared in the door and watched her go. She probably hadn't realized that Thys was sitting in the hall and obviously thought he might have overheard something. 'Venez ici,' she said, and when Thys stood to attention she asked: 'est-ce que . . .' but could not say more. She burst out in violent sobs, but stopped abruptly, staring furiously at him, clenching two chubby fists, but as she raised them they opened to cover her face. The sobbing resumed with renewed vigour and she seemed about to collapse weakly against the wall. Respectfully Thys lent her his support and for one moment her head rested on his shoulder. Thys did not move a muscle, but gritted his teeth. She pulled herself together, told him to go away and slammed the door of the drawing-room behind her.

If she had not after that made him atone for her momentary weakness, day after day, with even brusquer naughtiness than before, Thys might have shown a little weakness towards her in return. He might have confided in her, just for this once, in spite of his misgivings about her way of life. Where could she always be going? He did not much like her being driven home by liveried chauffeurs. He had seen enough by now to know how rotten high society was: who knows what Madame was up to? It was small wonder that the captain despairingly wrung his hands and said that nothing, absolutely nothing, existed.

Thys had landed in a world so full of disorder that he was at a loss to know where and how to begin.

The lesser world of the servants did not seem any better. These girls were careful to pick their evening so as to give their sweethearts a good time. They prepared small banquets, no less. Generous portions of chicken with salad and fried potatoes, wine to go with it, and followed by luscious cream cakes. Thys burned with indignation, it was downright theft. He didn't like the look of those two fellows at all. They wore creaking yellow shoes and were victims of the mutual rivalry between the two girls who fussed and nagged them till each had bought whatever the other had. One day they even turned up with identical walking sticks. They never took their hands out of their pockets, which were set far to the front on their thighs, until they sat down to their half-chicken. There hung a festive smell in the kitchen. Thys asked, with a stony expression, if Madame was paying for all this. They said yes, but he wasn't reassured. They picked up their chicken by the leg. The fat ran down their chins. They stuffed the potatoes whole into their mouths together with a large lettuce leaf and then they couldn't speak for a time. There was enough for Thys too, but he curtly declined. The girls helped to finish off the cream cakes and they weren't averse to the wine either. Presently things kept dropping on the floor and were picked up, providing opportunities to pinch the sweetheart's knee. Then the cigars were brought out. Perhaps they really had bought them, as they emphasized to Thys, but whether or not they had, they were the captain's brand.

Thys paced up and down the corridor. He knew his weakness and watched over himself; he walked up to the kitchen door with clenched fists behind his back, stretched out a hand to the doorknob, to chuck the two rascals out into the street with a clout and a thump, but thought better of it, reminding himself that he couldn't be sure of his case, and continued his restless pacing. Perhaps they *had* paid for it themselves, perhaps Madame *did* know all about it and turned a blind eye, perhaps the two young Messieurs paid the girls in return for their silence. He went down to the cellar and counted the bottles of wine so that at least he would be sure the next time. And indeed, when the next time came he was sure, and he mentioned it to the youngest maid first. Yes, she replied, the trouble was, in the beginning they

had spoilt their boyfriends far too much. If they now started
to stint the food there would be ill-feeling. But this cut no ice
with Thys. Ill feeling or good feeling, what they were doing
was theft and it should stop forthwith. She looked dolefully
at her feet and blushed. 'We wouldn't like them not to come
any more, Mathieu. You must think what it's like, a country
girl, all alone in the city, in service in a house like this, with
Madame always nagging and the others treating you like a
slave, Monsieur is the only one who is kind to us, and if you
then haven't got anybody to go out with sometimes in the
evenings, and talk, what kind of a life is that?' She gives
Thys her sweetest look out of the corner of her eye: she
won't marry that Fons anyway.

Thys is still as puzzled as before. How can she go and sit
in the nursery with Monsieur Maurice; it can't be because
she wants to deceive her sweetheart, so it seems, because he
only *thinks* he is her sweetheart, or does he think she is only
pretending and does he only come here to eat chicken, drink
wine and do with her what she will let him do? But before
honest Thys has disentangled this knot, she is nudging him
roguishly and asking him if he is jealous by any chance.
There's no need to be jealous, it's only kids' play. One day
she will marry a serious boy. But if she thinks she can lure
Thys away from his duty by womanly wiles, she is mistaken.
She may marry whom she likes, but those chickens are
stolen goods and so is the wine, stolen goods. If Madame
allows them to have these parties, well and good, but then
they ought to ask her first. That said, Thys walks off.

NINE

The second maid, forewarned by the first that the parson is
going to spill the beans, doesn't attempt to reason with

Thys. Two or three times he broaches the subject but each time she has just got to dash upstairs to 'do' a room. Thys is left standing. She tries to fob him off with a razor which Monsieur Paul had given her as a present for her sweetheart, but here, you can have it, it's yours, Thys. Far from mollifying Thys, it deepens his suspicion. Why doesn't she give that razor to her Louis, assuming, says Thys, it really and truly was a present, and he gives her a penetrating look. She ogles him with her sweetest, most innocent expression. Her next attack is an attempt at bribing him with wine, left over from dinner. Madame had told her specially to keep it for the batman, but Thys doesn't believe her glib talk any more. He feels like a big clumsy bulldog, she is a dangerous little cat. In the corridor she slithers past him with a large tray in her hands, and pushing the door shut with her bottom so that he can't get past, she offers him her daintily pursed mouth. Or she tells him he is needed in Monsieur Paul's room to help her turn a heavy mattress, but she doesn't get anywhere with him. Thys will find himself a girl some day and he won't do things by halves either, but he is not having a shopsoiled one, nor will he be bribed into complicity with injustice.

As he broods about all this iniquity to which he cannot resign himself and as he tries to think up the most impossible ways of bringing about some kind of order which satisfies his integrity, the maids have already made up their minds, long before the others, that he is useless. They exploit him as they have exploited his predecessors; naïve country boys all of them, they put up with anything. But none of them put up with as much as Thys. Now they try to get at him in a different way. Madame is told what a boorish, stubborn peasant they have got about the house now. He meddles in everything. If he had his way they would never eat anything but potatoes and vinegar sauce. Leftovers that would have gone bad anyway, that would have been thrown in the dustbin (and doesn't Madame herself always say that it's better to eat it rather than let it go bad?) are stolen goods, according to him. Oh Madame, you should hear him carrying on about it, a parson is nothing beside him. No, Madame, if he's going to stay here, the job is hard enough already, they'll have to start looking for something else.

The two young gentlemen are given a different explanation. Did they know why that parson kept coming to the door of the nursery? To spy on them. To tell their papa about it all, no doubt, at least he's always trying to creep into their papa's good graces. Before they know where they are, their papa will have another tantrum, like last time. By this they mean the captain's last frantic attempt to reclaim the role of father and master in his own house. Not a tactical move but rather a desperate bid. Banging on the table so that everything clattered and rattled, snapping at his wife, threatening his children, until finally, trembling with rage, he had taken his diary and written out a provisional set of rules. Point one: Nobody to come home after midnight. Point two: Three nights' absence automatically means exclusion. He wrote it down, jumped to his feet and shouted: and he will never darken this door again, I swear it! He sat down again and went on writing: point three: Each year's course will be paid twice only. No more third rounds for anyone. Finished. Point four: I must be told the names of anyone entering the house. No more unwanted guests.

Here the trembling became so bad that he could write no more. He stood up. If he had to do the ultimate, if he had to make a whip, a scourge, to flog them with, all of them, until they learnt in fear and trembling what their conscience had failed to instil in them, he would do it. And now he will calmly write down his plan, a complete code of conduct, and within two days each one of them will be given a copy.

It wasn't his fault, he said, that he, who had always been the most outstanding student both in behaviour and achievement, was now blessed with four children so dim that if *they* had been born in a poor man's hut like their father they wouldn't even have that left by the time they died. Blockheads, dilettanti, narrowminded nincompoops. But even the most wretched dog can obey and that is what he will demand of them, and if they don't know how to behave he will teach them, the way you teach dogs, military fashion, with the whip.

After all this he was still at boiling point, as happens with quiet people who only fly off the handle once every ten years and then get drunk on their rage. He would have gone on haranguing them much longer but for the way the youngest, the artist, looked at him. Not in fear but curiously, scrutinizingly, attentively, no doubt she looks at her models in that way, sharply observing a particularly expressive posture.

The captain fell silent, took a few faltering steps, blowing like over-pumped organ bellows when the music suddenly stops, and left the room. His sudden departure did not spoil the impression he had made on his audience, but instead of needing many weeks to develop a growing feeling of shame, he now felt ashamed at once. It seemed to him that he had taken the last step on the road to absolute pessimism and had reached the final point. Everything is useless, purposeless. Nothing exists. Man is lonely. Human society is held together by a host of senseless conventions: by truisms, duties, rights.

And now Thys challenges him, as a first start. Husband and wife should make peace with each other, says Thys. The children must accept their parents' authority and obey them. Together they can then take the servants in hand and teach them discipline and honesty. Happiness is there for the taking and Thys will hand it to them. He looks at the disillusioned man with guileless simplicity.

'Sir, I've thought hard about it but I still cannot understand how such a good and learned man as you can say that nothing exists. You exist,' says Thys, 'I exist. You can't deny that. Madame exists. Your four children exist. You're a captain in the army. Your house exists. You're rich. Your wealth exists. What more do you want? If you can't be happy no one can.'

Splendid, mon ami, laughs the captain, that's the way we talk in Brabant and very good talk it is, too. How about a cigar now? My grandmother always used to say that nothing is so easy as being happy, as long as you're happy with what you've got. I daresay your grandmother used to say the same, mon ami. Everybody back home says that. But then a child leaves home and goes away to study. He believes whatever they tell him, he becomes very knowledgeable, mon ami, but not wise. He sits with his nose in books, in ideas, he ponders, and thinks and reasons, but he doesn't live, because living is growing wiser. Life hits him on the nose; you remember the way they drive a cow or a bull along the road, back home? People are tapped on the nose in exactly the same way; they think and reason and when they've thought and reasoned right up to the very end, when they've thought and reasoned themselves empty, then they come back to what they were told in their childhood by simple, honest people. Do you understand me, mon ami, or don't you?

All Thys said was yes, there was no need for more, the captain is fond of soliloquizing.

And now I'll explain the difference to you, mon ami. For the purpose of living, we educated people know no more than simple folk and in many respects much less. They believe that outside the world they know there is another world which they don't know, and they believe in it, they trust in it. But we have seen that world and we know that it's nothing. Do you understand?

Yes. But Thys doesn't understand a thing, except that reasoning is a sad business. There's never an end to it and it is exhausting. You can prove anything with it, the maddest things best of all. He shakes his head disconsolately; the captain may be very learned, he says, but he will never believe that learned people know less than simple people. The rich say that money doesn't make you happy, people say that even the king is not content. No one is content. Learned people aren't content either. But they just say it to keep us ignorant.

'On the contrary, mon ami, the people must be educated.'

Here Thys senses the contradiction again. Education doesn't make a man wiser and yet the people must be educated. He asks for an explanation and receives a long lecture. Education of the masses is progress, liberation. This is such a slow process that some people can't even notice it and therefore deny its existence, whereas others can't notice it either but believe in it all the same. The captain is one of those who believe in it and it is a fact that backward people like the Flemish can grow so fast for a time that you can actually see it happening, until they have made up for lost time and then, mon ami, finish!

He smiles at Thys's helplessness and starts on another lecture. Why do we progress so slowly? Because we've got the past like a millstone round our neck. Discovering new things is easy enough but getting rid of the obsolete is a different matter. Look, he says, I want to do in one generation what it would take the world five hundred years to achieve. He explains at length. He needs a desert island and a group of children. He'll educate them. He will answer three questions: where do we come from, where are we, where are we going. The answers to the first and third questions: in the past everybody used to pretend they knew but nobody can know. Finish, not another word about it. Answer to the second question: we are here in a world which we should try to understand as best we can and which we should make as happy as we can for everybody.

Thys says yes! Thys looks round the room, trying to see where the light comes from which is pouring over him from all directions. Yes, says Thys, more loudly. He gets up from his chair, uplifted by a great emotion for which he has no words. Mon ami looks at him in surprise.

And fetches a bottle. No more philosophizing now. How far is Cobbezeele from Ternalfergem? When he was young he used to walk it in an hour and a quarter. Is that inn called Halfway House still there?

So they talk about Brabant, in dialect, all evening long. Mon ami laughs at every little thing. Later, when it is nearly time for the others to come home, he says that it was Thys who started talking philosophy and that he should not go on brooding any more. He only meant to say this, mon ami: when he leaves the army, a little while from now, he must go home, get himself a decent job, a nice healthy wife, and try to be content. There's nothing else worth bothering about. A good dinner on the table, a good bed to sleep in. And then, mon ami, come and visit me from time to time and I'll come and visit you too. Let me know when the pig is killed and I'll come to the tripe feast. He makes a half-turn and swears bitterly: nom de dieu. What's come over the poor man? Suddenly he laughs again. 'A soldier who thinks too much, boy oh boy, what shall we do with him?' His laugh bellows. He lights his meerschaum. The match trembles in his hand.

Then his thoughts leap to something else. He calls the Flemish people the North Belgian people. Talking of thinking, the North Belgians have never done any thinking; they have always simply believed.

Of course this is very interesting too, he won't deny it, mon ami, he's not a fanatic. But if ever they should start doing any thinking, that would be a good deal more interesting. Perhaps they would even begin to play some sort of role in Europe, as in the past. Only perhaps, mind you, no need to exaggerate.

On another evening he is quietly philosophizing about beauty and health. His gestures become delicate when he speaks of the beauty of animals. But human beings! Go and stand by the entrance to any church, theatre or station and see what they look like. Sixty percent of them are ugly, ninety percent are sick. He grimaces, as if he was in pain, and lists the squalid complaints of humankind: piles, obesity, varicose veins and on top of that, he says, we all have a touch of syphilis or a touch of consumption in our blood. He gives a slight shudder. And paints a picture of a healthy, happy, blooming human race. As before, Thys eagerly looks for a new light, but mon ami's thoughts are shifting again.

'Thys, you have two parents, four grandparents, eight great-grandparents, sixteen great-great-grandparents, thirty-two whatever they are called, and so on. Your ancestors double every twenty-five years or so. What I mean is this, we all have the same origins.' He gives Thys a sharp look, to see if he appreciates the full weight of this argument, with which his pride surmounts the humiliations suffered in his family, but Thys interprets it differently.

'I get your point,' says Thys. 'We're all one big family. The world', says Thys, 'must be like one big family, that's what I think.'

Then the artist daughter starts buttonholing him, there's always something! It's making him dizzy. He has noticed that the others are treating him even more coldly than before, so why should she get it into her head to talk nicely to him all of a sudden? Her brothers' sharp remarks against that big lump of a peasant draw her attention to the tall, quiet soldier. No slave could be more helpful, more modest. She finds him, when called, always ready to fetch anything, anyone, anywhere. And yet there's nothing soft about him. His faithful eyes look at you astutely as if they can see things that escape others. Papa's batmen are usually artless country bumpkins who try to behave like soldiers but feel like servants. This one is the most obliging servant of them all, but he has a strange dignity about him, a streak of independent strength. She loves the way he stands: looking into the room as if from a height: what's wrong here, I shall create order here.

She makes Thys happy by not passing in front of him as if she didn't see him when he holds the door open for her, but greeting him boyishly instead, with a brief nod and a wink. One day she says with a gesture towards the kitchen: 'you're out of favour, aren't you?' 'It doesn't matter, mademoiselle Corinne.' Then she sends Thys on errands; to buy a few tubes of paint or a piece of canvas, and one afternoon when

she is sitting in her studio painting a lobster, Thys enters
with two picture frames and she asks him whether he has
ever tasted lobster. No, mademoiselle. She says that this lobster has only been lying here since yesterday, it must still be
edible, go on, take it. The painting ends up on the floor and
together they eat the lobster after Thys has cracked its shell.
She sits opposite him with her legs crossed, receiving the
pieces with an open hand and stuffing them into her mouth;
she gives him a friendly nod and winks with both eyes:
'What have they got against you, teddybear?' He quickly
reverses the roles. Not he should be comforted, he is there
in order to protect others. So he starts telling lies. It looks as
if mademoiselle is pitying him. Good God, if only she knew
how little he cared. Ever since he was a little boy he has been
used to being kicked around and ill-treated. Once they had
to carry him home from school on a stretcher, half dead.
They had to work hard for three hours with vinegar and
artificial respiration to bring him round. Yes, honestly. Once
he was nearly strangled by the farmer he worked for because
the farmer's wife had given him some jewellery, worth five
thousand francs, on her deathbed. And after she was dead
they said he had stolen the jewellery. Later still he went to
work in a bakery where they didn't even give him his food.
It's too long a story to tell and anyway, rich people's children don't understand things like that, but he can assure
mademoiselle that he has never had such a good life as here.
A paradise it is.

Bending forward with his elbows on his knees, he cracks
the empty shells. She looks at his thick, closely planted hair
and says she supposes he must be a socialist. 'No.' Pause.
'As for me,' she says, 'I'm an anarchist.' He feels oppressed
as if she had told him she had secretly murdered somebody.
He doesn't know what an anarchist is and he daren't ask.
Not that it matters, for soon enough she starts trotting out
her theories. All the big bosses ought to have their heads cut
off, militarism and money should be abolished, all cities
should be burnt down and then: back to nature!

Close in front of her eyes rises Thys's alarmed face. Is that anarchism? She replies: 'I'm a terrorist as well' and Thys turns deathly pale although he doesn't know the meaning of that word either. She roars with laughter and roughly grabbles in his hair with both hands. Her flushed face approaches his, with clenched teeth. 'Poor duffer, they beat you and you let them do it. What a dirty world this is. It's because of teddybears like you that I want to put dynamite under it. I can't bear injustice.'

This puts a finger on Thys's wound. 'Nor can I,' says Thys.

'Do you hate it so too?'

'What, mademoiselle?'

'What? This whole filthy world.'

No, says Thys, and he doesn't understand why she pushes him away by the hair. To her he represents the dumb masses who do not understand, who endure and have no courage to stand up for themselves. To him she is one of the decadent members of this household full of nutcases and dissolutes and he does not know where and how to start his rescue work.

At night he wears himself out, brooding. He does not understand. Sometimes he sees the world as dominated by thoughts. He tries to disentangle them but never succeeds. He would like to go to the captain and tell him to stop thinking, it serves no useful purpose. Then he will discover love, which rules everything. The captain should sleep with Madame again, then everything will change for the better. He would like to make a soft bed for everyone in this house and say to them: look, this is what I have done for you, so now you can all stop jostling each other. No more pushing and shoving. But each time his insights fade again, he keeps discovering new thoughts. The world is divided between rich people who are not happy and poor people who would be happy if only they were rich.

Let the captain go and weave baskets if he thinks that life is so wonderful in Brabant and that simple folk are so much better off. Do Glorieus won't mind changing places with him, it won't bother him to know all the things the captain knows. Thys will go and study at the university and he won't take two years over each year's course. For hours and hours he ponders over the captain's assertion that nothing exists and tries to see the sense in mademoiselle Corinne's anarchism.

He no longer covets the little nursery to write his letters. On a corner of the kitchen table he writes in slow, elegant curves and loops: If you look around you in the big world, dear parents, you see people who are far less happy than us. There's nothing special about the way the rich live, and it's all very well to say that rich people who have the cheek to complain don't deserve their luck, but I think they ought to be pitied and I wish there was something we could do about it, because we're all of us such bunglers, but what can we do about it, it makes my heart bleed, I can tell you.

In the evening Do Glorieus rereads the letter which Dina has spelt out to herself at least ten times, with tearful eyes. The same big words as Uncle Dolf, always busy with higher things that should be no concern of his, and why doesn't he write any news? Why doesn't he write like Pol who tells them how many pigs they kill every week and one cow and one calf and how much the price of meat is rising? And that there has been an accident, a girl of fifteen has been run over and killed instantly, and he's not coming home this Sunday, the mistress has asked him to drive her to Weerde where there is going to be a procession and she doesn't like sitting in trains. She prefers to sit with Pol in the gig. Don't worry about Pol, he'll be all right.

TEN

Thys cannot give up, with tenacious patience he keeps coming back to the same point. Sir, he's thought about it a bit more; surely you can't deny that there is a God. Mon ami puts his fists to his ears: Crash! Yes, why not start with the easiest bit; per aspera ad astra! He tries to avoid the village philosopher. He is used to those dependable country boys whose hearts open out because their captain is a good chap with whom they can talk about the people at home, about the things that interest them. When he dropped those despondent remarks of his they understood nothing but that the poor man was married to a Jezebel and had four good-for-nothing children and that these were the causes of his undeserved unhappiness. They thought he was merely airing his sorrow in vague terms; they listened sympathetically enough and tried to distract him with jokes. But this brooder here wouldn't leave off; either he wanted to know more than he could digest, or else he wanted to convince and convert him. But he wasn't having any of it.

'Does hell exist?' asks Thys. 'If there is no hell there is no heaven either.'

'Wait, mon ami. I'll write it down. First question, posed by my batman Glorieus. I say, I used to know several Glorieuses living in Wolleghem, are they relatives of yours? No? Well then, first question: is there a God? Second question: is there a hell? And you added something, didn't you? If there is no hell there is no heaven either.'

'That's right sir, and if there is no God, no hell and no heaven, everybody can do as he pleases.'

'You'd have to ask the police about that, mon ami.'

'Yes sir, I've often thought about that, but if all these things don't exist then why should one man be allowed to make laws for another?'

'Have you any better ideas?'

'Yes, sir.'

'What then?'

'One person has nothing and another has everything. That's unjust. One person may do as he pleases and the other is punished for a trifle. That's unjust too.'

'Why are you asking me all these questions?'

'You told me some things sir, and I think a lot.'

'Tell me straight, mon ami, what is on your mind?'

'You shouldn't take it amiss sir, but, I am so unhappy about it.'

'About what?'

'This is such an unhappy house, sir, I can't bear it. I think Madame is a good woman, but you don't talk to her and she doesn't talk to you. And Monsieur Paul and the others, don't take it amiss sir, please, I know it isn't my business but it's a dagger in my heart, I would give anything . . .'

Mon ami slapped Thys on the shoulders, gave him a handful of cigars and said Thys was a good chap but everybody runs his life as best he can, isn't that so, mon ami, we'll never mention this again and now the captain has to write a few letters. See you another time. Another time that never came.

Because you shouldn't meddle in things that aren't your business, Thys counted the bottles of wine in the cellar, making sure to deduct the ones he himself put on the dining table because that was his job, and when he knew exactly how many there were he left the house before the girls' sweethearts made their grand entry. He'd stirred a cautious finger in the captain's pie, but with these two revellers he might forget himself and lose his temper. Thys remembered his weakness from his schooldays.

Usually the distinguished visitors had left by the time he returned. They were shown out by their lady-loves. It never missed: there was always a bottle gone. Then Thys would count his savings, he could ill afford bottles of wine and he always swore that this time would be the last, next time he'd sock them one. And he's not going to pay this time either. But the knowledge that there had been nineteen bottles in bin six and that now there were only eighteen, weighed on him more heavily as each hour went by. The impropriety, the unfairness oppressed and tormented him, he had allowed it to happen and knew no peace until he had bought another bottle and put it in the empty place in bin six. Hands on his hips he looked at it with satisfaction: he had put this right. He didn't ask why, it was stronger than him, a deep urge.

The anarchist sometimes asked him to let his hand hang limply over the arm of a chair so that she could draw it. Or again, she needed a bare foot. He didn't mind, it made him happy to be of use. But one day she told him that tomorrow she wanted him to pose in the nude. Thys's breath caught in his throat. Why, mademoiselle? She said curtly that that was none of his business and he said: she could ask him anything she liked, but not that. She flared up at him: perhaps he was afraid she would seduce him? Thys didn't know where to look in his embarrassment as she fumed that she knew well enough what a man looked like and that he shouldn't imagine that she found him in any way interesting. And that in any case he didn't know anything about painting.

He came. She gruffly told him to go and have a bath. Go and wash. He reappeared scrubbed. She became a bit friendlier and said mockingly how terrible it must be for him, having to pose for a lady. He'd better run straight to church and confess it to the priest. But listen here, big teddybear. She doesn't want to draw him, individually, but all people like him. She wants to draw the people that endure without revenge the injustice that is done to them. Good, noble people who have grown accustomed to the yoke, who have learnt to bend under it, who will have their reward in heaven. Do you understand? So she is not drawing a chest-out soldier, nor a rebel. Heavens, don't look at me like that. She gives him a worried, surprised look. Then she goes to the large attic window and stands with her back towards him, searching for words. Life is a huge, monstrous . . . no, life itself is good and beautiful enough but the world as it has become and has been made through our doing, is a huge monstrous beast, no, a machine, wait, she'll put it clearly and plainly: man abandons himself, body and soul, to life only to be crushed by it. Naturally, this means nothing to him.

She says: 'Come on, stand in a position you find comfort-

able and natural. Stand how you want me to draw you.'
Thys stands the way you stand in line, before and after
lessons, the way you stand before the tailor, a bit like the
way you stand up for roll-call in the exercise yard. No,
that won't do. It must be a beautiful position, a meaningful
position, full of expression. She can't explain it properly, he
should feel it himself what she means.

Slowly the soul begins to quicken in the man's powerful
body. While the young artist, who of course is attempting
something far beyond her ability, tells him encouragingly
that yes, it's a bit better this way, and better still, and still,
the torso rises above the pillar of his one leg, while the other
leg, more gracefully, forms the buttress; the chest moves forward, the eyes gleam with a soft, dreamy glow; there comes
a hint of movement in the slightly out-stretched arms which
present their broad hands in a gesture of giving, of offering
help. Unconsciously, Thys Glorieus's body becomes Thys
Glorieus's soul, conquering the shame of nakedness, just as
he always kept intact his will for justice and righteousness in
the face of all humiliations.

Silence falls, softly the charcoal scratches, with long
strokes. Her roguish eyes become feminine, wide, and misty.
To her, being artistic means swearing, smoking, an un-
willingness to be a bourgeois daughter painting pretty
flowers; but mere artistic airs cannot stand up against an
emotion which cuts off the breath; the breast receives no air,
gasps. On the large sheet of cream-coloured paper the dream
which was the inspiration fades; moved but helpless the
young artist gazes at the man. He is beautiful, great, good.
She clenches her teeth, and whispers: humanité. Thys asks:
'beg your pardon, mademoiselle?'

Sometimes she comes near him, the better to see a line or
curve, if the light is deceptive from a distance. At first this
alarms him, after three or four times he doesn't mind any
more, but at that very moment she comes up close to him,
puts her arms round him and kisses him long on the mouth.
Now they are both ashamed, like Adam and Eve, he because

of his nakedness, she because of her sentimentality. With her back towards him she starts rummaging around in a corner, amongst old, cobweb-covered paintings, while he gets dressed in the other corner. Of course, in his haste, something snaps, one of the loops of his braces. He mentions it placidly, this breaks the strain, she goes back to him. She has probably never held a needle in her hand, but no woman, not after twenty years of marriage, could have said more simply: 'I'll sew it on for you.' Art is forgotten as she sits on her stool, an old piano stool, behind Thys's back, sewing on the broken loop.

She feels she is becoming gentle, simple. How homely this is, how cosy. She says: you can work in the fields, can't you? Thys can, or could, if he had any fields. Quietly she continues. They will build themselves a little cottage, with enough land around it for him to make a living. Thys blenches. That was all that was needed! On the farm it was Rosa, and now this one! She says, he mustn't think she is a demanding person. She has been sick and tired of the city and of this whole insincere life for a long time. She wants to forget it all, she wants to milk the cow and have children. Here, your braces are mended. He goes back to his corner to finish dressing, she stays on her stool, elbows on her knees, hands supporting her cheeks. Thys is trying to think of a way to get downstairs. The whole idea is too mad to deserve a serious answer, he pretends he is treating it as a joke, she'll be grateful for it by the morning. But she asks with downcast eyes: don't you want me? She is trying to pretend that she is weeping, but she really is weeping. Moved at this, Thys ruffles her hair with trembling hands, and tells her that she is only a child and doesn't know what she is saying. He paints her a sombre picture of the realities of peasant life and assures her that he would never forgive himself for doing such a thing to his captain. And to her as well!

This makes her jump up angrily. What silly nonsense! One should dare to live! Before he knows what is happening her teeth are tapping against his. In the struggle to free himself she becomes a laughing, playful child, trying to shower him with kisses.

Thys's task is becoming complicated. He can usually manage to avoid being alone with her, but when she rings the bell, for instance, he has to go and answer the door. He cannot hide himself far enough behind the door but she pulls his head towards her with her left arm and kisses him, without the slightest concern for the half-open kitchen door. If he resists it only takes longer and makes more noise. If only he could find her a good husband. The kitchen maid from Brussels asks him if Corinne is making passes at him; she's such a hussy, you'd better watch out: today it's kissing and cuddling, tomorrow it's kicking and scratching.

It is from Corinne that he learns of Paul's engagement. A big party next week. His lordship her brother Paul, popularly Monsieur Paul, will be betrothed to Mademoiselle Marie-Louise Dumoulin, two to three million, fraudulently acquired in the manufacture of safety-pins, and like the rich brides in novels she's as ugly as sin. At home, Paul sleeps with the kitchen maid and sometimes in a brothel, soon he'll be sleeping some of the time with that dried fish of the safety-pins and that is what they call le mariage chrétien qui est indissoluble, mon ami.

Mon ami ... Thys suddenly hears the captain. This little wild cat suffers from the same disease. She scoffs: Those beastly bourgeois. Her parents are so stingy, they deliberately got workmen up at the castle so that the party would have to be held here. She asks what Thys thinks of that kind of marriage. Boy, we'll do it differently! She talks of a large, rough meadow where they will have cows grazing and a bull, and in the morning there will be a new calf. 'Yes,' laughs Thys, 'and the calf will come up to us and shake hooves, good morning you two, I was born just now.'

'And every morning,' she says, 'winter and summer, we'll run naked in the field and jump into the brook. And I want twelve children, twelve children like you, but revolutionaries of course, twelve revolutionaries.' He tries hard to go on laughing. 'Twelve? Why not eighteen, another half dozen.'

When the fiancée entered together with her family, Thys stood stiffly pressed against the wall, in livery. The hall was filled with kissing and welcoming. Corinne let herself be squeezed against Thys, took his hand unnoticed and whispered that this was Mademoiselle Safety-pin. She pulled his hand round her waist and leaned voluptuously against him. He was dying a thousand deaths, looked at each of the richly dressed people in turn, at the members of this dissolute family which he had tried to reunite. The thought struck him that he was in danger of causing an almighty row. He saw the fat safety-pin manufacturer, a blood-red face ready to burst, embracing Monsieur Paul and shuddered with horror at the thought of the captain ever having to embrace him. His wedged-in hand trembled on Corinne's hip.

Belowstairs they were allowed to drink wine. For Thys and the other manservant there were constantly refilled glasses on the kitchen dresser, and Thys drank. First he drank in order to conquer his feeling of depression and to keep his mind on his work, because a waiter must think of nothing but his work. Then he drank so as not to have such a dreary poker-face every time he came back to the kitchen, for while you must be as grave as a judge when waiting at table, when the meal is nearly over and most of the work has been done, the girls flop down in a chair and want to be amused, to laugh away their tiredness. So if the other waiter starts flirting and gallivanting and whispers what a sweet little popsy that little one is, the one that helps the cook, Thys doesn't want to stand there like a dry stick. The maids clear the table, everything is taken to the scullery where the charwoman will wash up the next morning, and now the servantfolk can sit around together and enjoy themselves, and 'pour me,' says Thys, 'some more of that velvet stuff.'

They look at him, he's pretty tight already, but it doesn't matter any more now. By and by the older guests begin to leave, and the Dumoulins, who have quite a journey ahead of them, to their castle far down into Wallonia, cannot stay very late. Everyone finds a reason to go, the party is thinning out, the tips bring cheer in the kitchen, and Thys drinks.

But the more he drinks the more serious he becomes. The gladness which had been lying at the surface of his mind blows away in gusts, his heart beats more freely and proudly, he becomes blessed with the gift of noble, fluent speech. Pour him some more of that velvet stuff 'because,' he says, 'at times a man should drink, in moderation to be sure, because it helps to drive away the gloom.'

'Are you so gloomy?' they ask.

It is a question like any other and anyway, why shouldn't servant girls and waiters, relaxing with a few drinks after a hard day's work, ask questions just for friendliness. But this question sends Thys right back to the doldrums. He gets up and leaves the kitchen, but after so many glasses of the velvet stuff he is a bit confused about the direction he takes, heading east instead of west, and he is half-way down the corridor just when Corinne puts her head out of the living room door.

'Darling' (she even calls him darling now) 'quickly, can we have some black coffee, very strong, plenty of coffee for papa, because he's ...' and here her hand makes a movement as of sawing, she laughs, blows him a kiss, disappears.

But the captain doesn't want any coffee. 'Why should I want coffee, Thys?' Thys puts his left hand on the captain's shoulder so that he is nearly holding his head in the crook of his arm, and solicitously urges him to take just a few little sips. He sees Madame getting worked up, furious at such gross familiarity, but Thys gives her a reassuring wink, the task can be safely left to him, he'll sober down his tipsy, beloved master. They can be sure that any threat to the festive atmosphere will be skilfully averted, they have called him in the nick of time, and if he has not at all times been able to bring comfort and relief, as he would have liked to do, they should not therefore doubt his skill and tact in nipping slight disturbances like this one in the bud. He pours some coffee into the cup, lifts it to the captain's lips, still holding his head carefully against his shoulders. 'Have a sip of this, sir,' says Thys, 'you'll be asking for more.'

Madame rises from her seat. 'Mais enfin, soldat!' Thys puts a finger to his lips, ssh, to assure her that he is on the point of succeeding. A little more patience and everything will be all right. But then comes Corinne; Thys thinks she doesn't realize that he is trying to rescue her papa, but she wants to rescue him instead. She snatches the coffeepot out of his hand. Thys makes one last attempt. He whispers into the captain's ear that he would like to speak to him, confidentially, just for a moment, and again he winks reassuringly at Madame, who is seething.

'If you have anything to say to me, mon ami, say it now.'

'Sir,' says Thys, 'Madame,' says Thys, 'Monsieur Paul, monsieur Maurice, mademoiselle Irène, mademoiselle Corinne,' says Thys, 'I am an ordinary country boy and I have had a few drinks, I admit it, but if we all pull together things will go better from now on. Just a bit of good will, because happiness is what we are here for, so what's the point of making one another unhappy? Kindness, love for one another, that's the secret. This world could be so happy. My aim in life is to see nothing but happy people, that is the purpose of my life.' He looks around in surprise and wonderment at the sound of his own words as if he cannot quite place the source from which they come.

The two boys burst out laughing both at once, as if on command, but their laugh, quickly spent, makes the silence all the more embarrassing. Thys's eyes fill up with tears, he feels intense pity for these people. He turns to Madame, excuse me, madame, but the captain is always so unhappy; he says to the captain that madame is unhappy too, but she tries to hide it. To the children he says that it must seem to their parents as if they didn't have any children. He wrings his hands: please stop making each other so unhappy!

T–D

The silence becomes deathlier still; a perplexity of rage and contrition at once; the boys are suddenly worried. Is he perhaps more than drunk, has he gone mad? He is certainly not like any other orderly they have ever had. But the others feel that the drunken boy is speaking as if from a higher level, and it is the captain, the upholder of order and duty, who is the first to bow his head. It is the only movement in the room and it gives the woman, still livid with rage, strength and voice again. 'Sortez!' she shrieks. 'Sortez! – je vous dis, sortez.' Corinne helps him leave the room.

After that, they sit in silence. Anyone attempting to speak hears his words fall vainly and uselessly into the silence. Madame is literally eating herself up with vexation because the captain did nothing and is still doing nothing, he is not even holding his head high any more. His rambling story of the poacher attacking his father, broken off in mid-stream, is forgotten. At last the crackling of a match, lighting monsieur Maurice's cigarette, eases Madame's strained nerves. Two sobs, she stands up and flees to her room. And then something happens to the captain. He gets up too, and, ignoring the last seventeen years, he kisses his children good night, one by one, making the sign of the cross over them as he used to, with his thumb. For seventeen years he has not believed in the cross, for ten years he has had no children, and now, once more, he believes in what has been irrevocably lost. Looking at Corinne, his youngest child, he lifts her chin and rests his cheek against hers for a long while. 'Ouf,' says monsieur Maurice when he has left the room. 'That puts the lid on it.' And stretching himself languidly: 'Good God, what a madhouse, with yokels and dotards that can't carry their drink.'

ELEVEN

His dismissal the next day and a return to ordinary barrack life would no doubt have been hard for Thys if, sobered, he had not remembered what he had said. But he remembered every word of it. He was glad to receive the order to go back to the barracks through the Brussels kitchen maid, because this meant he did not need to see anyone else. And he was gladder still when he thought of Corinne; in the barracks she wouldn't be able to get at him.

But she did write to him. The briefest of notes in illegible hand-writing that slanted upwards; she asked him to meet her at the entrance to the academy, Corinne. He went and they walked. And as long as they walked they found nothing to say to each other because Thys had no desire to discuss what had happened; any attempt at amorous talk he quietly diverted and an ordinary conversation he couldn't have with her. She took him to a park and he sat on a bench with his arms and legs firmly crossed, an attitude she vainly tried to make him give up. Not for long though: suddenly she flew into a temper. If they had been at home she would no doubt have hit him in the face. She wanted to say something hateful to him, or simply tell him, between clenched teeth, I hate you, but instead she tamely said that she had to go home, stood up and left. Thys had learnt once again that it is no good meddling in other people's lives. People simply don't appreciate it.

He looked closely at life in the barracks, hoping to find a purpose, a meaning, which he felt was escaping him. For the first time in his life he realized that he was not like others. Had he been wearing blinkers all these years? Most people think chiefly of themselves, he always thinks of others. He watches three soldiers rushing to the same chair and the one who gets there first sits on it. Thys looks on in bewilderment and thinks: how odd that I would get more pleasure out of giving that chair to a complete stranger rather than sit on it myself. The simplest everyday trivialities become revelations. One day he is standing with his back against the wall that surrounds the barracks. A delivery man who has just finished loading bricks kicks his horse in the belly and a pain pierces Thys's heart, he suddenly hears the head of the cat he once murdered crack and he feels ashamed. Do the others scorn him because he was sacked by the captain or do they too feel that he does not belong to them? Whichever it is, he becomes lonelier day by day. He has a longing for somewhere but cannot name the place; it is a longing for a better world, but he has not grasped this yet. Lieneke sends him a short letter, the first and only one. She doesn't ask how he is, doesn't mention father or mother, but Pol is getting married to the woman he works for. That this woman weighs fifteen stone and is at least seventeen years older than Pol seems not to be worth mentioning but she stresses that Pol has secured himself a good spot. Pol is now rich and Pol is his own master and Pol rides in a carriage on Sundays and Pol this and Pol that.

And then a brief sentence: 'Another one who has got married: Rosa and that schoolmaster. Best wishes, your sister Helena.' Thys feels a stinging pain. So Pol has done well and he hasn't, he's not even somebody's servant any longer.

But Thys never loses his self-confidence for long: he smiles at the thought of how he will amaze them all one day when he has become a great man. So Rosa, the youngest of the family, married last of all and just in time too: on Saturday.

For on Sunday the farmer died, at least a month earlier than they had expected. Rosa would actually have preferred him to have died sooner still, because the farm had been emptied by marriages and she was no more inclined to keep Ridge Farm going than any of her brothers and sisters, who had all turned their back on farming. They could have sold everything as soon as the funeral was over, as promptly and profitably as possible and she would have been able to move into her dream house with her schoolmaster. The disadvantage of his early death would have been that the marriage would have had to be postponed until several months of mourning were over and that all that time she would have had to stay with one or other reluctant brother or sister, far from her Karel. Now she had got him.

The worst of father's untimely death was not that the honeymoon fell through but that Karel, on the evening after the funeral, talked with the others for hours about selling and dividing and then, when he was alone with Rosa, suddenly hit himself on the forehead as if a long-held thought had only just occurred to him: he called it first-class folly to sell the farm.

They would get barely half the value for it; each one of them would have a little mound of money which they would have no idea how to invest properly. Nothing but a miserable bit of interest. But if he and Rosa kept the farm, they could buy out the brothers and sisters who would be sure to agree in principle that whoever stays at home the longest and remains there after the parents are dead, should benefit most. That's the first gain. And the second gain . . .

She cuts him short. How can he say a thing like that? Is he, a teacher, going to play the farmer here? Is he going to resign his headmastership? Surely he knew all along that she didn't want to go on farming. Has he forgotten that they have already rented and furnished a house? It takes some while before he answers: 'I don't want to remain a schoolmaster.' On the fourth day after her wedding a young wife does not yet blurt out: you have deceived me – but she may think it. Her love is still too ignorant of life to withstand a violent shock. Her illusions will have to flake off under small daily knocks, like a glaze. If the first blow is too hard, her love will shatter altogether.

Even for the most amorous woman, and Rosa is not the

most amorous woman, there are moments in the early days of marriage when male tact has to remove her qualms at going to bed with a stranger. She becomes apprehensive because she is in his power; she thinks: suppose he strangles me tonight. This feeling takes possession of Rosa, she cannot shake it off. It used to be so different between them, so different, too, between her and Thys. 'Come to bed,' he says, but she is afraid. There are many women who daren't sleep in a house where there is a dead body, but they don't normally have this fear once the funeral is over.

All night long she lies awake beside the cobbler's son who courted her merely to get his hands on the farm. The more she thinks about the plans he has secretly been hatching, the clearer it becomes to her that he has not yet achieved his aim completely. Why did he never mention what he had in mind, why did he never tell her that he didn't like teaching, that he would rather be a farmer? She remembers the many times when she told him quite plainly that she was glad to see the last of the farm and all the dirty work, but never did he give her as much as a hint that one day he would change his mind. Two days before the wedding she was still busy getting things ready in the rented house. She went to school to meet him, it was prize-giving day. He showed her where some new classrooms were planned for the future. A house for the headmaster would be added as well. She was so happy about that; a new house for which they wouldn't have to pay rent. And heating and light all thrown in. Now she remembers that he did not react, that he did not say: this is where we shall be living one day. He just nodded. Why? Surely he knew that her father had not much longer to live.

Probably he was persuaded that she wouldn't have wanted him if she had suspected anything of his plans. But then he must also have known that her love for him would crumble if he came out with it after the wedding. What did go on in that square head of his with the small, deep-set eyes? Either he must have thought that she would agree, or that he would soon teach her who was boss, or else that it didn't matter one way or the other. Or did he imagine that their married life would only be a short-lived misery anyway? Did he perhaps have someone else in mind and had he only married her in order to get hold of the farm? But how did he think he was going to get rid of her? You sneaky fathead, don't you dare touch me, your mouth tastes of shoe leather.

'Karel, I am ill.'

He embraces her ardently. Surely she knows, women often feel ill at first, perhaps they are already expecting their first child. His joy is a knife in her heart. He probably knows the law. He must have made careful inquiries, maybe it stipulates that there must be a child first, before he can have full ownership rights. She is going to find out about the law herself, tomorrow. As long as it isn't too late. He is not to touch her any more until she knows. She implores him not to, it's because she feels unwell, she says.

Yes, in the early days women often feel unwell. And behave strangely too. He is made to get up in the middle of the night and unchain the guard dog, because she wants it to lie in the bedroom. If the law does not require a child and if he tries to murder her tonight she will have Black to rescue her; he'll make short work of you, you cunning fox.

He is surprised that she makes no further objections to his new vocation. He hadn't suspected so little resistance. After all, it must be hard for her. He knows how much she was looking forward to their new life. She laughed so happily: I shall be a lady from morning till night, and she was going to train Lett to be their maid. On the farm, where the work is scattered over so many different places and where you have to take independent decisions if you are to be of any use, Lett never did anything properly and was only in the way. But in an ordinary town or village house all the work is contained in three or four rooms and is repeated day after day in the same routine. She could be taught that kind of work, and in any case, she would be under constant supervision. Think of it, Karel, an unpaid maid, moreover a maid who makes no demands, never asks for a day off, who is content with wearing old clothes and who later, when there are little ones, will be a child among the children because playing with children is about the only thing she is good at.

Karel comes to the conclusion that a woman is an odd creature. Love gives her an unsuspected, unpredictable strength. Or could it be that she had reluctantly resigned herself to a new life with him because she had never dared hope that he would wish to become a farmer? Only one possibility he does not consider: the disappointment is so great, the surprise so painful, and she knows at once that this is a fait accompli, already determined at the start of their courtship. It is useless, she thinks, to fight against it. Anyway, if you have been lured into a marriage to a man you have come to hate and despise, what does it matter whether he is a headmaster or a farmer?

The next day she had already found something better than the guard dog: Thys. They are sitting at the table with the maids and men, and looking at Karel one would think he is not too pleased to see his wife jump to her feet with happy surprise: 'Look who has come to see us!' She goes to meet Thys but realizing in time that her surprise betrays her, stops in her tracks and anyone with a bit of charity can believe that she was merely going to pull up a chair for Thys, although there was no need for that. None at all, because Thys has just eaten, he has only come to say hello, he has come back for good, arrived only yesterday. He has heard about the farmer's death but he has come especially, he says, to wish the schoolmaster and Rosa every happiness, and everybody is amazed at the dashing way in which he goes up to them and shakes hands. His left hand in his side, his right shoulder slightly forward; smiling broadly, warmly. All my best wishes, says Thys. Thank you, says the schoolmaster, and Rosa remains gravely silent. 'Hello Lett, and how are you, aren't you going to talk to me, you?' She smiles faintly at him and he notices that she still sits with drooping shoulders and a sunken chest, he'll have to remind her about that presently. Because he has really come for her sake. The farmer is dead, the farm will be sold, what is going to happen to Lett? Never has the promise at the deathbed oppressed him as much as now.

The maids and men have hardly left the table and gone out of the kitchen when Rosa astonishes Karel by turning cheerfully to Thys, bidding him welcome to Ridge Farm where he has always been so well loved, and how often haven't they said to each other, how we miss our Thys. Yes, honestly! And now Thys has come just at the right time. The farm isn't going to be sold after all, Karel and she are going to be master and mistress now. She doesn't want to speak ill of any of the workfolk but he knows well enough how things are, doesn't he: one is too old, the other is too young and when it comes to it they are always short of a man they can rely on. And they all know one thing: they can rely on Thys, no trouble is ever too much for him.

Thys doesn't quite know what to do. Now that father has no longer got Pol to help him, he could work at home, but he has another dream, of which he knows no more as yet than that it is not basket weaving. And now that Rosa has asked him to come back to the farm he knows that it certainly is not farming either. It is a yearning for independence, a strange feeling of being destined for something better. Disappointments have prevented the dream from taking form. So why should he come back to the farm and be in the way of this young couple? The look in Rosa's eyes warns him to be on his guard.

He says he needs time to think about it and talk it over at home. He lies a bit. He will probably go back to the city. The owner of the bakery where he used to work before he went into the army keeps writing letters to him asking him to come back. The captain whose orderly he was has also offered him a job in a safety-pin factory near Nijvel. The captain's son is married to the owner's daughter, you see.

Last night Pol was at home and he said: come and work for me, I could do with your help. But mother was against it. There's no hurry she said. Thys can help father and take his time looking for something that suits him, he needn't take the first thing that crops up. Still, to be honest, Thys has always liked working on the farm and he is not saying no.

'You must not say no, Thys.' Karel looks wonderingly at his wife and Thys doesn't know where to look. Karel gets up and says he's going to the fields. If this is the tone she uses when engaging farmhands she has probably got other things to say for which she would rather be alone with him. Well, he washes his hands of it, kiss him if you like, then he's sure to stay. But the day after tomorrow I will sack him again. He stalks off, jauntily because he is sure that nothing will come of it.

She did indeed want to be alone with him, Thys mustn't go away, she's got to tell him something. He must come and work at the farm, he mustn't refuse, he must not.

'I'm not refusing,' says Thys. 'I've got to think it over.' But even that won't do. He has got to accept now, he's got to say yes, right now. He's got to because she asks him to.

'Rosa,' says Thys, 'you are married.' But she replies that this is exactly why he must not say no. He doesn't understand the logic of this but it doesn't take long to discover the reason: she is so frightened that Karel will do her harm. She hardly knew her mother but she doesn't think she would have dared take her own mother so completely into her confidence as Thys. She knows that one can tell him everything, and be sure that no one will ever hear of it. Well then, yes, she is frightened of that man. She doesn't even call him Karel any more. He married her only for the sake of the farm, he has deceived her, they had rented a house, furnished it, and yesterday he suddenly told her he was giving up his job as a schoolmaster to become a farmer. He doesn't love her. Thys. And now she is afraid he will want to get rid of her. Does Thys know what the law says in these matters? If she dies childless, will the farm be his? Will Thys please

go and find out for her, as soon as possible? Here is someone who knows and understands Thys. In a few words she
deals him the final blow: 'now you see what you've done to
me, you didn't want me.' He senses that there is something
wrong with the argument, because he didn't want to marry
her, that's true, but neither did he want her to marry the
schoolmaster. However, the appearance of guilt is enough to
burden Thys's oversensitive conscience.

Now and then, a busy-bodying maid comes hurrying
through the kitchen so that Rosa, in order to give herself an
appearance, pretends to be carrying or fetching things and
Thys pokes around in the fire. When he speaks it sounds
gruff: this has to conceal the happiness of being needed by
her, of being taken into her confidence. He says it's nothing
but silly talk, she is imagining things. Yes, she should be
ashamed, talking about her husband like that, that's no way
for a newly wedded wife to talk. Fortunately she has only
said it to him, it will be buried in a tomb of silence for ever.
But watch it, don't you dare say such things again, not to
anyone, Rosa.

Are you coming? she asks, for that is the only thing she
wants to know. Of course, he has already made up his mind
that he will come, but he tells her coolly that he shouldn't,
just to prove to her that a woman ought not to talk about
her husband in this manner and that it is all imagination
anyway. But all right then, he will come. And now she must
leave him to sort things out. Good Lord, if she knew what he
had been up against in the city, very different that was and a
good deal worse. Yes, he has seen life, Rosa, he knows what
goes on in the world, because she is not the first one who has
taken him into her confidence, he can tell her that. So many
times he has thought: there is no hope here. And yet it
turned out all right in the end. Well then, see you
tomorrow.

'Thys!' she runs after him. 'Thys!' and she wants to
thank him, take his hand, perhaps more. But no, she
mustn't.

Dina asks him if he has gone out of his mind, going back to that place, poking about in the muck from morn till night, for a piddling wage. Has he forgotten how they treated him, and her as well, the dirty skinflints? We may not be rich but her child is too good to be a farmhand. All the same, Thys goes. He can't explain it to mother, why he is going, he doesn't admit that he cannot explain it even to himself, why he always follows that same urge. In any case, it won't be for long, she may be sure of it, and soon she'll be surprised at him, when he has found what he is looking for. Do stops whistling for a moment to give his comment. When Thys walks behind the cows and they drop something he'd better give it a good stir, it's bound to be in there, whatever it is he is looking for.

TWELVE

And then Uncle Dolf arrives to give his opinion. For thirteen years he has been gone without a trace, that is the longest time he has ever been away. At dusk he suddenly looms up in the lonely fields, he stands in the doorway, pushing his bowler hat against the lintel so that it sags over his eyes and they see nothing but a hat and a beard; Dina screams. He always makes sure he looks different. Thirteen years ago he had shaved off his enormous moustaches, now he stands there, as big as Do, but two hands broader and a good deal heavier, with a dense, frizzy, short, square beard. Hello, everybody. As if he had only left the day before yesterday.

He has been to see Pol. Dina and Do enjoy talking about Pol, so this is an excellent opening, but Dolf shrugs his shoulders doubtfully and says 'yes, yes' a couple of times. Killing a piglet and a calf, cutting them into neat little pieces and selling each piece at a nice little profit, fine, splendid, nothing wrong with it, he's not saying you can't live on it, but my dear children, that's no way to get rich, is it now.

And yet he's going to be rich, you mark my words, says Do, and he is already rich, says Dina, but again Dolf says yes, yes. Anyway, he told Pol what he thought of it, but what's the use of wasting your breath on that duffer who doesn't know chalk from cheese? What does he know about business? I say to him, Pol, have you got any money? 'That all depends, Uncle Dolf.' So I say to him: buy yourself a shipload of Spanish donkeys, there are seven shiploads on the way here. In the whole of Brabant there aren't two donkeys to be found, they're all such peasants here, the kind that would but can't. Well, asses of peasants. I say to him, boy, go and fetch your donkeys from Antwerp, sell them on the way back, you'll come home alone and in two days you will have earned more than you now do in a year with your ears and trotters. That's business. And what about young Thys, what does he do for a living? They tell him, he answers: Good Lord. And what do you do? asks Do.

Nothing. Uncle Dolf is travelling for pleasure. He has earned enough money, in wool.

'Why don't you buy those donkeys yourself, then?'

Thanks very much. Do they think he's going to walk all the way from Antwerp with two hundred and fifty donkeys when he's got piles of hundred franc notes in the bank? When they've all gone he'll start thinking of work again. Then he sees Thys, who is just coming home, walking towards the house in his clogs. He jumps up and calls out in a voice that makes Dina put her fingers in her ears: watch your front! Steady! Forward march! Right wheel, right! Attenshun! Halt! By this time Thys has arrived right in front of him and Dolf's voice suddenly seems to have run out of steam. 'Goodness me, look at this fellow, and he can think of nothing better to do than ride around with a muck cart. Shall I . . .' and he make a broad gesture as if to hit him but instead he hooks his right arm round Thys's neck and by way of embrace he briefly holds Thys's head against his breast.

Do whistles a little louder and a proud mother, tingling with happiness, stirring the porridge with feigned concentration, steals a glance at the two robust figures: father and son. In what way does the boy resemble his father's unusualness? He is different from all the others, different from his father and yet the same.

Lieneke seems hardly flattered when Uncle Dolf tries to catch her in the same way with his arm. She wards him off and two pairs of parental eyes are already on their guard. They know this brother: cunning enough for ten and always a merry customer, but nothing that wears a skirt is safe from him. Thys can ask him what the law says about inheritance: when there is a child and when there is not. He knows all about it, and he asks if Thys has perhaps got his eye on some fat old woman too, like Pol, or maybe a bonny millionaire's daughter.

On the third day Karel tries to get rid of Thys. What is he doing here anyway, explain it to him, what do they need him here for? But whilst he got off his resignation to the local council without a murmur from Rosa, getting rid of Thys is not so easy. Rosa resists with a ferocity that alarms him. He is getting more and more baffled. The decision to stay on the farm she accepted without protest and for a farmhand she will fight to the death. How could she give herself away so easily, how stupid can a supposedly shrewd woman be, how naïve, like a child. She asks him what he knows about farming, he, a schoolmaster who has never seen anything at home except shoemending, who has been wearing out his trouser seats on schoolbenches for four years, teaching children to read and write; what does a man like that know about farming? How should he know whether Thys is superfluous here? Has he ever seen him with idle hands, or wasting time? Thys works from morning till night, he is already busy when everybody else thinks it's too early and he is still busy when the others think it's too late; he works as if it was for himself, Has Karel ever known of any other farmhand who would do the same, if so, let's hear about it. Karel says he knows plenty of people like that but he doesn't think she'd be so keen on them. It's Thys she wants, nobody but Thys, isn't that so? It is obvious enough, but this doesn't put Rosa out of countenance. Yes, sure, she wants Thys; Karel wants the farm, so now they've both got what they want. Such brazenness makes him bang his fist on the table, for the first time but not the last. Each time it happens again, she will startle a little less, but today she bursts out crying, before he is able to shout that here on the farm he will have his way, 'in spite of everything'. There are no two ways here, has she got that in her head? He thinks that only women betray themselves unwittingly but he does not see how he is unmasking himself: a cobbler's son laying down the law at Ridge Farm. He has slept with the youngest daughter for a week and imagines that therefore his position must be safe. She is beginning to think that perhaps she ought to call all her brothers to defend her against the intruder who is acting like a tyrant.

An opportunity to talk quietly to Thys, alone, he had allowed her only once, on the first day, and that but grudgingly, against his better judgment; now he is no longer so generous. It suits Thys not to have to talk to her, because her interest in the law seems suspicious to him. It isn't his job to inform her whether or not she should refuse to bear Karel a child. He prefers the job of teaching Lett to be a hard-working girl who knows how to make herself look pretty on a Sunday, because Lett must find herself a husband.

One evening, at supper time, Rosa decides off her own bat that one of the farmhands and two maids, who sleep in the knocked-up rooms in the outhouses, had better be in the house in future. Her brothers' and sisters' rooms stand empty anyway. All under the same roof. Otherwise it's too lonesome on the farm at night, especially now that winter is closing in. And you, Thys, if you'd rather not sleep with Soo, you can sleep in our Louis's room.

Karel and Thys answer both at once: Karel that Thys can sleep at home as he's always done, and Thys that he prefers to sleep at home. Not Thys's answer but Karel's instant, curt intervention makes the maids exchange a quick glance, but they don't turn a hair. A silence falls. Soo, the farmhand, shatters it with a laugh: why can't Thys sleep with Lett? The maids find this a priceless joke and nearly split their sides with laughter. But Lett doesn't find it ridiculous at all. She gazes at Thys with eyes a little less dull than usual and bares her teeth in a grin as if to ask: well, Thys, what about it? It is so unmistakeable that Soo becomes still wittier: 'You see, she'd like it.' The maids nearly fall off their chairs. Thys merely casts a stern, reproachful look at the stepsister who doesn't know how to behave herself. Karel is pleased to see his subordinates enjoying themselves, albeit in that crude way of theirs, but Rosa says with a cross, red face, that it's not funny. And she reflects in sudden anxiety how she could have forgotten that Thys once spurned her in favour of that dimwit. Now she herself has asked him to come back, and a thought stabs her like a sharp, swift lance that perhaps he has come back because of Lett. Everything that repels her in Karel, everything that Karel wants, his desire for pleasure and love, makes her long for Thys, because it is with Thys alone that she wants to enjoy all this.

A second time Karel bangs on the table and again Thys is the cause. One of the maids has complained about him. Servant girls are always ready to bring their quarrels to the master. She's a quick one, that girl, but her work shows the signs of haste, and Thys is pernickety. They were sorting potatoes and Thys said she had been throwing sound ones on the same heap as the bad ones so that they had to sort them all over again. Such complaints had never been taken much notice of at Ridge Farm, with the old man she would have got into trouble herself, because nothing must ever be wasted. But Karel holds forth at length about it. Sorting those potatoes a second time might have saved a bucketful of pigs' fodder at most, hardly worth the precious time that was wasted on it. Working hard isn't everything; working with foresight and proper organization, that's what matters. Rosa lets him carry on, maintaining a disdainful silence, but when he reaches the conclusion that someone who knows he is surplus to requirement will naturally try to keep himself occupied in any way he can think of rather than squat by the wall rolling cigarettes, she calls to him from the sink that she can think of others around here who are surplus to requirement. In a flash he stands before her and asks who. Who? Use your eyes and you'll see. As gentleman farmer of Ridge Farm and master over everything, he should surely be able to find out for himself if there's anyone surplus to requirement.

'I've already said who.'

'And I'm saying that there are others who are a good deal more surplus to requirement.'

'Who?'

'Look for them yourself, I told you.'

He clasps her wrists as she stretches her arms to lift a tub. Who? You need better preparation than teaching a class of infants to hold down a sturdy country girl; she jerks free as if he was nothing. It humiliates him. He tries to be stern with her in a different way, and says he will sack the first redundant worker on the spot. Now it is her turn to grab hold of him, but by the arm. Her voice begs and threatens. 'Karel, don't do that' and 'Karel, be careful, I warn you.' If she had released her grip he might have calmed down outside and changed his mind before finding Thys. But now begins a dangerous game; he tries to wrench free, is unable to, nearly succeeds, is clasped tighter, gets excited, furious, suddenly being reminded, in the hold of a woman he cannot control, of all the humiliations of a schoolmaster without authority, a cobbler's son who is hit in the neck by a worn slipper while writing on the blackboard. He thinks: am I going to let myself be bossed around forever? He feels his back pressing against the wall and while it flashes through his mind that he must not push his knee into her stomach to struggle free, he grabs her by the throat.

Every evening she has shuddered at the thought of being strangled, now it has come. Her strength flags, she screams Thys, Thys, Thys! Karel releases her and goes out to look for Thys: sometimes the weak are braver than the brave. Thys is called back from the fields and is told to come in: the mistress wants to see him. She shows him her neck: he nearly strangled her, I was already turning blue!

Thys's blood begins to rise but he watches himself and tries to remain calm. He asks her to tell him first what she had done to deserve it. 'You can be vicious too,' says Thys. But he is itching inside, he is tearing at the bit, she can tell.

'What's this, Thys, are you going to stand back and let him kill me?'

'Be quiet, Rosa,' says Thys. He feels his destiny approaching.

'Be quiet, be quiet, why should I be quiet? Are you a coward or do you simply not care about me? I have got to be quiet, have I, and let myself be murdered.'

'Rosa, before it ever got to that I would have smashed his brains in ten times over.'

She doesn't understand why he leaves, as if in flight, but he is trying to escape the urge to fight a hopeless battle.

His words have reassured her, for on his word you can build churches, but this flight seems odd to her. It is as if he had promised to protect her, but not out of love, as in the past. His concern for himself she interprets as a defection and this she can only explain by assuming he has set his mind on Lett. That he will give succour and protection to anyone, not only any woman but anyone who suffers or is troubled, even if it costs him all he has, she still has not recognized. That he consciously, yet only half knowing why, neglects to build up a life of his own because she has made an appeal to him, nothing in her suspects it. All she sees is that he does not love her enough and that Lett must bear the blame.

Sometimes she asks herself what it is she wants. It would

be wrong for him to love her, after all. There is no solution. Whether he takes Lett or someone more suitable, it should be all the same to her, considering that he can never have her. There are moments when she firmly makes up her mind to encourage him to have a talk with Lett, insofar as one can talk seriously with that slattern. She might tell Lett that Thys means well with her and that she should try to get him to marry her, the sooner the better. At this thought she overflows with magnanimity and she decides that the young couple could surely stay on at the farm, why not? She convinces herself that she would feel happy for Thys's sake because it would be such a good life for Thys, and that it had never crossed her mind that it would be very agreeable for her to have him near her forever.

However, these are merely noble reveries in the darkness of the bedroom, or at dusk while she tends the fire, alone in the kitchen, whilst by the cowshed the milk pails and churns clatter against each other. When she is faced with Lett she cannot refrain from speaking gruffly and instead of sending the girl to join Thys she deliberately tries to keep them apart. She cannot help herself.

One Sunday Thys comes to the farm with Uncle Dolf and Lieneke, to fetch his ward. Uncle Dolf loves going round all the best cafés with a retinue for which he pays and Thys says 'they should see more company.' Besides, Lett and Lieneke will have each other for company; it is better if Uncle Dolf talks only to him. Rosa watches them go from behind the window, jealously biting her nails.

The sinful thoughts come upon her more suddenly. Like a headache or gout they are there one moment, gone the next. Her hatred is as fierce as her love. They assail her for the first time when she discovers that she is pregnant. How she used to dream, long ago, of the happy anticipation which would unite husband and wife in a bond of prolonged, dizzying bliss; now her first thought is: I hope he will never see the child. Of course she feels ashamed immediately and reasons until she has persuaded herself, that it was an unconscious thought, therefore not a guilty one, therefore not one she will have to confess. Besides, how could one ever confess such a thing? Yet this reasoning brings home to her for the first time that she desires her husband's death.

Nothing agitates her more than Karel's professed interest in her condition. Those intimate moments when no tender allusion to these things seems reverent enough to a newly wedded wife, she no longer tolerates. He has therefore no choice but to ask about it bluntly. He puts the question while she is standing with her back to him, ordering Black to lie down on the mat in front of the bed. She replies curtly that there is no question of it. The absence of any tenderness between them has made him as irritable as her; every evening the slightest snappiness would be enough to make them flare up savagely and violently; the big dog is not there for nothing.

When weeks later she can no longer hide the truth, she tells it to him with such churlishness that he asks a second question: and is it my child? Too late he realizes his mistake; one does not gain authority, not even over a woman, merely by assuming it. Too late he makes a last attempt at reconciliation, aware at last that her constant petulance was not a passing stage. He tries once more to be tender, asks her to tell him what it is that stands between them, but again, he cannot help adding: or who? And again she turns away. But he bashes on, already beaten, injured. If it is because he sent in his resignation, why didn't she say so when there was still time, then he wouldn't have written the letter. No, certainly not, Rosa. But she appeared to take it so light that he had thought that after a few days' sulking she wouldn't have minded any more. When she went on moping he had imagined that it was the usual irritability of pregnant women and that she with her passionate nature was more susceptible to moodiness than other women, that was what he had said to himself.

Oh, she knows what he is after all right. It's too late to withdraw his resignation, the child is on the way, everything has gone according to plan, if she is now going to be all sweetness and smiles for as long as necessary, he will have all he wants. But he has unwittingly given himself away by asking if the child is his. She says: 'Why are you so keen to make it up between us if you don't even know if the child is yours?' She would have made herself clearer if she had said: while you pretend you don't even know if the child is yours, but it isn't her fault that she has never studied to be a teacher and naturally, he chooses to put the least favourable interpretation on it: it is not certain whether the child is yours or not. It is hard for a man to contemplate such a thing but the fact that it has been said is enough to make him sick and savage. 'Aren't you even sure of that?' he asks, 'are you such a trollop?' She wants Thys to kill him.

But if that is to happen Lett must be out of the way first and never mind about the housework that morning, the breakfast things can stay on the table till ten o'clock, Rosa must write a letter. Would her dear sister please have Lett to live with her. On a farm where it is impossible to keep an eye on her all the time she is useless, but in a house in town she could be properly trained. Dear sister knows how good Lett is with children. Dear sister has already got three children and would no doubt be pleased to have such a nursemaid. How in the world is it possible that Rosa has never thought of this before. This morning, as she was getting out of bed, it suddenly occurred to her and she lost no time in writing quickly to her dear sister. Let us know your answer soon, then Rosa will take Lett to her house herself.

Dear sister replies coolly enough to this hasty request, but still, she is willing to give it a try for a few months. If it doesn't work out, she will send Lett back, because they did agree, after all, that Lett's home would be on the farm.

But Lett herself replies even more coolly. She understands enough to know that she is better off near Thys. Every one of her brothers and sisters used to beat her and snarl at her and these are the things that children and simple-minded souls remember. Rosa heightens her apprehension by

forbidding her to ask Thys for advice; Thys has got nothing
to do with it, he's not one of the family, do you hear? Whatever is decided about her, if it is done without the knowledge
of the only person who is good to her, it cannot be right. She
doesn't want to go and when Rosa asks her why not, she
replies: I don't want to. But why ever not? Stubbornly
she repeats: I don't want to.

THIRTEEN

For Rosa this is no more than a slight hitch in her plan.
With feverish zeal she applies herself to making life hell for
Lett. By keeping out of Thys's way as much as possible she
hopes to reassure Karel who now spies on her with burning
eyes and is too restive to settle down to any work. For the
time being, Thys does not matter. As long as he keeps hovering around Lett, constantly concerned for her welfare, she
cannot rely on him anyway; but once she has got rid of Lett
it will not take her long to win him over. But she must be
quick. This must be a brief period of committing sin upon
sin; she must get it over with quickly, without thinking
about it. Thys will be the first to hold her child in his arms,
then she will make her confession, they will forget everything and she will make amends by a pious, godly life.

At first Thys suspects nothing when Rosa announces that
she needs Lett in the kitchen to help her with the heavy
work. He hears Karel agreeing at once, hears him say to Lett
that she must be specially helpful, for remember: Rosa is
expecting. Rosa exploits her pregnancy to wear Lett out, at
the butterchurn and dragging heavy kettles to and from the
hearth. She slaps Lett flat in the face. She makes a frightful
fuss over trivialities. It doesn't matter if the workfolk see
her, they are bound to make allowances for her now. She

rages that the lazybones had better go to her sister in Tieleghem if she doesn't like the work here, but she, Rosa, can't be
expected to tire herself out, in her condition and the work
has to be done.

The ill-treatment soon attracts comment. One cannot
blame the mistress; one can see the change in her, day by day,
one hardly recognizes the old cheerful Rosa as she scurries
about like a hunted animal with distorted features and wild
eyes. But woe betide the person who has to live with her!
They themselves have never felt much affection for Lett, the
tiresome dimwit. Often enough they too have pushed her in
a corner and the maids are not above pinching her viciously
in the arm so that she doubles up with pain and sighs, but
she never screams. But this is going too far.

Thys hears of it last of all because Rosa's pregnancy never
bothers her when he is around. She even becomes friendlier
towards Lett in his presence.

Is it true, asks Thys, that she beats you? Rosa had shown
him her neck, Lett shows him her arms and says: you should
see my back. What a house this is; even at mon ami's things
were never as bad as this. Anger rises in Thys. Is it the same
everywhere then, the same damned malice and injustice?
And do they think he is going to stand aside and watch it
all? The farmer beats his wife, the wife beats Lett and he
sees it happening right in front of his eyes and doesn't lift a
finger. He is always holding back, always exercising
patience. But it has been going on long enough now. Fate
will have to run its course, come what may.

Let me have a look then, says Thys. He takes her behind
the barn door, he wants to see her back. Expertly he presses
on the three blue bruises which can't have been caused by a
mere twist of the fingers and she flinches with pain. Still he
tries to deflect his anger: you'd be better off in Tieleghem. –
No, she doesn't want to go there. – Why not! She keeps her
back turned towards him and doesn't need to remember his
lesson about the way a girl should behave, timidly, with a
pursed mouth, for she now feels this timidity herself.

'Why not, Lett?'

She answers softly, looking at a large cobweb in front of her: 'I'll wait here till we get married.'

'I'm not marrying you,' says Thys, 'go to Tieleghem.'

'No.'

'Why not?'

'I'm staying with you.'

He is touched. Kindly he tells her to pull her dress straight. He would have liked to caress her back. A great flow of compassion fills him. He puts his strong arm round her and hears himself say that she may stay with him forever, always, he promises her and you can rely on his promises. So nothing, absolutely nothing can happen to her, because he will be there. He will be good to her. Is she crying, is she sad? Her sadness is a child's sadness and cry she never does. And yet she hangs her head and nods, yes, very sad. Thys says he'd like to see who would dare raise a hand against her now.

The one he would like to see suddenly appears in the doorway, raving and screaming. 'Ha, necking behind the door, hey, back into the kitchen, you trollop!'

'What was that you said, Rosa?'

She knows Thys better than anyone and immediately begins to weep, the only way out of her blunder. She is so tired and so ill and Lett is driving her crazy, she doesn't know what to do with the girl. Just now, she was nowhere to be found for over half an hour.

'Less than ten minutes,' says Thys.

'It's all the same, she's got no business here.'

'Why not? All right, Lett, you can go dear, I'll be along.'

'Is she your sweetheart by any chance?'

'Yes.'

'Is she your sweetheart?'

'I just told you, yes.'

Her whole plan lies in ruins. Before she has nipped this in the bud the child will be born. Despairingly she comes close to Thys and suddenly clings to him, but he is better at fighting her than Karel. 'We're courting,' says Thys, 'and we're going to get married.' He goes to the door. She clutches at his clothes, she wants to talk to him, ask him something, it's very urgent, come back, just for a moment. No one ever makes such an appeal to Thys in vain but she cannot ask him, in the two minutes he gives her, not to marry that half-witted Lett, because she, Rosa, will soon be free if only he will kill her husband. Now that she has this chance to talk to him, she has lost her nerve. She asks him at least to wait for a while. Her tone surprises Thys but if that is all, all right, why not. There is something else, she says, but this something else, when uttered, becomes only the same again: wait a while. He leads her outside by the arm. Come, you're ill.

It seems to Thys that to this day he has lived in half-conscious confusion, what else is youth? He has only acted like this and like that, blindly following his impulses, a bit muddled by ideas picked up in the captain's house, and a bit tormented by a vague but deep yearning for something great, unnameable. Now at last he has done something: he has promised to marry Lett. Of course, it's folly, but he is destined for such follies. On the way home he throws pebbles at the arms of the signpost and defiantly whistles the Brabançonne. Let them all bully him as much as they like: he's marrying Lett.

Mother, he's getting married! There they sit, the four of them, the ones who will laugh at him. Let them! There's Uncle Dolf, he'll be the worst, tilting his chair back, Do, whistling softly as usual, Dina and Lieneke, knitting. They look up briefly but Do goes on whistling until Thys mentions the name of his chosen one; then he swallows the wrong way and coughs splutteringly, Dina pretends she hasn't heard properly so that Thys has to repeat it. At first she thinks that her serious Thys is making a joke. It's his first joke ever, but it's a good one.

I thought, says Dina, it might have been Fina from the

bakery. Fina the baker's daughter is a fat hunchback, a milliner who hobbles about on two crutches and under her skirt there hangs a thin little baby-foot beside a thick clumsy leg. 'No,' says Thys in full earnest, 'it isn't her, it's Lett from Ridge Farm.' They are all dumbstruck, speechless.

At last Do says that mother had better put her little boy to bed, he must be feverish. Thys folds his arms on his chest and says that father can try if he dares. He has never spoken like this before. 'Come here,' says Do. 'Come here,' says Thys. Uncle Dolf, sniffing a tempest: 'Watch out you don't hurt each other or you'll have me to deal with.' But he promises fifteen francs' prize for the winner.

Do lifts his son by the waist and carries him five, six paces towards the bedroom but Thys wedges his arms between Do's, forcing him to release his grip. Swerving, Do tries to pounce on him again but Thys grabs him by the wrists and pulls him with a swift jerk down on to his knees. It is tough for this father no longer to be the stronger one after twenty years; he is already panting and curses between his teeth. Dina wants them to stop but Dolf pushes her back. Lieneke runs out of the room and Thys says calmly: 'We'd better stop now, father.' 'Come here,' growls Do and clasps two iron arms around Thys's neck. When Thys wriggles his head out of that grip it feels as if all his hair has been left behind. Thys becomes wild; he pounces and now it's all the same what Do does or doesn't do, he is bent like a tree over Thys's thigh, further, still further, his feet lose their hold, he lies horizontally in Thys's arms and Thys asks where he wants to be carried. Mother's eyes glow with pride. Her admiration remains silent, to spare the feelings of the defeated.

Uncle Dolf's tongue loosens. Marrying is the daftest thing anyone can do in his life, that's why he himself has always remained a bachelor, but Thys is right. Uncle Dolf knows the girl. He's only seen her once and that was more than enough. He doesn't need any more time than it takes an express train to flash past to know all he wants to know about a girl. This particular girl looks as dumb as the back end of a donkey, she probably can't count up to ten. But what of it, those are the best ones.

'To you,' says Do, 'all of them are the best ones.'

'Shut up, you fathead, or I'll have you tucked up in bed. A simple-minded clot picks you up under his arm like a sucking pig and you dare throw your weight about. Here's fifty francs, go and get soaked and then come back shouting your head off. For me there aren't best ones, I'm telling you, there isn't one that is any good.'

'Why don't you keep your hands off them, then?'

'If they keep their hands off me, you numbskull, you get my meaning?'

'What? You dare say that again.'

'I'm telling you, you keep out of my way. If you've got anything to say to me, come and say it outside, not in here.'

Dina calls out: 'Dolf, if you must quarrel, get outside.'

'I was talking about Thys, why should he start on about something else? I said that Thys is right in marrying that girl. I'm allowed to say so, aren't I, why shouldn't I? And I'm saying that no woman is any good and why shouldn't I be allowed to say that as well? And Thys can do as he pleases and snap his fingers at the rest, fine, that's what I call a man.'

It isn't easy to get Uncle Dolf on one's side. The usual things, the things other people approve of, he scoffs at. He's got to stand alone and take risks. But once you've got him on your side you've got an army on your side. He says he'll help Thys get set up and after that he'll have to prove what he can make of himself. He'll set him up in town. If he's a bungler we'll find out soon enough but if he's got something in him, it will come out. More I won't do, says Uncle Dolf. The next morning he's already off, to Brussels.

Rosa's hastiness now takes hold of Thys as well. Two feverish journeys crossing each other. She now promises she will treat Lett better than a true sister if he will give up the marriage; then she promises to do the same if he will only wait. It is all so frantic and inconsistent that she spoils her case. He sees in it the despair of a love which he must not return, as well as the capriciousness of her pregnancy. Those supposed intentions of Karel's to murder her must have been pure fiction too.

Thank goodness he didn't walk into the trap altogether. Her impatience only makes him all the more eager to get away and in order to make it quite plain to her that she should have no illusions about him he asks her advice about Lett's wedding dress. Karel, maids and men are sitting around the table when Thys turns up with a fashion magazine. They ask him if he's going to cut and sew the dress himself, and try it on her. Amidst the merriment trembles the finger, trembles the hand with which Rosa points at the patterns she thinks would look nice.

That Saturday evening she looms up in the dark, by the signpost, in front of Thys and whispers that Karel will be away all day tomorrow and that he must, must, must come, she can't say any more just now. See you tomorrow!

And she runs away, behind the barn, to enter the house by the back door so that no one will suspect anything.

On Sunday afternoon she is alone. Lett is playing across the road with a crowd of children. For years she hasn't been allowed to do this. Rosa's heart beats, the child stirs. She is sitting far enough from the window not to be seen from outside but will be able to see Thys coming down the road. When he arrives he's bound to ask for Lett and she'll tell him to go and look out of the basement window, you'll see her from there. That will show him that the bride whose wedding dress he is about to order is skipping with the little girls. Or maybe she's squabbling over a marble with kids no older than ten. She will tell him that Lett has escaped her. 'She's run off, Thys. I daren't leave the farm to fetch her and anyway she wouldn't have come back with me. She's not afraid of me any more. For your sake, Thys, I have been good to her, too good, and Lett knows that and now she won't do anything for me any more.' Feverishly she debates with herself. It must be bitter for Thys to have to pick her out of a group of children, to tell her to throw away her marbles because she has to order her wedding dress. Then Rosa will say what she has on her mind. She will ask him if the marriage can't wait, what's the hurry, and then she will burst out crying, he won't be able to resist tears. And she'll say that she'll tell him everything; spelling out Karel's cruel behaviour in every detail, asking Thys for protection. Once in his arms she will prevail on his conscience. I know you still love me like you used to. He will forget everything else, he'll go out to meet Karel. Between the village and the station there is a ten-minute stretch of lonely road, there he will slay him. Luckily everybody has heard about his wedding plans; no one will suspect him therefore. If he abandons the marriage afterwards, that will appear more natural and more sensible than if he actually does marry Lett.

A man comes sauntering into the yard. He is carrying a basket, like the shrimp-hawkers who come down on Sundays from Scheldt-side, but it isn't the time for shrimps. He starts pushing at the barn door. Then he goes to the house and rattles at the closed door. Rosa becomes frightened, why isn't Thys here yet? The man knocks at the window, Rosa presses herself close against the wall. He peers through the window, shielding his eyes with one hand, and pushes at the pane which gives slightly. He calls and listens. Something scratches as if he were picking at the putty with a knife or a fingernail. He walks by the side of the house and disappears through an open stable door. This way he can get past the stables into the orchard; a little window in the wash house is open. Rosa runs to it, bars it. He'd only need to push the pane out, no one would hear or see it on that side of the house. She hurries in her stockinged feet to the bedroom, fetches the double-barrelled gun, sits down at the top of the stairs and aims. The man does not break the window pane, all remains silent. She walks down the stairs with the gun, still aiming. The man has come out of the stable. Again he approaches the house. When he pushes at the front door Rosa is standing in the corridor, ready to shoot. The door is old. The lock and the two bars are strong but the sockets in which they rest are slack. The door gives by a finger's width, then a slit of light appears through which he sticks his fingers, pointlessly for not even a crowbar would open the door like this. The man goes away. She thinks: I should have stayed in the bedroom. The window is straight above the door. To hit him I would only have had to hold the barrel flush against the window ledge, if need be without aiming, simply shooting straight down. Of course I wouldn't have fired at once; the sight of the gun would have been enough to scare him. Or I could have shot into the air to raise the alarm. But maybe he could press himself so close to the door that I would never have hit him?

She goes to the bedroom and aims. When she steadies the barrel against the underside of the window ledge, holding her finger on the upperside, she can even shoot into the doorway.

Dusk is falling and still there is no sign of Thys. The end of the road, where he should appear, is beginning to fade. Perhaps it is better if he comes in the dark, then no one will have seen him. The sound of children playing stops abruptly. They have gone indoors, perhaps their parents have called them to come in to eat and go to bed, and have told Lett to go home. But even if Lett stays out, she needs time to make sure Thys goes where she wants him to go. Lett returns. She is counting marbles from one hand into the other, knocks, and hides them behind her back as she enters; there are nine of them. She finds herself some food; Rosa can't eat. Lett slips upstairs with a sandwich to hide the marbles in her bed; she hasn't had such a Sunday for years.

Rosa can find no rest anywhere. The wind gathers, everything begins to rattle, the weathercock on the barn squeaks. She fetches the gun and with her woman's fear of weapons leans it against the wall with the barrel pointing down. There is no more sign of the shrimp man than there is of Thys, but gusts of wind rattle a door here, a window there. A metal bowl hanging outside by one handle bangs against the wall from time to time. At the front of the house the shutters tap at intervals as if someone was knocking at the door. She calls: who's there? Only the wind replies.

Rosa goes to the bedroom, taking the gun with her. The window is still open. It can stay open: south-westerly winds come from behind the orchard. She had better leave it open, she thinks, in order to shoot the shrimp man. But suppose the shrimp man puts a ladder against the wall and clambers into the room by the window? She sits down with her back to the bed, the barrel on the window sill. He'll be hit full in the face and topple backward from the ladder.

Suppose it was Karel; he can't get in, the doors are barred. No one would ever think it was a crime, any woman would shoot in a panic at a man climbing through her bedroom window. For some minutes she holds her finger on the trigger, determined not to wait till she recognizes the face as it appears. If it is Karel, so much the better.

At the entrance to the yard the gates slam, the cross-piece drops with a thud: Karel. He walks down the narrow brick path alongside the barn, then along the front of the house. This is the path of those who belong, of those who avoid the cart ruts in the dark and the shafts of the thresher. His key is in the lock.

Rosa stands up, very calmly, rests the barrel against the front of the window ledge. Karel has turned the key, but finding the door slow to open, bends down to see if he has pushed the key in at the right depth; you have to be familiar with these old locks. Rosa shoots him in the back of the head and neck.

FOURTEEN

She remains standing bolt upright by the window. If the shots have been heard, someone is sure to turn up and she will call for help. She leans out of the window. Karel must be lying on his back for she sees his shirt gleaming white. As long as he is no longer alive! If he can still see, he must now see her head like a black shape sharply outlined against a dark grey, fast-drifting sky. She calls: who's there? and looks sharp to see if he still moves an arm, but she sees nothing. She waits for an hour. Then she wakes Lett and tells her she has shot a man who was picking the front door lock. Even when wide awake Lett would need time to absorb such strange tidings; half asleep she does not take it in at all. The poor in spirit sleep soundly, like children. She says: all right, and turns over. Rosa shakes her: it is already one o'clock, Lett, and Karel still hasn't come home. She shakes even harder to tell her that she is afraid she may have shot Karel and that she is too frightened to go and look, but Letts answers yes to everything. Rosa returns to the bedroom.

Two things occupy her mind: whether she should now undress and go to bed, and how, when the workfolk arrive at half past four, she will make a sufficiently heart-rending noise.

But the latter problem solves itself. When the two farmhands enter the yard in the half-dark they hear, through the open window, the cries of a woman in labour, even before they have found Karel's body.

It isn't too hard for a woman giving birth to make a heart-rending noise. She tosses and turns on the bed, her screams are heard all over the yard, that she has murdered her husband and that this is her punishment, they must let her die like a dog. About noon she falls silent in the indifference of the totally exhausted to whom it is the same whether they live or die. But when the hospital ambulance rumbles into the yard and when through briefly opened eyes she recognizes Thys among the men who have come to fetch her on a stretcher, she remembers everything clearly and thinks: keep it up.

Thys takes charge of the proceedings, he informs the police and the relatives, keeps out the crowds that are jostling in the yard and receives the gentlemen from the court, offering them coffee and brandy and making sure there is food for anyone who wants to eat. A strange agitation makes him be everywhere at once, thinking of everything, taking care of everything. It is the agitation of an animal sniffing danger, it is also a thirst for justice.

The gentlemen from the court say that this village is getting a reputation for shooting people down. Less than eighteen months ago a woman did exactly the same thing, but she had eight young children, so it was a bit late in the day. Earlier this year a young man who had only been married a fortnight shot his wife through the heart. His friend next door was getting married that morning and he was going to give a salute. He came downstairs with a revolver, one of those old-fashioned stubby ones, to shoot an elephant with, and sat down by the table to clean it. His wife jumped up in alarm, like all women when they see a gun; it might be loaded. Look, he said, to prove it wasn't loaded, and he shot her straight through the heart, in front of her own parents.

The gentlemen interrogate Lett. Of course she doesn't remember at what time she came home last night, she noticed nothing unusual about Rosa, she heard nothing all night and in the morning she was woken up by the maids.

The two farm labourers heard Rosa's cries and they found Karel's body. Rosa's and Karel's was a good marriage, but Rosa had been nervous and irritable during her pregnancy. They say it must have been an accident. Are they sure of it? Absolutely. Do they think their mistress was capable of murder? Absolutely not. One of them says to the examining magistrate: no more than you, your honour.

There is no need for them to ask Thys any questions. He tells them painstakingly of his relationship with Rosa from the very first moment that there was something between them; he tells them that he did not want to marry her because he wasn't of her class. Then he tells them how he came to be back at the farm, what he has heard and seen here, how she talked to him about Karel, her request to him to come on Sunday, even her appeal to postpone his marriage. They ask him why he is telling them all this. Because the court ought to know about it. Does he think Rosa is capable of murder? He cannot believe it as long as it hasn't been proved. Does he want to send her to prison then? No, but justice must be done.

They are so little accustomed to such testimony that the examining magistrate leads his interrogation into a different direction. Is he telling them this because he is afraid of becoming implicated? He has to produce his alibi, which is enough. He was in Brussels with Uncle Dolf, they visited such and such acquaintances of Uncle Dolf's, viewed vacant shops in this place and that, and back in the village they stayed in the café till one o'clock. After that they went to bed. The examining magistrate begins to think he is probably dealing with a compulsive worrier. He asks questions that astonish Thys. Whether he often goes to church, whether he often goes to confession, and when he doesn't seem to get anywhere, whether Thys reads many books? No, not even that. He looks at Thys puzzledly.

It now looks as if Rosa is damaging her case by not mentioning Thys at all. She keeps stressing the suspicious behaviour of the shrimp man. That was what upset her. Fortunately, this shrimp man has been seen elsewhere in the village, by some children at play and also by two old people who were watching them. It was true that he had been loitering about looking for something. They ask whether Rosa had expected anyone that Sunday. No, nobody. Was she happy with her husband? She would have preferred him not to give up his post and they had occasionally had arguments about this, but she had more or less got over it now. Had it always been merely an argument, the sort of quarrel that occurs in any family? Had he ever beaten her? No, he was much too well bred for that.

The examining magistrate makes her go over the whole evening once again, in detail. It seems as if he is only half listening, reassured that there has been no crime. And weary. He looks at his watch and puts his leather briefcase in front of him, as if he will be leaving as soon as this formality is over. However, he says, arranging his cuffs, he just wants to hear a clear and straightforward answer to two questions. Naturally, it goes without saying, doesn't it, that Rosa has given all her answers in perfect honesty, without omitting anything?'

Yes, she sighs, the torture is coming to an end.

Now the second question: why had she asked Thys, the farm labourer, the evening before. ... He looks at her sharply. Well, there is no need for him to tell her who Thys the farm labourer is – why had she told Thys the farm labourer that she wanted to speak to him urgently and what did she want to say to him? She thinks: I'm turning red, my hands are trembling.

'Don't think about it so long,' says the examining magistrate. 'Is it something you are afraid to say?'

'No.' She wanted to ask him to postpone his marriage to Lett.

'Why?

Because they couldn't spare either Lett or Thys.

And yet she wanted Lett to leave.

That was also in order to postpone the marriage.

So she could spare Lett.

Rather lose Lett than lose both of them.

Why didn't she want to lose Thys?

Because Karel didn't know enough about the farmwork

yet and because Thys is the sort of person who works as if it was for himself.

And because Thys would prevent Karel from strangling her.

That's a lie.

Does the examining magistrate lie?

No, but he has been told lies.

By whom?

She doesn't know. Perhaps by one of the maids or men.

Has she spoken of this to any of the maids or men?

Not as far as she knows.

Who could have told him these lies then? Thys?

No.

Is she quite sure of it? Can she swear to it? Has she never shown him her neck?

Oh yes, that! But only as a joke. She and Karel had been fooling about and Thys happened to walk in and asked her why she was so red in the face. And then she had shown him her neck and said: he'll strangle me one day.

And asked him: are you going to stand back and let me be strangled, Thys?

Yes, she had asked him that too. Also as a joke, because he always takes everything so seriously.

That is why Thys came back to the farm after completing his military service, isn't that so?

Yes, your honour. She had to tell him these fibs because he didn't really want to come. He's such a deep one and always makes such heavy weather of everything.

And he had to find out for you what the law says, isn't that so?

Has he told you that too? But she knew it better than he.

And she wanted to marry him, didn't she, run away with him one night and sleep somewhere on a bench in Brussels?

Rosa laughs nervously. Had he believed that seriously?

Yes, yes, Thys had believed it all seriously. She is very good at making people believe things and now she is trying to make the examining magistrate believe things, but he isn't such a deep one as Thys, he doesn't believe it all so seriously. He sees that Rosa is tired and therefore he will now make things a bit easier for her. He will tell her exactly how it all happened. She was in love with Thys for years and Thys was in love with her too, but his conscience wouldn't allow him, the son of a poor basket weaver, to abuse his position at the farm to turn the head of the wealthy farmer's daughter. Thys looked after the interests of Rosa's not very bright half-sister because he had promised her dying mother to do so. Rosa was jealous of the girl. She started going out with Karel when she had lost hope of getting Thys. Everything would probably have been all right if Karel hadn't given up his post. It was just at that time that Thys returned and Rosa began once more to entertain a foolish hope. She hated her husband and was afraid that he would murder her, so that he would have the farm to himself and marry someone else. First she wanted Thys on the farm to protect her against Karel, and then gradually she began to have other dreams. She became jealous of Lett again and she wanted to get her out of the house to stop her from marrying Thys. On the day of the murder she had asked Thys, who had already promised to kill Karel if ever he tried to strangle her, to come so that she could make him carry out his promise. Thys didn't come and therefore she did it herself. So why be in tears now? It's better to speak the truth because only the truth can save her. No punishment will ever ... And her punishment will not be very heavy because there are many mitigating circumstances. For instance, it is quite obvious to him that she committed the murder on a sudden impulse. Didn't she? On impulse, surely, because her pregnancy had made her restless and constantly on edge. This is another mitigating circumstance and there are more. Her husband's unreasonable behaviour, for instance. And above all Thys's testimony that he does not think her capable of murder. That is bound to make an impression and create a mood of compassion: even Thys, who has been forced by the facts to acknowledge her guilt, cannot believe that she is capable of doing such a thing. No, she must not be afraid of the punishment and this is what he wanted to say just now: no punishment will ever be so hard to bear as the remorse of those who bear their guilt in loneliness. She is a Christian, isn't she; her conscience would take revenge sooner or later if she tried to escape justice by lying. She would not succeed anyway, the evidence is too overwhelming. Is she still finding it too difficult? It isn't as if he wanted to force her to own up. He knows that with honest, upright people a confession will come anyway. He is even prepared to go away until she calls for him, until she is ready to free herself by saying yes, but she must realize that this will have the disadvantage that the court will be less sympathetic towards someone who goes on denying till the last moment, in the face of all the evidence. Why not now? He stops for a moment, then repeats: why not now? And then peacefully find the sleep which her conscience has denied all this time.

Rosa despairingly throws up her hands. She didn't do it on purpose, your honour!

'Poor woman', how deeply he pities her. He would understand it if by these stubborn denials she could escape justice, but no matter what she says, she will still have to appear before the Court of Assizes. Does she want to stand there as someone whose guilt is obvious to all and who will be punished all the more severely because she lies like a hardened criminal? But come, he will leave her now to her conscience. He hopes it will speak to her while there is still time because the longer its voice is stifled the more cruelly it will one day torment her. Think of it. He is not speaking to her as an enemy who wishes her harm. Her best friend could not advise her better. If the murdered man could still speak he would say: my dear Rosa, I forgive you, but save yourself from remorse. Do penance and start your life afresh. Not only Karel would say this, but Thys says it too, that grave young man who loves her more than Karel ever did.

Through his testimony he is showing her the road of penance and recovery. He knows that this is the only road that can ever bring them together. At the end of that road, which will be short and purifying, he will be waiting for her. Do it for his sake or for the sake of you both, do it for the sake of your love.

Rosa's teeth chatter as she repeats that she did not do it on purpose. This cannot save her from prison, nor from the gruelling torments of the Court of Assizes.

And it is all Thys's fault: it says so plainly both in the Daily News and in the Antwerp Gazette. We read our newspapers with zeal, in the evening we discuss them, at home and in the bar, and small clusters of people gather in the doorways, talking. We are honest folk and we stick together like brothers against all public authorities.

They can't have our interests at heart, we know it. They demand taxes from us which they squander, soldiers whom they corrupt, and for whom we have to pay money to boot. They give us rural constables who spoil our fun on Sundays and at the fair, foresters who begrudge us the odd hare or two, policemen who meddle in our quarrels and what business of theirs are our quarrels. Lawyers who trick us out of money and judges who make a living out of punishing us. We try to keep out of all their clutches and only the meanest scum among us would ever take pleasure in playing someone into their hands.

Take this Thys, for example, we don't understand him, the mind boggles when we ask ourselves how for God's sake anyone could slap his employer into the nick like that. Granted that she had flirted a bit with him, youth will be youth, why should he go and split on her like that? You must be worse than dumb to go and tell tales to the judges, those unscrupulous foxes who'll make out of it what they like, the worst soonest of all. And if it's true what he told them about Karel, then Karel got no more than he deserved. We don't need anyone to tell us that it's wrong for one man to shoot another as if he were an old dog with one foot in the grave, but if a poor pregnant woman loses her self-control in anger and does something bad, you're not therefore going to clap her into jail. What she did was rid the world of a scheming scoundrel, and of course it wasn't right, but after the event, it wasn't such a bad thing either. Those who know anything about it ought to keep their trap shut and not give the girl away. That is common decency. Now we have seen once again what scum live out at the Leas. We always thought that Thys Glorieus was better than the rest, but now we know that even he is no good.

We think there's more behind it, we think the papers aren't telling us everything. We've heard that that ne'er-do-well from the Leas had set his mind on Rosa and that he was actually jealous of Karel. It may well have been that he goaded Rosa into doing it because he was too cowardly to kill Karel himself. In our opinion he suddenly got frightened that Rosa might squeal and so that's why he spoke up, because he was scared. The one who talks first is most likely to be believed, naturally, even though he miscalculated in his fright. If he had had a scrap of sense he would have realized that Rosa would never betray him, because that wouldn't have lessened her own guilt. Some people have been told by one of the men working at Ridge Farm that Thys betrayed Rosa out of revenge. When he had lost all hope of getting her, he started making eyes at that half-witted Lett, would you believe it, goodness me, that goose. He probably thought he would get into a nice bit of money that way, but at Ridge Farm they weren't born yesterday. They've all had a good education or they have married people with education and it seems they wrangled and haggled till there was hardly anything left for Lett. They say he was furious about that, and that is why he did the dirt on Rosa.

You hear all sorts of things and who knows what really did happen, but one thing is certain, the villain of the piece is that ruffian from the Leas. They ought to have . . . but we're sure he will get his due before long. Run as he may, he'll come a cropper one day, his chickens will come home to roost.

We were disappointed in the Court of Assizes; it was all over in two days, luckily with an acquittal. So at least they were sharp those fellows of the Law, to see straight away: there's no proof, not a shred. But we felt like tearing our Daily News to shreds when we read about the testimony of that bastard Glorieus. The people who went to the trial say he looked as if he had swallowed a broomstick; he never blushed, he never wavered, it all came out raw. Rosa, they say, covered her face in shame, but he didn't flinch. Did you love her? asked the judge. Yes, said the wretch. Didn't you know, asked the judge, if you loved her, that you are the one who has brought her before this court? Why did you do it? And wouldn't you have skinned him alive; he answered that he wanted justice to take its course! Let him come home if he dare! The defence didn't mince words: conceited farm-hand who thinks he is the law. Fine words, but what do those rogues from the Leas care about that, you've got to beat them over the head, otherwise they don't feel it.

Wallop them good and proper, that's what we say.

FIFTEEN

Thys didn't even have to wait till he got home. On that same lonely stretch of road where Rosa had wanted him to waylay and attack Karel, he himself was waylaid and attacked by three men. One of them jumped on him from behind like a huge beast. He managed to jerk himself free but as he bent down the two others overpowered him and hit him with cudgels and kicked him till he lay on the ground, stiff and still.

Uncle Dolf had not gone with him because he didn't agree with what Thys was going to do. He hadn't said much because he only defended opinions which were not shared by

others and Do and Dina had given their view forcefully
enough already. But he despised everything that smacked of
authority, of officialdom. Whenever I see an official cere-
mony, says Uncle Dolf, I count the decorations and the one
who has the most is the biggest scoundrel, it can't fail.
'Simpleton,' Uncle Dolf had said to Thys: 'do you still believe that justice is just?'

But at midnight he gets up and finds Thys's bedroom
empty. He is seized by anxiety, his great voice rouses the
others from their sleep, he calls out ominously: why isn't
Thys home yet? Dina gets nervous, a lioness sensing her nest
in danger and Do's wisdom is inadequate: Thys is old
enough to find his own way home. So he is, but what if it's
one against many, what if he's come to harm. Uncle Dolf is
already outside, he's off and Dina follows him at a distance.

There is hustle and bustle in the village: the old gig from
Ridge Farm has gone past, people have cheered Rosa, poor
betrayed, innocent, acquitted Rosa.

There is no need for Uncle Dolf to knock at doors to ask
if anyone has seen Thys; everybody is outside but no one has
seen him. He casts silence all around and has gone some
distance before one plucky soul is brave enough to call out
that they've no doubt given his Thys what he deserves. And
look, there is Dina Glorieus too, coming after him, that big,
bold woman. She doesn't look left or right, doesn't talk to
anyone, but stalks on, calling anxiously at intervals: Thys!
Behind her back they call mockingly: Thys, my sweet darling Thys! Uncle Dolf turns into the lonely dirt track. There
are no people here, of course, the gig must have taken the
paved road. And there is Thys, lying across the track. Uncle
Dolf turns him over so that he faces upwards, he says his
name, shouts his name, touching his hands, his chest, stands
up, calls for help, kneels, listens for his breathing, listens for
his heart-beat, jumps to his feet, pulling his hair and tugging
at his beard, banging his fists against his temples, rushing off
in one direction, ready to tear into the first person he sees,

then in the other direction; he goes back to Thys, lies down beside him, sobbing, kissing him; he stands up and curses, in a raw, croaking voice. He lifts Thys up as if he were a child and starts carrying him back to the house. Dina approaches. He says: 'Our child is dead.' She stands still in front of him, petrified like Lot's wife. He has to walk round her in order to continue his way. After a long time she catches up with him and begs in a strangely soft voice: 'Dolf, let me help you carry him.'

Dolf does not let go of his burden, nor does he answer. She implores him: 'Dolf, please, he's mine too.' She sees Thys's hands hanging over Dolf's shoulder. 'Dolf,' she says softly, 'he still gives me his hand.' Then she is unable to go on, she stands still, looking around in the dark with one hand to her cheek, as if there is something odd about the spot she is standing on. But by the first houses of the village she catches up again.

There are still people about, intent on jeering at those from the Leas. Uncle Dolf sees them sticking their heads together. He lets out a roar, like a huge, injured beast. He shouts at them: cowards, riff-raff, murderers, and then: that he has got Thys here, this here is his Thys!

The leaden body seems to burden him no more than would a baby on the arm of a sturdy countrywoman; his voice thunders untiringly. Cowards, they were in a crowd, attacking the boy, he'll find out who did it. Even if there were a dozen of them, he'll mow them down, he'll tear them limb from limb, he'll break them over his knee, he'll trample them underfoot. Come on, all of you, anyone calling himself a man, they have murdered his Thys.

They cower against the walls and those who can sidle in by a door, holding one hand on the handle and a knee against the door. They fear that at any moment he will lay Thys headlong across the street and lash out at whoever is nearest, murdering them one by one. But as the threats grow wilder, ten bodies he is now demanding for this one body, his voice leaps into a raw, harrowing wail, that this is Thys, this is my Thys. Dina still walks behind him, without knowing where she is going, her beloved child still offers her its hands, there is nothing else left for her. When they have gone past, the people dejectedly slink back into their houses. Dolf's voice has called down a terrible retribution on them, in silence they climb the stairs to their bedrooms, wondering who will have been slain by the morning, asking themselves what blind folly could have induced them to lay their hands on one from the Leas.

But when Dina and Dolf have laid their child on the bed, have unbuttoned his clothes and washed him with water and vinegar, they are amazed to see the lips moving and in Dina's hand the fingers begin to stir hesitantly. From somewhere in Dolf's large body a thin, quavering baby laugh gurgles up and at last Dina is able to cry. She comes perilously near to embracing Dolf, just in time she reaches out to Do who is standing bolt upright with his back stiffly against the door. She hurries out of the room when Dolf has brought Thys round, his broadly smiling face bent over him, wanting to be recognized. Thys whispers: father.

Slowly Thys recovers, slowly the feverish wanderings, the bouts of dizziness, decrease. So do the fruitless conversations with the captain, with mademoiselle Corinne, with Rosa, and the even more fruitless searches for a job for Jef. The dead farmer's wife, Jan the foreman and always again mon ami, offering advice as he struggles desperately to catch the meaning that flutters away from their buzzing words, visit him less and less often. The pains ebb away, the dull headache lifts like a mist and Thys smiles because he is alive.

Soon he begins to tell lies, a good sign. He talks about the heavy crowbars which they used on him, anyone else would have died a dozen times from less than half the blows. But he counted every blow down to the last one and he lost consciousness only after the attackers had all gone. There were twelve or fifteen of them, he wasn't able to see accurately, he was too busy warding off the worst blows with his arms. They ask him why he couldn't recognize anyone if he was conscious all that time. That is easily answered: they were masked. But there is another question to which Thys does not know the answer, it is a question asked by Uncle Dolf: have you found out at last, you wind bag, where you end up with your prattle of justice?

Thys withdraws into himself and admits that he is alone. But he doesn't worry about it any more. It is his lot, he will go his own way and if anyone wants to get rid of him he'll have to do better than those seventeen, for by now their number has increased to at least seventeen. 'Fear,' says Thys, 'I have no fear. I could easily have run away and they would have had to be quick to catch up with me, but they might have thought I was scared, hoho.'

They have told Lett that Rosa has been in prison and that it was Thys who sent her there. He had told so many lies and said such bad things about her that the court believed him, the scoundrel. Lett had better watch out and not be seen with him again, or she'll end up in the nick herself. Nothing but bread and water, and beatings every day.

She listened and said nothing. What matters to her are children, her mother and Thys. With the children she loves to play, for her mother she loves to pray and Thys, who knows everything, who can do everything, Thys she loves. The others are vicious, they tell her lies and beat her. She lets them jabber. Thys won't send her to prison, it's the others who wanted to send her to Tieleghem and when she said she didn't want to go they made Thys leave, but he will come back. Did he not stroke her back and say, go to the kitchen, Lett, I'll be along? She'll wait for him. She listens when they mention his name. They never do so without using the most terrible words, but she doesn't care a bit. One of the maids gives her a punch in the loins: and you, stupid bitch, you nearly got yourself married to that reptile. She endures this thrust as she has endured so many others in her life.

When she is sent to work in the fields with the others she can easily see Thys's house. She would like to steal away, as she often does, disappearing without a trace, to emerge somewhere amongst a group of children in the road. The beating she is sure to get as a punishment does not deter her, but the thought of Thys's face does. For if Thys does not come of his own accord it means that he cannot and must not come.

One evening there is a party because Rosa is coming home. It is nearly morning and still more wine is being fetched. Lett does not notice that when she forgets to empty her glass no one reminds her; she is waiting to hear Thys's name. But her brothers and sisters refer to him as 'the other one.' The other one, they say, didn't get very far with his slander. The other one was taken to task by the second defence counsel, do you remember him saying: 'Is this your gratitude to your masters, you knave, your masters who took you in when you were a child, who paid you a wage when your work did not justify it, that you now accuse your mistress of murder?' They nearly shouted bravo, up in the public gallery. Rosa is silent and withdrawn. Lett cannot follow the conversation, she waits for the name which is not uttered. The next morning she waits for Thys to come. Now that Rosa is back, surely the quarrel will be forgotten, he will come back now and make her his wife. Every morning she looks surprised at his empty place at the table. Nothing is mentioned because Rosa does not wish it. It is all over and done with, and yet Thys stays away. The days are long, her mind moves but slowly, until at last she gives voice to her loss: when is Thys coming?

One of the maids kicks her on the shin under the table. Rosa turns pale and gets up as if suddenly busy but one of the farmhands, the jester, saves the situation. He says: Thys will never come back, Thys is dead. They quickly change the subject, discussing a cow that has gone dry, and pay no more attention to Thys's betrothed who chews her bread even more slowly than usual and leaves the bacon on her plate congealing in its fat.

The farm work resumes its normal routine, except that in

the kitchen the atmosphere is more subdued around Rosa who in prison has lost the habit of chattering, who no longer shouts at Lett, who does not even notice that Lett has surreptitiously stolen out of sight. Lett goes straight to Thys's house. His father is sitting in the open door of the little shed, weaving a wicker stool. She goes up to him and asks if Thys is dead. He replies that it's the first he's heard about it. If he is dead, it must have happened in a flash, because a moment ago he was still alive. Why not step inside and ask? In the house there is that terrifying Uncle Dolf with the beard. Is Thys dead? In reply he calls out to the back of the house: 'Thys, there's somebody come to ask if you're dead.' Thys is just washing his head under the pump, he appears with his bare back and chest covered in blue and yellow bruises. 'Hello, Thys,' she says, 'who did that?' And Uncle Dolf: 'Oh, it's only the mosquitoes, my dear.' He goes outside to have a laugh and a grumble.

Thys pulls a navy-blue jersey over his blotched body. He looks at her, not quite knowing what to say. She is standing before him, a whole head smaller, and there is something about her which makes her beautiful and sweet. Thys, she whispers, with a happy, longing smile, showing her marvellous teeth. Thys, throwing a quick glance around to see if anyone is looking, puts his arms round her and gives her a kiss. She is the only one who has remained faithful to him. It is Uncle Dolf who does the rest: when are they going to get married? They might as well be quick about it, no need to waste any more time. One week is enough to get everything ready in Brussels. What exactly you have to do in order to get married he does not know, he has no experience in that respect, but come along Thys, you sort that out. There is only one real difficulty and he solves it on the spot. If Lett stays at the farm till the wedding day, she'll arrive at the altar even blacker and bluer than Thys. Uncle Dolf is of the opinion that this can easily be avoided. Lett should go to the farm at once to fetch her clothes. If they won't give them to her, she must come back without, she'll have to call out to them in the yard: 'Bye bye, everybody, I'm off, I'm not wait-ing for you to tattoo me before I get married.'

I'm going with you, says Thys, but Uncle Dolf asks him, hasn't he had enough of a tanning yet, otherwise I'll give you some more, to save you the journey.

Lett was just tying up a bundle when Rosa came into her room to see what she was up to. There was no need to turn Lett inside out with hundreds of questions. The new bride was able to string just enough words together to leave Rosa in no doubt what was going on. In three weeks' time she is getting married to Thys and she has come to fetch her clothes because otherwise she might get beaten up. She thinks: if you want to beat me you'd better hurry up, soon you won't be able to any more, soon I'll be with Thys.

But Rosa does not beat her, she says softly: I'll help you, although there is not much help needed with the few odds and ends Lett is packing. It doesn't take them long. Lett must hold her finger on the knot so that Rosa can tie it. The two women's heads approach each other as they bend down.

Rosa asks: are you happy? Yes, whispers the other bliss-fully.

When the two bundles are ready, she asks Lett into her own bedroom. She looks in the wardrobe, takes out a few plain dresses which Lett must try on. As if she didn't know yet that whatever fits her, fits Lett. She goes on looking through the clothes, more in thought than really searching. She takes out her own wedding gown, a white dress covered in little pearls. Look, this was once Liza's wedding dress, but don't tell anyone that Rosa has given it to you. Have it dyed blue, light blue.

Lett has to try the dress on. Rosa sits on the bed and makes the bride walk up and down. This is the dress in which she should have married Thys, now this other bride will be on his arm, one who is more worthy of him than she. Her eyes grow wide and staring, her heart thumps, she shivers, her teeth chatter, she says she feels as if she is going to have 'flu.

When the clothes are lying on the bed ready to be packed, she looks in a drawer for a small golden watch with chain, golden earrings and a narrow golden ring with a corallite. She says these too are Lett's. It is as if she is trying to delay the girl. She asks her when she is getting married, where they are going to live, whether they have found a place to rent yet. The wardrobe door is stiff. As she pushes it, trying to shut it properly, she suddenly asks if he's quite better now. Lett asks: who? She presses her full weight against the door and utters his name: 'Is Thys quite better now?' Lett says that his body is all covered in blue and yellow bruises, who could have done that? Rosa coughs: 'I can't get this door shut, you turn the key while I push. There we are.'

And Lett, there's something else. Did Lett know she has got a money box? Did Lett know that ever since mother's time they put her New Year's money in it every year? That will come in handy now. Wait and I'll get it.

Rosa disappears to another room and returns with a heavy tin, the old man's idea. He used to put coins in it from time to time. Then, if the brown friars came, or the nuns, or the ladies collecting for the missionaries or selling almanacs, or the priest for St. Peter's Penny, there was always something or other, he could give with a lighter heart, he didn't notice it so much.

Rosa quickly filled the moneybox with heavy coins. Like all children, Lett was more pleased with this than with a bigger sum in neatly counted notes. She hurriedly rolled the moneybox up in a dress and couldn't get away fast enough, in case it would be snatched away from her.

Rosa said: 'I won't see you again, good luck.' Gently she took the meek girl in her arms, kissed her on the cheeks and said, with her lips close to the other's mouth: 'I hope you and Thys will be very happy.' And now Lett must go downstairs alone and leave by the gate in the hedge, at the side of the orchard. Rosa will stay upstairs. Then she throws herself on the bed and sobs.

SIXTEEN

That Sunday in church we could scarcely believe our ears when we heard our old priest announce from the pulpit: 'shall unite in holy wedlock: Mathias Ludovicus Glorieus and Coletta Hendrica Johanna van Doorslåeren, both of this parish; this is the first time of asking.' If they had been names like Desmet, De Clerq, Peeters or Janssens, we might have thought we were mistaken, because there are so many people with those names, but Glorieus and Van Doorslaeren aren't names you hear every day, and we clearly heard the Christian names: Mathias and Coletta, that is Thys and Lett.

There fell such a deathly hush in the church that even the priest, who is hard of hearing, noticed it and looked wonderingly over the heads, as if he thought somebody had called out or something had happened that had escaped him. Then the congregation began to mutter among themselves and no one heard anything of what the priest read and preached after that, our thoughts were miles away.

Thys to be married to Lett! She could be as dumb as she liked and have no idea what she was doing, but wasn't there anyone at Ridge Farm who could make her understand what she was letting herself in for? No matter how sick and tired they were of her, no matter how glad to get rid of her, that was still no reason to deliver her into the jaws of that vicious serpent. Her name is Van Doorslaeren isn't it, haven't those people any sense of family honour? The old man always found himself too good for farming, the girls all wanted educated husbands and now they marry Lett off to a labourer who has never even learnt a trade. It seems he used to cycle around Brussels with a bread cart, maybe he knows all about making bread, you've got to put it into the oven before you can eat it, it won't amount to more than that. We don't suppose he could even weave the simplest laundry basket because he's never done anything at home with Do. So what are they going to live on?

But never mind, that sort always make a living somehow, if it can't be done by fair means, then by foul. What we are puzzled at is this: how about the trial? The Van Doorslaerens can never claim they didn't agree to this marriage. They must have agreed to it; that girl is no more than a child and if any of them had said: look here dear, we don't allow it, then nothing would have come of it. But to come back to the point: what about the trial? Was it libellous what that fellow from the Leas said, or was it the truth, that's what we should like to know. We wonder whether we would allow someone who had done that to us to marry our sister, and we're not even called Van Doorslaeren. It isn't surprising that the tongues are wagging. There are some say bluntly that Thys didn't tell all at the trial and that they bribed him in the nick of time by threatening him he wouldn't get Lett if he didn't hold his tongue. Otherwise things would have come to light that would have made the outcome of the trial rather different. As we turn it over in our minds it becomes crystal clear to us that Thys knew more than he said. We said at the time: what have all those tales got to do with the accident, but of course, the reason they seemed to have nothing to do with it was because Thys was hiding what was most important. If he had told everything, according to some people, Rosa would have gone to jail for twenty years. Today Thys has his reward, and did you see that blue wedding dress? They don't do things by halves, over at Ridge Farm. The Glorieuses must have been open-mouthed.

Uncle Dolf had taken over a small grocer's shop, the most humdrum little shop you ever saw, he was embarrassed about it himself. But not for long. He shrugged his shoulders when he looked at the shelves. Two or three worthwhile properties on which he had had his eye had escaped him at the last minute. There was no time to be lost, so therefore he had taken this dump, but it wasn't a bad proposition, really. There's nothing better than a grocer's shop: you eat at wholesale prices, and however little you sell, you soon make as much as you spend, and that's all that is needed for the present. Now he can look at leisure for somewhere suitable to start a small lemonade factory; on the other hand, however, he might take out a patent for a new kind of polish. You put a little on a piece of shammy and you rub the furniture always in the same direction and never more than three times in the same spot. With a sponge it works very well too. And in any case, he whispers in Thys's ear, I wanted to find out whether that girl of yours is any good in a shop, do you think she can serve a pound of sugar? But Thys says he doesn't think so, he lets him get on with his demonstration, one hand in his pocket, while he himself carries on getting things ready in his little shop.

Lett is gentle, sweet and obedient, he is happy. She wakes up beside him and thinks: Thys must have coffee, she gets up and love gives her the knowledge to do what she has never been able to learn. As he eats she keeps her eye on him, when he looks her way she beams all over her face and smiles. Then Thys goes to the market to buy vegetables and she thinks: Thys will have to eat again soon. She tastes if the soup is good enough for Thys, rakes about in the stove because the fire must burn well for Thys, and cuts her own piece of meat much too small so as to have a large piece for Thys. When Thys comes in, waiting hopefully behind the glass door for an old woman to be kind enough to come into his shop, he naturally sees what she is preparing for him. That big piece is for him. And he says that it is for her. She: no, for you. He: no, it's for you. And they hold each other tight.

When Thys has eaten, he will have to eat again soon, and then he counts the money he has received, deducting the amount he has spent that morning, calculating the present and the future, his honest, earnest eyes on the ceiling. Admiringly she looks up from her darning at this wonderful man who has it all in his head, who does everything so well and who is so good to her. She waits till he tells her to come and sit by him until Uncle Dolf returns from his important, mysterious journeys. He remarks how neat and tidy everything looks, he likes that; no, he never knew she was such a good housewife. Heavens of bliss open up in her otherwise dull-gleaming eyes, everything has been fulfilled for her when she can rest in Thys's arms, waiting for Uncle Dolf to return. Then begins the joy of the night.

Thus pass days, weeks, filled with the same bliss, which Uncle Dolf's boisterousness fails to disturb. One day he has heard where to rent a café with five billiard tables and behind it a large garden, beautifully situated, where he would put tables and cane chairs and swings for the children. Make a fortune, Thys! Another day he stumbles in with a suitcase full of bottles of varnish and polish. A friend of his makes it but he will teach Thys to make it better and more cheaply and Thys can start a business of his own and make a good profit. Does he want to get rich or doesn't he?

What he does himself, Thys doesn't know, nor does he ask. He never earns money in the same way twice, sometimes it comes in dribs and drabs and sometimes at such long intervals that one can tell by his clothes and shoes, but then he suddenly appears looking like a lord dressed in brand new clothes, pays for his board and lodging in handsome round sums and makes sweeping speeches about politics, that jiggery-pokery, the stupidity of the people, the advantages of a republic over a kingdom and the more delicate question: industry or commerce. But there is no response from the two who have each other and need nothing else. He has a few quick drinks and then: 'good night.'

And good it is, the night in which Thys lays his hand on his wife's waist. It's going to be a wild one, laughs Thys, when I come along it starts kicking. As for her, the more it kicks the better. Sometimes it moves so violently that it catches her breath and she takes Thys's hand to make him feel how excited it is. When it remains quiet for too long, she holds her breath, listening. Go on, kick me, hurt me, child of Thys.

But Uncle Dolf sits down by the table with a broad gesture, takes out a leather notebook and silver propelling pencil, and this is all well and good, but we'll have to do a few sums now. Come on, let's have a statement of incomings and outgoings. No beating about the bush, what does Thys earn in this doghole. Thys falsifies all his figures exactly by the double amount; he states both his purchases and his sales as twice their true value. But even this is not worth Uncle Dolf's while writing down. Thoughtfully he draws a large capital D and points his finger to his forehead, asking whether Thys is stark staring mad, slaving his guts out from morning till night for next to nothing. But Thys is not to be shaken out of the slumber of his happiness. 'It will improve, Uncle Dolf, you'll see.' Uncle Dolf shrugs his shoulders; is this his son, this bungler, with his pea-brained wife? Sleep well!

Less than two weeks later he comes to say good-bye, for he's off to the coalmines in Wallonia, Brussels holds no attraction for him at present. It vexes him a little that they let him go so easily. He has always been the happy wanderer, tossing any regret and sorrow into the laps of those he leaves behind. He was always a free man, living for himself, making wide, sweeping gestures, a man used to people but never needing them. Ever since that night when he carried Thys through the village his heart has become imperceptibly caught in the noose which binds us to a place, a house, people, and which prevents us from following our impulses. He felt it when he stood by the glass door between the kitchen and the shop, unconsciously acting as if he had forgotten something. He put down his two suitcases, fumbled in his pockets, and on his lips was the unspoken question how Thys could let him go, just like that. As nothing so childish could ever pass his lips, he said he had run out of matches and took the box from the mantelpiece.

Once outside he was filled with rage and pretended to himself that he was leaving simply because he was ashamed of having such a son, because he couldn't bear it any longer, having to watch that big lumbering idiot, who was surely strong and shrewd enough to do better, grubbing around all day for half a loaf, and in between times playing about a bit with an imbecile wife. He swore behind his teeth, he didn't even want to see their child, it was bound to be an imbecile too. And yet, it was no good, for the first time in his life freedom weighed heavily on him and he felt he had left something behind.

When the first pains begin, Lett crawls away, like a mother animal, seeking solitude in which to suffer the pain which is the price of her happiness. She closes the door, raises her arms, clenches her fists, and grits her teeth, but utters no sound, for this is her part, not Thys's. All he must do is take the child, washed and swaddled, in his arms and rejoice. Stabbed and racked she throws herself on the bed, clawing at the blankets and sheets, and tearing at the cover with her teeth. Then she kneels, protecting her belly with her arms. Then she falls on one side, curving herself like a bow, raising her hands; then she rolls over on her back, her nails scratching the sides of the bed as they seek a hold. She jumps up and tiptoes round the bed, bent double, cradling her belly in her arms, like an animal trying to escape into a hole which it cannot find. Then she lies motionless on the bed, her temples clammy with sweat, not daring to breathe lest the slumbering pains are awakened, but at ever shorter intervals they overpower her and tear her apart.

Added to this there is Thys, anxiously banging on the door. There are moments when her voice fails her, so that he thinks she is dying. He does not believe her when she calls that it is nearly done, that he may soon come in; he rushes into the street to find a doctor, who comes too late but in time: he is there to receive the child and give it independent life. He teaches Thys one or two basic principles of maternity care and then leaves them on their own.

It is a son. And Thys's first thought is that he must start a bakery; he stands absent-mindedly between the two sleeping bodies in bed and cradle, a man of strength on whom fatherhood has conferred importance, peering into the future with sharp eyes.

But she is only pretending to be asleep and as he is still holding himself aloof she opens her large, wide-awake eyes in which the struggle for life still smoulders faintly, and she asks him if it's all right. He kneels by the bed and it is very much all right, she is a good girl and he is going to start a bakery. He whispers in her ear that he will start in a small way, with butter cakes and currant buns. His whipped cream will be the best in town. Before long he will build a little oven in the basement and while he is still explaining his splendid plan to move the fireplace from the basement into the kitchen, she drops off to sleep. But she wakes up again to ask if he is pleased. He is very pleased, she is a good, sweet girl and that fireplace will cost him no more than a length of flue two metres long. He'll also bake the cheapest rye bread in the whole of Brussels and even supposing that he will find no other customers for it but farmers coming to the early morning market with their horses and cows, just imagine, Lett, how much extra that will bring in.

And don't forget that he will do the baking at night, so they won't have to give up the shop. She's fast asleep again, naturally, but he skips lightfootedly over the first ten years of toil and arrives effortlessly at the day when the ten-year old boy starts helping him. What do you say to that, he asks, I always told you I would look after you and what I say, I will do. I am not a man of empty promises, says Thys, I do what I say. Of course they will be moving house one day and take a larger shop, but that is still a dream and he will therefore not say much about it yet. He raises his head from his dreams in the groove of the pillow and at last notices that she is asleep, just when she wakes up again and asks him to show her the child, and, anxious question of all mothers, if it has got everything. It is a well-formed full-term baby with the usual displeased old man's face. It makes her laugh because Thys looks just like that when he is asleep. Thys does not think at all that it looks so much like him, at any rate it has got her mouth, exactly, look then. He doesn't please her by saying this; the child must look like him, it's his child, she wants it to be completely her gift to him.

Together they put it to her breast, but under his guidance. He decides by how much she may depart from the order to lie still and yield to the need to lie on her side while the child suckles. A little bit over this way, but don't move the hip any further. She mustn't talk either, and she must breathe softly through her nose, because breathing draws up the milk. Go on, says Thys encouragingly to his son, go on then. Trying to tempt him to greediness he presses gently on the breast. At last Nic sucks. It becomes so quiet that they can hear him guzzling. Blissfully her head rests back in the pillow and Thys's dreams are now of a son of nineteen, about to become a soldier, and how are we going to manage in the bakery?

SEVENTEEN

According to Rosa, there was nothing they could have done to stop Lett. She had been aware of it for some time and she had warned Lett repeatedly, but anyone on the farm can tell you that when that girl has made up her mind about something it is impossible to talk her out of it. No, she hadn't slipped away unnoticed, Rosa herself had caught her in the act when she was ready to leave with her baggage. My dear, she had said for the last time, you're heading straight for your downfall. But she hadn't even answered. She had walked past her without a word, sullenly and wilfully.

Yet not a day goes by when she does not think of the poor

girl, she says. Not because they couldn't do without her, on the contrary. She has gone and the work gets done just the same, even better. They used to give her some small, simple job to do and thought they could rely on it being done. Then of course it wasn't done properly and when they thought all the work was finished they would have to do her part all over again. This doesn't happen any more now; in short, as far as the work is concerned they're better off without her.

But dear me, you would never believe how much she misses Lett. After all, we were used to her being there. She was always around, never went out, she always used to sit by the others, quietly, and withdrawn. She never complained, never argued, never asked for anything, never disagreed. We got attached to her without realizing it. Yes, every day Rosa thinks: I wonder how our poor Lett is getting on. She can't write of course, and even if she could she still wouldn't. And here we are not knowing how she is getting on, it's awful. Rosa keeps thinking: Lett has gone and we don't hear anything, dear me. Whether she is happy or whether she is miserable, Lett is silent. The maids look up in surprise. For her sake, not a word is ever said about Thys and yet she is always talking about his wife. It's perfectly obvious that she cannot keep quiet about it. Even though she never mentions Thys, his name hovers in the air whenever there is talk of Lett. At first no one dared reply, it's so easy to mention accidentally the name of a husband when one is talking about his wife. One day one of the maids turned up with the news that Lett had had a baby, and here at last was something that could be discussed. And she lived in Brussels in such and such a street, in a mean little shop. As Rosa still remained silent, because she was literally dumbstruck, the girl added gratuitously, and it's got a harelip.

Then Rosa wrote a letter. That she had heard, dear sister, that she had had a baby and that it was such a wonderful baby, warm congratulations, she hopes that mother and child are doing well. As soon as you're up and about again, dear sister, I hope you will come and visit us and show me your lovely baby. But perhaps you would find it difficult to make the journey at first, so maybe I will come and visit you instead to see your lovely baby. But there is always so much to do at the farm, I can't say for sure if I shall ever get round to going to Brussels to see your lovely baby. Has it got brown eyes like you? I would like to buy it a pretty little outfit, as a present from its aunt who loves it so much. I wish I knew someone I could ask to take a parcel for you because I don't really think I shall be able to come. Good-bye dear sister, and once again, warm congratulations. Your sister Rosa.

Then she tears up the letter, for she has caused Thys enough pain already without having to send her sister, whom she has always treated badly, these honeyed congratulations as if he didn't exist. But with this letter all possibilities are exhausted; there are no other means of seeing Thys's child, of ever being near Thys again, of ever hearing his warm voice again. There is no one in the village or among her acquaintance whom she can ask to go to Lett on her behalf. All she can do is ask the maids, by roundabout ways, to find out more about mother and child.

Either she feels remorse, think the maids, for having treated Lett so badly, or she is hoping to hear that Lett is not happy. Rosa has been much quieter and more devout since the trial, she does good deeds, never speaks ill of people as she used to, and never flies into a temper either, but resentment can hide deep down and when all is said and done she can't really be blamed for wishing ill on Thys and Lett.

But the happiness of a small shopkeeper in Brussels has no story. Lett and Thys have a child, there is little more to be said about it. It has got a harelip and there is no more to discover. Rosa desperately writes a second letter. Dear sister, I have heard you have had a baby and I congratulate you with all my heart. I am writing in haste, please let me know when it will be convenient for me to come and see you because I would like to see your baby.

She tears up the letter at once. Thys would guess straightaway that she is writing to him, because Lett can neither read nor write and he knows that she knows this. Suddenly she thinks: he wouldn't chase me away, he would never do that. It is as if he is actually standing before her.

He looks into her eyes and does not move. She says: you won't chase me away, I know you well enough to know you won't.

It is like a dream. Thys vanishes. Bit by bit she recalls his life at the farm. He was never spiteful. Up till now she has always repressed the desire to see him again, now she unwittingly prompts it by wondering how he would receive her if she came to see his child. She tries to convince herself that she is irresistibly curious to see the child.

In the end she announces that tomorrow, Sunday, she has to go to Tieleghem, but she travels to Brussels instead without any clear idea how she will contrive to see the child.

In the shop she buys, in any event, a little vest, a bodice, a singlet, a frock, leggings, bootees, a bonnet. In the shop-window lies a doll in a cradle. Rosa wants to have whatever that doll is wearing. And even if she didn't want it, the nice lady with the beautiful grey curls would talk her into it; there is nothing more willing than a woman's heart in a shop full of pretty things for the newly born. The customer smiles and beams as she holds up the miniature vest, puts it down gently, spreads out the little bodice on top of it, then the dainty little singlet, then the pink frock. As if she was already about to cuddle the baby. Spreading her fingers she tenderly holds up the unbelievably soft bonnet, she would wish to press the bootees to her breast, so sweet they are. With a boldness permissible and flattering among women, the lady asks if it is for Rosa herself. Her happiness overwhelms her, blushingly and proudly she casts her eyes down: yes. But madame, well, how shall I put it, isn't it much too early? In a flash Rosa remembers that she is not wearing a wedding ring, but never mind, she blushes: another four months. And lets herself be complimented because it doesn't show yet, there are not many women who carry so well. In a whirl of pain and happiness, flushed and breathless, Rosa leaves the shop.

In Thys's narrow street it is busy. Girls cross the road hurriedly, in slippers, boys loiter with their hands in their pockets, older people stand on the pavement, chatting. Twice Rosa walks up and down the street, first on the left, then on the right. When she is still a long way from the shop she hopes that Thys will be standing behind the narrow, small-paned double door but when she is level with it she is afraid and hurries on. The third time she daren't go past again, inhibited by her countryfolk's suspicion of being watched by everyone. Diagonally opposite the shop there is a café, a large, modern window under a sweating pointed gable several centuries old. She runs inside for cover. Three habitués in shirt-sleeves, and the fat landlord himself in trousers and singlet are playing billiards. She sits down by the window; not even a scrap of paper can blow past Thys's door but she will see it. Perhaps he will be going out soon, on an errand, then she would bravely go into the shop, she might even wait till he came back.

She takes her time over her glass of beer. She should leave now. Or else order a second glass. The landlord brings it to her and asks her bluntly if she is waiting for someone. He doesn't mean any harm by it but she turns dark red and says that friends of hers live in the shop across the street but the door is shut, they are probably not in. In his opinion they are bound to be in, they never go out. The door may be shut, but there is a bell, has she tried that? Yes. Ready to oblige and self-assured, he tells her to come with him. She follows him across the street, he opens the door without further ado, and with knocking knees she stands before Thys, he with his back to the kitchen door, she leaning against the street door, ready to go straight back to the farm at a sign of his finger. I heard, she says, that our Lett has had a baby and I would like to see it if I may.

She hears his warm voice from afar: 'Come in, Rosa.'

There is no grudge in him, she looks pale, and she is trembling, he wants to do something for her.

Thank you, she whispers, she walks past him, through the door he is holding open for her. There is Lett, sitting by a wicker cradle, Do Glorieus's work, on the other side is the chair Thys was sitting on. She kisses Lett, who gives her a fleeting smile without getting up; the beatings have not been forgotten. Then she bends over the cradle, starts laughing and crying at the same time; she has to sit down on Thys's chair and now she is no longer laughing but crying.

Thys's heart turns and turns inside him; he has to do something for her, he takes the child from the cradle and puts it into her arms. Now she even starts crying out loud. She gives the baby big, smacking kisses, with open mouth, and Lett looks on in stunned alarm, wondering if she is going to eat it up. At last she can speak again. It is the most wonderful baby she has ever seen in her life and these words unite the three of them. Thys asks who does it look like, and at once she replies, like you, and kisses the child again, with tightly shut eyes. But it has got Lett's mouth, says Thys, which Lett denies with great conviction and Rosa says that on the contrary, it is absolutely Thys's mouth, and she kisses that mouth of Thys's.

Then Lett must open the present she has brought for Nic, what kind of a name is that, you never hear it in the country. 'Dominicus,' says Thys, 'like father,' but they didn't like 'Do' and Thys himself thought Nic was a nice name. When he was in the army, in the captain's house, a friend of the young gentlemen used to visit them and his name was Nic. He had asked the captain what kind of a name that was. Mon ami, he said, at home in Brabant they would call him Do or Domien, Nic is a bit posher but it's Dominicus just the same. Thys hadn't forgotten.

His kind voice is soothing, he makes coffee while the two women put the new clothes on the baby against its will. Then they all sit round the table and Rosa talks all the time about her train but she doesn't leave, she daren't ask what she wants to ask. Whether they are doing well, whether they would please be so kind as to treat all that is hers as if it was theirs, whether they wouldn't want her as their maid, she'll polish their shoes, she'll look after their baby when they go out, arm in arm, calling each other sweet names, she'll make their bed so that they will sleep softly; for herself she will spread a straw mattress in the attic. Thys asks: how are things at home? 'Ah,' says Rosa. That is all she is able to say. The remorse and despair that gnaw at her heart are a matter between her and her God.

While Lett is giving the baby the breast she quickly says good-bye and when Thys takes her to the tram stop she asks his forgiveness. He answers that they won't talk about that ever again. They say no more and there is the tram. 'I know,' she says, 'that no one could ever forgive such a thing, I deserve no forgiveness.' Thys says simply that all is for-given.

'You must not be so generous, Thys, you've always been far too generous, you ought to throw me under that tram. You ought not to forgive me, I don't deserve it.' Thys laughs that there is nothing she can do about that. Why harp on it? It's finished, it's all over and done with, and that is that. Does she think he has never had troubles before? Good heavens, this was only a triviality. If he worried about things the way she does, he would have mouldered in his grave long ago. So they won't mention it again. And if she is too lonely at home, she can come and visit Lett, always welcome. Shake hands now, and cheer up. She's no longer a child, she ought to know by now what life is like.

Crushed by his magnanimity she daren't even offer him her criminal hand.

By the church of Finis Terrae she gets off, to confess her murder, in French because then the priest won't connect it with the murder in Flemish Brabant about which he has no doubt read in the paper and 'j'ai assassiné mon mari' does not sound quite so terrible to her as 'I have murdered my husband'. She cannot understand how she can have kept her secret bottled up for so long. When she talked about it with Thys just now it all seemed so simple. Everything she has been taught about God's mercy makes sense to her at last: He is like Thys, she would wish to go from one confessional to another and confess the same everywhere: j'ai assassiné mon mari, for the sheer relief of being able to say it, knowing that someone is listening.

A priest comes strolling through the aisle in the direction of the altar. Reading his breviary, he walks three steps past her, turns round and looks straight at her, asking with his eyes if she sits deliberately so near the confessional. Her heart stands still, she grabs her handbag and flees.

EIGHTEEN

At night Thys bakes his butter cakes and currant buns in the kitchen stove and in the evening Thys builds his oven. All he lacks is customers. He and Lett have to eat half the stuff themselves, but when he halves his production there are sure to be two or three customers who for some far-fetched reason suddenly want a large bag of cakes and then Thys works to full capacity again.

The owner of the café offers to put a plateful of cakes and buns on his counter. He says there is a demand, from people who don't want to go home to eat because they would never get away again without a row. Mind you, it's sale or return, that's understood, isn't it? His experience is the same as Thys's: sometimes the dish is empty by the evening, but usually half the buns come back and if one day Thys sends him fewer, he needs a lot more. Thys has to make complicated calculations: the price of flour, milk, butter, a few eggs and the buckets of coal he burns, deducted from the proceeds. In order to maintain any profit margin at all he does not bring his labour and lack of sleep into account and sets all his hopes on the oven. It is strongly built and is given an old oven door bought at the flea market. There is a small hole above the handle which he has to fill up before each baking. In the end the oven probably costs him more than the proceeds of all the cakes he has sold so far, but Thys now bakes bread. He bakes rolls, and his own speciality: horse bread. In the window he pins the cardboard backing from an old calendar on which he has written, in ink: 'we specialize in horse bread.' In the left hand corner he has drawn the head of a little known breed, half sheep, a quarter donkey and a quarter horse. He launches his speciality at the early morning market, buys vegetables only from those farmers who come with horse and cart and is able to dispose of some bread with the people he buys from. If he neglects one customer in order to recruit a new one, the one he ignored buys less, or nothing at all from him, and the sale of vegetables in Thys's shop remains too slender to push up the sale of horse bread. No matter how Thys calculates and piously raises his eyes to the ceiling, he can neither prove that he is making a loss nor that he is getting a fair return for his labour. He therefore doesn't count the labour and neatly demonstrates to Lett that from the start he has been making a small profit. She believes everything.

Her profit does not require so much demonstration, nor does it keep in step with his. The fecundity of her gently blossoming body puts a Leo in the cradle which Nic still needs to hold on to, faltering on the adventurous journey to the nearest chair.

Dina is godmother. At her side is Lieneke, like a guard. The once so proud Dina appears to have surrendered to this hard, merciless spinster. She daren't even be amiable under Lieneke's lack-lustre eyes. Thys busies himself to make them feel at home. Thys lies a bit, boasts a bit, Thys even tells jokes because he knows how fond mother is of laughing, but each time he has nearly broken the ice, Lieneke starts talking about Pol. Pol has been on holiday, Pol has bought a new cooker, twice the size of this one here. Pol has bought a carpet.

And again Rosa comes, again she gives the child a present of vest, singlet, frock, bootees, leggings, and she presses an envelope with money into Lett's hand. This is for the two children, better not say anything to Thys.

Because Thys would refuse to accept it, whilst she tries desperately to mollify her God who will not forgive her her sin and her wickedness as long as she has not confessed. And she dare not confess, she cannot. Nor does she dare stay away from the communion rail on Sundays, for what would people in the village think of her if she did. She goes to communion to prove the purity of her conscience. With the host in her mouth and her hands covering her face, trembling lest God will strike her dead on her chair in punishment of the sacrilege she is committing, she weeps. The people think she weeps because of what she has been made to suffer, but she weeps because of the terrifying accumulation of sins and sacrileges. There is no forgiveness but she frantically mortifies the soul and does good works, putting money in the offertory boxes, giving to the poor, to Thys. Thys shows her his hand-made oven, but she can tell at a glance: this is poverty, a lot of worry and work for nothing. She asks him cautiously whether he is always firm and ruthless enough with his customers. He shouldn't be too soft-hearted and too honest. He has always worked himself to the bone for others and never thinks of himself. She hopes he is making sure his city customers pay him properly? Has he never thought of taking over a well-established bakery?

This is what Thys intends to do as soon as he has earned enough money, but he's not going to get himself into debt for it.

How can she offer him money? She says she is sure that he could easily get a loan. Everybody trusts an honest, hard-working man like him.

But he is a Glorieus, an independent spirit, he tells her

again that he won't borrow any money. Just let him be, the beginning is always hard. Yes, she knows, but if it is in one's power to make it less hard, what is the point of not doing so? She herself, for instance, she has the farm all to herself now, she didn't have to start all over again with a little one-horse holding, did she? If only Thys was willing to borrow money, he could skip ten years' hard toil.

'In appearance,' says Thys, 'Only in appearance. The money would cost interest, wouldn't it?' 'Not at all,' asserts Rosa. And Thys: 'It would still have to be repaid one day.' And she: 'That could be discussed later.' And he: 'That's not the way moneylenders talk, you know.' She fumbles at the oven door handle. 'It's the way I talk. You said: we'll never speak of it again. That's what I say too.'

Thys stands even straighter than usual, puts his hands on his hips and looks in disdain at his troubles. He says, she is talking like someone who doesn't know what he has been through. She thinks he had a hard time of it on the farm, but if she knew what he was up against when he first came to Brussels! And hasn't he come out on top? He's had plenty of jobs offered to him, but all of them working for a boss. He wants to be his own boss, he doesn't want to be dependent on anyone. He is already his own boss now, but you wait. He's only been at it for two years.

She looks into the oven and her voice resounds: 'I'd like to do it for your children, Thys, for your children's sake you should accept it.' But he answers so proudly that she looks up with a start: He can take care of his children.

And Thys goes on baking and selling his vegetables, rice, flour, noodles, tinned food; he does his sums every evening, sleeps only half the night and awaits the birth of his third child. Let's hope it will be a girl this time.

A respectable gentleman with a small twirled moustache calls. He has been a verger in one of the suburbs for two years and he comes from Brabant, like Thys. He says he sometimes cycles down this street and he has heard about Thys through some farmers from his village who come to the early market. 'Good morning, madam, what lovely kiddies, bursting with health I see. Good health is all that matters, isn't it, madam, it's all that matters? But what a lot of worry they cause us before they're grown up.'

From parental worries he nimbly jumps to a proposal which will ensure the prosperity of Thys's children for many years to come. As verger of a newly established church in a parish largely consisting of factory workers he doesn't earn very much, he's sure Thys understands, and so we won't talk any more of that. Now, in his church they preach sermons about *Rerum novarum* and a fair wage for the labourer, and it all sounds splendid, but paying a fair wage themselves is another matter, isn't that so, madam. Still, he's not complaining and he's trying to make a bit on the side here and there; he's married too, and he's got two kiddies, so you can imagine. Anyway, to come to the point, he's running a dairy business with his brothers. That is to say, his two brothers, both of them still bachelors, come to town every morning in a lorry and he's looking for customers for them so that they can expand. He has already obtained the custom of several big shops and bakeries. He also advertises door to door, well, yes, it's hawking in a way, but these days one can't afford to be too particular about the way one makes an extra penny as long as one makes it, that's the main thing, isn't it, and he has always been taught that hard work is no disgrace. So now he has fixed up several delivery rounds, which are looked after by eleven agents. This is the way it works, you see, if you listen carefully you'll get the point straightaway. He, the verger, goes over a certain district, let's say the district Thys and Lett live in. He goes from door to door, leaving a sample of his milk, and he chats to the people. They see at once that his milk is first class, and so it is, first class milk, madam, he can vouch for that, this is milk such as nobody else sells in the whole of Brussels. This milk has not been baptized, there's no chalk in it, madam, it boils in one minute flat, madam, it froths up in a jiffy like three-year-old Brabant beer. First of all the brothers take the rounds themselves, because they do as much of the retailing as they can handle, but as soon as they can no longer cope they start looking for agents and that's why he has called on Thys. They have two kinds of agents. Some of them work on commission; they get so much for every litre sold, and then there are others who work on their own account. They buy a milkround from him, because he has recruited the customers, you understand, and they can get it cheap because they sign a contract to buy milk from his brothers for a period of at least three years.

Thys needs only to ask the price of such a milkround to know, without doing any sums, that he can't afford it. And work for someone else he won't.

He begins to dread Rosa's visits, and visit them she will, because the third child is on the way. Most of all, he hopes that Uncle Dolf will stay away! Rosa treats him with a kind of pity which wounds his pride, Uncle Dolf with a contempt that exasperates him. When he visits his parents Do boasts, like Lieneke, about Pol, who kills so many pigs, calves and cows per month. They don't tell Thys to his face that he is daft, having married a slow-witted wife who spends what he earns and prevents him from getting on in the world, but that is what they think, he can sense it. There are days when he deliberately torments himself with the question whether or not he really is daft, an inferior person. Ever since his childhood he has felt himself to be the stronger one, the one who is helpful and good to others out of his abundant strength. He always gave himself to others because he didn't mind what happened to him, and because wherever he went he wanted to put things right. Was that daft, was the great Thys Glorieus who always helped other people too daft to help himself?

He found a cruel pleasure in tormenting himself. Bending over the loaves as he pulled them out of the oven he sneered at himself that he was clever enough to bake them but not clever enough to sell them. Standing in his shop, hands in his pockets, he pondered upon what Uncle Dolf had said and

looked dispiritedly at the tray of spinach and the tray of
chervil and the miserable-looking salsify. These were hard
days for him, who had never doubted himself. All his pre-
vious disappointments had left him unscathed because he
knew that his strength was inexhaustible. But now, for
example, they didn't have a pram and he couldn't afford to
buy one. Were his children not even to have what he, a poor
basket-weaver's child, had had? Had he not assured Lett
that she would have a good life with him, and did she have a
good life? No, she did not. Thys bowed under a burden that
was too heavy for him.

When Rosa came he put up a brave front in order to stave
off her pity, and to make sure he would receive no further
covert propositions. Yes, he had had another splendid offer,
a milk round. He'd have to borrow a small amount, so
much, but then, he'd have his bread and butter, and more.
But she knows his principles, he doesn't borrow. Perhaps he
might, if he saw no future in his shop, but he's confident in
that, he's as sure of his shop as he is that tomorrow there will
be another day. While Lett is putting the little ones to bed,
he defends her; why should she always be blamed for his
lack of success, it could equally well be the fault of others.
People say, he tells Rosa, that Lett has no idea about house-
keeping and saving, but she does save, says Thys. She saves,
and he doesn't even know how much, but he knows where
she keeps her moneybox. He gives Rosa a confidential wink
and says that of course he could easily find out how much it
is, but he doesn't want to, because she wants it to be a surprise for him, and so a surprise it must be.

Rosa has a bright idea. When Thys has gone to the basement to see to his oven, she in her turn gives Lett a
confidential wink. She is going to give her the money for that
milk round and then Lett will have to tell Thys that she has
saved it. You see, Rosa has no children, all her other brothers and sisters have married rich, it's a pleasure for her to
be able to help Lett's children.

Lett has no scruples, she accepts presents like a child. And whatever is good for Thys and the little ones, is welcome, no matter where it comes from. Put it under your mattress, says Rosa, and give it to him at night, then he can't see from your face that you're telling a bit of a lie. And Rosa laughs out loud. She is suddenly very happy. Because God is like Thys. He does not demand confessions either. She has come to him and this sign of repentance was enough for him. Words are idle. She does penance, she does good works, he does not demand from her that terrible confession, on the contrary. He thinks: you would give anything to free your soul by confessing your sin. Keep your secret and suffer, that is the penance I want of you.

Her gaiety makes Thys feel happy. One day she will get over these brooding moods of hers, one mustn't lose hope.

Then there is another cause for happiness. At first he jumps up as if stung: where does all that money come from, he has never earned that much. But she has learnt Rosa's lesson well: saved up bit by bit from the first day. He doesn't believe her capable of a sustained lie and the joy of having miscalculated to his own disadvantage every evening is too tempting. You see! Hadn't he always told her that he would look after her and the children, Letty my sweet! But he adds, it's all her work. He may have earned it, but she has saved it and remember this: earning money is nothing, but hanging on to it! Now the verger may come.

Don't buy a pig in a poke, says the verger. Thys must come along on the round for a week with the agent he has recruited for it at a commission of so much per litre, then Thys can see for himself that it's worth the price. If you're doing business, both parties must be satisfied, honesty is the best policy, isn't that so, madam? Madam, isn't that little boy of yours tall. How old is he? Three and a half; well, well, so is his little boy, a month older even, but he's a good head shorter. This little chap here is going to be like his dad, you can see that, but I hope mine is going to be a bit taller than me, madam, it's tough luck for a man to be too small.

It's cheap for clothes, but that's all, a man wants to show a bit. Anyway, we're all agreed then, next week they can sign the contract and see about the payment.

Cash, says Thys.

Oh but, well now, he means to say, well all right if you insist, it's all the same to him, if you prefer it that way, then cash. It's not for this or for that, he really wouldn't have minded at all, but cash *is* best of course. Buying, knowing what you're buying, and then paying cash for it, that's the way honest people do business. But these days you'd sometimes believe that there is no honesty left in the world.

Of course, Thys and Lett probably know the city fairly well by now, but if they knew half what he knows, he who has been inside so many houses! And the poshest are often the worst, madam. Yes, yes, but dear me, he's kept them chatting far too long, but then, when you're having a pleasant conversation with people you can trust, time flies, doesn't it. See you next week then, Saturday morning around eight o'clock, how's that?

When Thys had familiarized himself with the milk round and knew what he was buying, he paid cash, with the pride of an honest man counting out his own hard won pennies; he cancelled the lease of his shop and rented further down the street a large garage at the back of which there were stairs leading to three poky rooms under the eaves. It was part of the outhouses at the back of a large house in a more elegant parallel street, dating from the days of the carriage-and-pair. The gate to the stable was bricked up, and the stable itself, converted into a wash house, was used by the big house, but through the kitchen window Lett and the three children could breathe the fresh air from a large garden. Thys, with little Dolf on his arm, Leo and Nic running about his legs, and with Lett by his side, turned his face to that garden which reminded him of the meadows and trees at home; he talked of buying the whole building and converting the garage into a shop, with white tiles:

LAITERIE M. GLORIEUS
BEURRE ET OEUFS
EN GROS   EN DETAIL
MAISON DE CONFIANCE

of raising the building to four storeys, with spacious balconies running all along the back, for the fresh air and the lovely view. How happy he would be to give all this to his wife and children. He reminded Lett of the wretched little dump they had just left. She blissfully rested her cheek against his broad chest, and even more blissfully he said that this was only a first beginning. He was thinking of the future, when his father and mother would be old, and Uncle Dolf too, perhaps even Lieneke who didn't seem to get married ever. His foreman would be Jef, who would earn a wage more than large enough to rent a better place for his old grandma. He would train the children of his poorest schoolmates to be wholesalers. Vaguely he foresaw a future when his benefactions would flow abundantly over many and he would bring happiness to all, for that was his destiny, that was the purpose of everything.

NINETEEN

But once he had paid up and the job was about to begin for him, it was finished for the verger, finished and done with. He got his biggest profits from chatting up new customers and getting new milk rounds going. These new recruits had to be coaxed with first class milk and the only means of selling them first class milk was by pouring all the water into the churns intended for the previously established rounds. This was only done after a time lag of a few months, just long enough for Thys to be convinced that here at last he was on the right track and could start thinking of the little white tiles. Two workmen came to place them at a height of one and a half metres and the second row from the top was a frieze of red flowers. He himself was standing on a ladder, covering the rest of the walls in oil paint. Once this was done he would start selling butter and eggs.

The first customer to cancel her order was an old woman living alone, who couldn't keep her teeth in position. She snapped with those teeth in Flemish and in French and Thys didn't trouble himself too much to keep her custom. Quality is its own advertisement, she was sure to come back.

The second one was an elegant lady, with two children, who said it was irresponsible to sell such milk, didn't Thys have any children of his own? She would never argue about the price, all she asked for was first quality milk. That's why she had started buying from the verger, but since he had left the business she had had reason for complaint. She was not going to put up with it any longer.

That day there were ten complaints and Thys passed on the message to his suppliers. They assured him that the milk was always the same, but the season might have something to do with it. In spring, when the grass is new, the milk tastes different and looks a bit bluish. But Thys knew enough about milk, he wasn't born yesterday. Then they told him sharply that for their part they delivered pure, unadulterated milk but that they could not, of course, guarantee the quality after the churns had left their truck. Thys's eyes were sharper still when he replied that maybe he hadn't understood them properly. They should get down from the truck and explain to him what exactly they meant. They were chubby, little men, as short as their brother but twice as fat and courage wasn't their main failing. All right, all right. Thys earned enough money didn't he, why should he bother about the belly-achings of a few fusspots; come and have a drink across the road, man, come on.

Thys continued to lose customers and when the two fat men began to realize that neither by smart stratagems nor by feigned joviality could they avert Thys's slowly gathering rage, they suddenly made a quick dodge: if Thys had anything to complain about, he should go and see their brother, he was the one he had signed a contract with, not them.

However, the brother was nowhere to be found, even postcards urgently requesting him to call at the earliest opportunity did not appear to reach him. Thys decided to make an all-out effort to win back the customers lost from a sadly dwindling list, not only because of the milk sales but also in view of his first-class butter and eggs. He did not have to go far; from the very first one, the woman with the false teeth, he found out everything. She was now buying milk from that monsieur si gentil again, the verger, and now she knew who was to blame, c'est vous. 'Moi?' asked Thys. Oui, vous, she said, you're a swindler, she knew all about his tricks, ce monsieur had explained it all to her. He had been in too much of a hurry to get rich, but ça ne va pas comme ça, vous savez. Elle connaissait son numéro, she knew his kind, but the monsieur had advised her to buy milk from him again, then she would soon see that he sold excellent milk and that it was the agent who watered it down. She had taken his advice and now she had once more du lait comme avant. And she slammed the door.

Thys wasted no more time on postcards, he went straight to the verger's house. A huge fat woman asked him if she could take a message because her husband was still in church for a late burial service. Thys said he would call back another time, but waited outside. After he had seen the verger going into his house the fat woman told him again that her husband had not yet come home and that he probably would not be back till quite late. That's all right, madam, said Thys, you can call him anyway, I saw him go in. She apologized most politely. She had been busy tidying the rooms upstairs and her husband must have come in without her hearing him. One moment, please.

The verger apologized even more profusely. How unfortunate, this had happened once before, with another good friend of his, but luckily, the man had seen straightaway that it was a mere misunderstanding. Thys quietly let him talk until he had finished. Thys had come to discuss the milk round. He had bought it, he had paid for it. Ever since, he had been supplied with poor milk and he had gradually lost his customers.

The verger had then gone to his customers behind his back, telling them that Thys tampered with the milk and winning them back for himself, no doubt with the intention of selling the round which Thys had bought first, to some other poor sucker. But Thys is no sucker, Thys wants his money back. He wants to see it counted out here on the table before five minutes are up. After that, we'll talk again.

The verger laughs like a trumpet. Thys says: I see you don't know me yet. I can't bear injustice. I will give anything to squash a scum like you underfoot like a caterpillar. I'll strangle you here in your own room. He says it perfectly coolly, he has learnt how to control himself.

Tut tut tut, what a nasty fellow we've got here. Liza, quickly, go and ring the police from next door's, and tell them there's a fellow here who wants to murder me. The fat woman turns pale and grabs at her heart but Thys tells her it's no use 'phoning the police because her husband will be dead before she is back. He once tried to obtain justice from the police, madam, but ever since then he has looked after his own justice. And Thys calmly explains to her what he has already told the verger. He wants his money to be paid back to him immediately.

At this the fat woman bursts out. Isn't Thys ashamed of himself to suspect and threaten an honest man?

She clearly knows nothing about his shabby tricks; her defence is sincere. She gets excited, shouting louder and louder; she says that she thought at first that Thys was a madman who had escaped from an asylum somewhere, but now she has found out that he is no more than a trickster. All right then, he can have his money back, if he thinks he can get anywhere with it.

And I thought, madam, says Thys, that you knew that your husband was a crook. But I see that you are an honest woman. Give me the money and if he has the nerve to call the police and take the matter to court I shan't deny that I've had my money back.

She shrinks back in consternation, her mouth hangs open. There is a deathly silence. Suddenly the verger starts up again. All it says in the contract is that Thys has to buy milk from him for three years, it does not say anything about the quality of the milk. Just in time he notices how his wife is looking at him; he immediately veers round and pretends to be angry. What kind of manners are these; this man is trying to blacken him in front of his wife. Go and ring the police, Liza, quickly.

Head forward, Thys lunges towards him, his hands stretched out behind him, ready to lift him up and fling him on the floor. The woman places herself between the two men, one retreating, the other advancing.

I'll give you the money, she says. There is an instinct which unfailingly betrays to a woman what a man is worth. There is nothing verger-like about her verger. He is a crafty little crook who wants to fill his pockets at any cost, she has known that for a long time, but she had never thought him capable of such blatant deceit. Suddenly she has seen through him, because with her feminine instinct she believes Thys: he is honest.

The verger thinks she is only pretending, and will quietly slip out and ring the police; he chatters busily. Yes, that will be best. He will give Thys the money back and then they will go to the law to have the matter settled amicably. Then it will all be straightforward and above-board, won't it? Naturally, he is concerned about his good reputation and whichever way it goes he will insist on a decision by law so that nothing can be said against him, he is acting in good faith. The longer his wife stays away the more he is convinced that she will presently return with a policeman. Smart work, that; stamping hard on the stairs to give the impression that she was going upstairs to fetch the money and then quietly opening the front door.

The verger even starts talking about the weather, but when she appears with the money in her hands he explodes that she must have gone out of her mind. She snaps back that he can lodge a complaint if he wants to.

When Thys has got the money in his pocket and is turning his back on the verger, something stops him: the thought that this is the way tricksters extort money. He asks for pen and paper and with steady hand he writes out a receipt for the sum of so much, returned to him by way of annulment and cancellation of the purchase-contract.

He leaves silence behind him. That evening the woman fills the silence with sobs. The verger tries to explain to her that the real rascals are his brothers, who tamper with the milk, if you can call it tampering. Is there anywhere in Brussels where they sell unadultered milk? There is not a single country in Europe where the inspection of milk by state and city is so bad and so slapdash. This is just what he always says to prospective customers, and then he always adds that there is nothing they can do about it except buy from an honest supplier. But his self-defence is feeble. She retorts, between her hands, that he must have known the milk was being tampered with, because he had tried to win back the customers behind the poor man's back with the aim of selling the round to somebody else later. I am ashamed, she sobs, I daren't show myself in the street any more.

Then Thys took a basket full of eggs on one arm and on the other arm a basket full of butter, he joined his hands together and with each hand he picked up a churn of unsold milk, looked around the garage, saw that there was nothing left except his pushcart, steadily climbed the creaking stairs and deposited everything at Lett's feet. It was all for her and the children, he said, eat it all up, don't let it go bad, and he swore in a most unchristian way: blast this and damn that, now we shall see! As in an afterthought he took the money out of his pocket, placed it in two little parcels on the eggs and the butter and said: and here is your money back too. Now she had remembered Rosa's lesson, but she had not been taught what to say if he should ever give it back. Or maybe it was because he said 'your money'. Whatever the reason, she replied spontaneously that it was Rosa's. That was all that was needed! But today Thys didn't fuss about trivialities. He didn't waste any words on it. All right, said Thys, this here we'll eat and that we'll give back. He sat down by the table and wrote a letter: Rosa, we have the money ready here. I hope you will come and collect it as soon as possible. You will be welcome. Thank you for the money. Thys.

Even more promptly, Rosa sat down by her table. Thys, so Lett did tell you after all, I was afraid she might not be able to keep it a secret. Thys, the money belongs to your children and you cannot in good conscience rob them of it, and surely I can do what I like with my money and please don't do this to me, it would make me very sad. Rosa.

Rosa, the money must leave my house, come and collect it, the children won't go short of anything. Thys.

Thys, you're still as crazy as ever, but all right, I will come and collect it, of course I know you can look after your children, that wasn't what I meant. You are a man and it will be done as you wish. Rosa.

TWENTY

Twice a day Thys came home with a cartload of empty bottles: wine bottles, beer bottles, vinegar bottles, liqueur bottles, champagne bottles, medicine bottles, perfume bottles, bottles of all possible and impossible shapes and sizes, bottles in which petrol, paraffin, oil, ammonia, syrup, dye, glue and goodness knows what other muck had been kept. He unloaded these bottles into vats and in the evenings, late into the night, he washed and rinsed them with methylated spirits or hydrochloric acid. It was a dirty, disagreeable job, but at least Lett was able to help him with it. He warned her, though, that methylated spirits and hydrochloric acid are dangerous poisons. One tiny sip and she would drop down on the floor, she would just have time to squirm a little and then, dead! It made her laugh, he didn't know why, and he was afraid she didn't take it seriously enough. He forbade her ever to touch those poisons and stressed it again and again. Watch out, she couldn't be careful enough, two drops of it and she's had it. Every evening he pointed a warning finger at the poison. Remember, don't ever touch it.

More, he didn't tell her about his new occupation, nor did she ask; he always knew what was best. Thys meticulously boiled the corks, left them to dry and sorted them into trays: whole ones and damaged ones, big ones, medium ones, small ones. He put deep shelves up in the garage, all the way up to the ceiling, on which he arranged the equally meticulously sorted bottles, and over the door he painted

BOUTEILLERIE M GLORIEUS

It was a good business: it cost nothing and it brought in nothing. He collected the empties from the rich houses, where the servant girls were glad to get rid of them for a small tip. If the girls were greedy and asked for payment, Thys advised them to get a bottle washer to call. They would soon find out how much that cost and they would have all the mess to put up with. And in any case, he always gave them a tip, didn't he? He rarely needed to bother a second time, for such arguments strike home with snooty servants in posh houses. But his cart was always quickly filled. For his wine bottles Thys found customers without difficulty; a few wine merchants were glad to buy them. He collected enough empties to sell them a fair supply every now and again, but wherever he collected them he was obliged to take all the other rubbish as well, so he had no choice but to fill up his shelves with the most bizarre trash. One day soon he would have a fair-sized stock of everything, but in expectation of that day the business consisted of collecting rubbish, selling little or nothing; poverty; and in this time of waiting for better things, there is a knock at the door one evening: Uncle Dolf.

He has had no need to change his appearance this time: the beard itself has seen to enough change: it has grown grey. He pinches his nose and gasps for air. He's been all over Brussels to find Monsieur Mathias Glorieus, next time he'll no doubt find him in a stable. What the hell is Thys doing here? Well, well, bouteillerie Mathieu Glorieus, is it? He chuckles.

Yes, it is, says Thys and sullenly carries on working. Uncle Dolf scans the shelves and shakes his head in silence. He lifts Lett's chin and asks her how she is, he thinks she has become prettier. Fine, says Thys. They show him the three children in the shabby little bedroom and he shakes his beard more dejectedly still. Of the third child, the one that was named after him, he says: 'Let's hope he's going to be another Dolf Glorieus', in a tone which leaves no doubt that the child of such a father cannot possibly be worthy of him. Thys replies proudly: that he wants the boy to become another Thys Glorieus. This is not the moment to humiliate Thys; if anyone thinks himself too good for Thys, then let him stay away.

Behind his back Uncle Dolf makes a sign to Lett: listen to that good-for-nothing, that gasbag. He winks, she looks at him in wide-eyed surprise.

There is hostility brewing. Uncle Dolf feels irritated by his reception. He is angry because the longing to see his son has had the better of him, for days he has dreamt that Thys would say: hello father. That would have been enough, just that. Grey hair makes a man soft. He had expected the poor son to look up admiringly at his clever father, but Thys doesn't even ask him how he's been, what he's been doing, whether he has earned a lot of money. In the end he has to ask them himself what they think of his looks: grey as a dove. Fine, says Thys without even looking at him. Uncle Dolf pulls off his shoes, lights a cigar and asks if they have at least got a room for him. Yes, they have. A strange sadness comes over him, he aches for a kind word and more gently than he has ever spoken to anyone he asks Thys to tell him, seriously, between the two of us, how much he makes with that business downstairs. He is not trying to mock Thys or humiliate him. He is sitting comfortably, smoking, his warm feet on the stove, and in spite of everything he feels at home with his son.

A single word, a complaint, a sigh, and he will say things at which he himself will be amazed. Am I your father, or am I not? Didn't I carry you home that time, Thys, didn't I bring you round, didn't I look after you better even than your mother? Would I let you live in poverty, my boy? But Thys turns pale at the humiliation of not even being able to earn his bread and butter after all these years, now, as the father of three children.

He could have answered that father has come six months, at most a year too early, but he is conscious of the feebleness of such an excuse. He is afraid Uncle Dolf will offer him money. That is why he calls him emphatically Uncle Dolf. It's none of Uncle Dolf's business what he earns.

There follows a long silence. At last Uncle Dolf says slowly, with a sigh: 'to be stupid is nothing, but to be pretentious as well, that is bad.'

Immediately Thys retorts, without twitching a muscle: 'to be pretentious is nothing, but not to be able to guard your tongue, that's dangerous.' All that is needed now is for one of them to move a foot or raise a hand just a trifle too quickly, for both of them to tear into each other in a fury. The air around them is tense, loaded with suspense. Lett senses it intuitively, she suddenly calls out anxiously, don't do anything to Thys. Thys asks quietly who would do anything to him and Uncle Dolf answers scornfully that they'll leave him in peace, he's doing nicely, my dear, let him be.

The next day he asks Lett if she was really afraid that he was going to do something to Thys. Of course he wouldn't, my dear, he's not like that. He loves Thys far too much and moreover, he loves her and the kiddies far too much as well. Come to your uncle, you little roly-poly. He wants them to be doing well, that's all, and last night he was annoyed because he doesn't think they're doing well enough. What do you think, and he swears, what do you think it's like for him, for him, and he swears louder, who can stamp money out of the ground, to have only one child and to see that child, and here he swears like a thunderclap, grovelling about in a dump like this. And then the blithering idiot is too damned proud to accept a helping hand!

The only way to get a word out of Lett is by talking about Thys, or about the children and especially by talking ill of Thys. She says it isn't Thys' fault, he works like a horse. Dolf admits this readily, then he sinks away into his silent bitterness but bounces up again when she lifts a kettle on to the stove, resting one hand on his knee.

She is not pretty, he thinks. Why should he put himself out for something he doesn't even want. She's too narrow in the shoulders and too broad in the hips. And she stoops, he doesn't like such lack of spunk. Yes, why does he bother to look at her. If he met a girl like her anywhere else, a girl he would only need to wink at and she'd come, he would turn his back and never give her another thought. And yet this one he wants, just because she is Thys's wife. He pinches her arm and winks at her. Waves of anger sweep through him, he doesn't know why.

One really has to hate one's son deeply to want to steal his wife from him, not for love, nor for belated lust, but only to show one's contempt. Sometimes he wonders why he wants to hurt Thys like this. He finds no other clear reason except the gruff welcome, yet this is only the least of his tangled motives.

Thys is the only child he has ever taken any notice of, the only one he is fond of. And unconsciously he resents him for it. He assumes that here and there his blood lives on in illegitimate but no doubt extraordinary people, at least as superior as he feels himself to be. He wants to avenge his disappointment on this son, whom he has chosen out of many of his kind. And it is precisely in this miserable wretch, this pathetic little plodder, with his taste for domesticity, that he has taken an interest. He is fond of this bungler, it is for his sake that he has come back. He watches Thys playing with the children for half an hour after lunch and supper. He enjoys it just as much himself, but when Thys does it he is consumed by a savage urge to pick up each of those pups by one leg and chuck them against the wall: poxy little housefather, go on, why don't you work and live like a man!

The poverty around him in the three little rooms is a personal humiliation to him. That his son feels happy here, because he sleeps with a simpleminded woman who adores him and smiles at him in stupid amorousness, becomes unbearable. He could grab the girl in front of Thys's eyes and shout at him: look, you bloody fool, this is how much she's yours, I take her and I've got her. He walks out into the street and passing through the garage he feels like pulling all those orange-crate shelves from the walls so that the whole caboodle will crash and clatter to the ground: there are your toys, you fumbler, for God's sake do something that is worthy of me.

He has to go and sit on the terrace of expensive cafés with a fat cigar, to shake it off, that his son lives in a garage. Sometimes he orders an expensive meal, with two wines, has the waiters rushing to and fro and nothing is to his liking.

When Rosa comes to collect her money he stands bolt upright by the stove, not out of politeness but dumbfounded. He doesn't utter a word until Thys comes home, because he wants to see how they greet each other. Nausea rises in his throat and he asks, isn't she the youngest daughter from Ridge Farm? Rosa confirms it. Well then, if he's not mistaken she must be the daughter who was on her own at the farm at the time when he was staying with his brother Do for a few months, when Thys was still working at the farm. Thys braces himself and Rosa blushes: yes. He doesn't remember any of the young people in the village, it's so many years ago since he left, but she must be the one that was married to a schoolmaster. This time it is Thys who replies, yes, and forestalls further awkward questions: Rosa, what do you think of Nic, has he grown? Uncle Dolf puts his shoes on and downstairs he kicks the support from under the pushcart, but the bottles are piled up too securely, only three or four break with a clatter.

The gate of Bouteillerie M Glorieus slams, although there is no wind on that side.

At suppertime he's back again. He asks Rosa if she hasn't remarried yet. Again it is Thys who answers for her: surely Uncle Dolf can see she's not wearing a wedding ring. Then he is silent and eats as if he was alone in the room. But later, while Lett is washing the dishes and Thys has gone to the garage with Rosa, he approaches Lett from behind. Does Lett know what those two are up to downstairs? This. And he takes her in his arms and kisses her. Angrily she pushes him away.

Meanwhile Thys is explaining to Rosa that pretty nearly everything she can see on those shelves has already been sold. He has so many orders that he can hardly cope with the demand. That whole shelf over there is going to a big pharmacy, he tells her the name and address of it. He's got liqueur distilleries, breweries and wine merchants as his customers, big firms all of them, which pay well. My word, if he compares it with that beggarly little shop he used to have, Rosa, where everyone bought on tick and where he couldn't even remind people for fear he would lose their custom!

She is so happy to hear it. He has never complained, it's true; when he was still in the shop which he is now portraying in such a disparaging light, he also used to say that he was doing well, but this time it somehow sounds more plausible. It's so original, this business of his, just like him. He is sensible and hardworking; she has to be able to believe that he is doing well. She says seriously: It'll make you rich one day, Thys, I know it will.

Thys is in no doubt, just leave him to it. Back on the farm Rosa confesses for the first time that she has been to see Lett. There are two new maids, still young, who were not there at the time of the murder and the trial. The men keep quiet. She utters Thys's name for the first time and nobody looks up, there is no embarrassed hush. Feeling secure, she talks about Thys's bottle business and adds to it double what Thys had already added to it himself; and Lett has three lovely children. Yes, they're doing fine.

Sweet is the thought that God blesses Thys. She dedicates her torments to him. If she is to be doomed, then may her good deeds be of benefit to Thys.

One day Uncle Dolf bumps into his daughter-in-law in a cheap department store. He calls it a coincidence. She is buying cheap flannelette by the yard, for the children. After that her purse is empty. Doesn't she need anything else? Yes, but she will come back for it another time, on Saturday, when Thys will be at home all day and she can go shopping in the afternoon. But he makes her recite all the things the children need, she has to choose and he pays. Pleased as a child she walks beside him through the store. He points at a pretty apron. She has to put it on. Smilingly she admires herself. Listen, he'll buy it for her, but not a word about it to Thys, she must promise him.

No need to tell her anything about Thys's sensitivity on that point, and the remedy she knows already: she will say she has bought it out of her savings. By the exit there is a display stand with nothing but hats. He takes her by the arm and says as if to a child that now she may choose herself a hat too. Rapturously she looks at him as he points at different hats, and he is her mirror: she chooses the one he likes best.

Why has she never asked for anything before? She only needs to say the word and she can have whatever she wants, a dress, a coat, shoes. He stumps on ruthlessly towards his goal, what does she know of a man's wiles. Any other woman wanting to remain faithful would have bitten his nose off straightaway, this one smiles gratefully. And smiles more gratefully as their poverty increases. When Thys has filled the shelves with all manner of bottles and jars, arranged according to make, size or destination, he has still got to find customers for them. Occasionally someone offers a derisory price and goes away until Thys is forced to call on him. His business will thrive as soon as he has found a set of loyal customers who know that they get a good bargain with him, that he hasn't just accidentally got a little lot in that happens to suit them but that he is able to meet their requirements regularly. He is still too much a collector of unwanted rubbish; it takes time to become a supplier of empty bottles.

It vexes him no end that Uncle Dolf is there to witness his struggle; how gladly he would refuse the money Dolf pays him every week for board and lodging, just as he used to do at home, to Do and Dina, but he can't afford it.

That Uncle Dolf sits alone with Lett for hours would normally have worried him, but not now. When he is around he is always proud and haughty and Thys suspects that Uncle Dolf, like everyone else, partly blames Lett for their poverty. Never mind, let him sulk till Thys has come out on top.

There is constant friction; a sharp question answered equally sharply. Or Dolf calls out at the top of the stairs: 'Hey, Thys, are you in the warehouse?' Even though they still call it the garage. 'Yes, I'm in the garage.' Sometimes Thys asks her if Uncle Dolf ever gets fresh with her. No, no. He thinks he probably does at times, but that she is too simple to understand.

Uncle Dolf dangles a banknote in front of her. To buy herself something with. She prefers it that way, because coats and dresses she can do without, but what she has to buy is indispensable. And she won't spend all of it, because Thys likes her to be thrifty. But Uncle Dolf doesn't let go of the note which she is already eagerly holding by a corner. 'First a kiss.' She obliges at once, it's for Thys isn't it? Thys would be very cross if he knew, but he won't know and in this way she can save, for him. He's been wanting to have a leather coat for a long time, but he can't afford one yet, first they must all be better dressed and fed. All the same, he has said, a leather coat would save on other clothes, and spare him colds. Now she is going to give him a surprise. With childish happiness she shows Uncle Dolf how much she has already saved up. He would prefer to see her spend his money on something else rather than on a leather coat for the bungler who doesn't even deserve to have the coarse shaggy jacket in which he traipses along the Brussels boulevards, but he says nothing. If she can be caught as easily as this, stupid bitch, why not? He can fling it into his face afterwards: 'and that leather coat, you numbskull, that's what your wife has earned for you, and how!'

One Saturday morning she asks Uncle Dolf of her own accord to give her just a little more money, then she can go and buy the leather coat, after dinner. The guilelessness of it, it's enough to kill yourself with laughter, he thinks, what a couple they are, those two. He pretends he wouldn't dream of giving her any more money and surely she can't go and buy the coat on her own, shouldn't it be tried on first? But she wants to buy it herself, just like that, and then give it to Thys as a surprise, he will be so pleased. If it isn't the right size he can always go back to the shop himself and choose one that fits. Dolf thinks it's hopelessly stupid, altogether what you would expect of those pitiful little bunglers. A leather coat for his lordship the bottleman while his wife goes around in rags, the children in smelly nappies and on the table herrings today and herrings tomorrow. Leave him alone.

She comes up to kiss him. 'Please give me it, Uncle Dolf.' Despising her and Thys, he feels her breasts. Come and see, big mister bottleman from down below, your missus is working for your leather coat. She hits him crossly on the hand. He chuckles: 'but you'd like the money, wouldn't you?'

Then she fights a hard battle. But only until noon: a longer fight is not within the power of her dull mind. He might have given her the money if she hadn't hit his hand. It's not allowed, it's sinful, Thys has told her. But what about Thys's happiness, what about lying in Thys's arms again tonight, like that other time, when she had given him Rosa's money. He will stroke her again like he did that other time and whisper good girl. And talk about work and being thrifty and the future.

As she stands by the cooking stove she watches Thys from behind. He is sitting by the table with Nic on his left and Leo on his right. He serves them their stew of potatoes and gravy and tells jokes so as not to have to talk to Uncle Dolf. Guiltily she approaches him, like she approached Uncle Dolf a short while ago, and kisses him long. It means: I love you alone, I love you so much, but not him. Uncle Dolf grumbles in his spoon, a brobbling noise as if he was blowing in it from too nearby, but she wants him to see, she is doing it partly for him: I love Thys, not you. He watches with grim relish. Go downstairs, bottleman, then she'll come to me all the sooner.

Never before has he sneaked his way into a family in such an underhand manner. His style has always been bold: surprise attack. This kind of petty, furtive comedy is just right for these two dunces.

After dinner Thys asks her if she has to go out, if she has any shopping to do. If so she had better go early, while the children are having their afternoon nap, because he has a lot of work downstairs; he doesn't trust the children near the tubs and he hasn't got the time to keep running up and down the stairs to make sure they don't get into mischief. Uncle Dolf says: 'I'll look after them,' but Thys says: 'No need for you to stay at home.' So it all happened in a hurry. Thys has barely started stirring the vat below, when she comes begging again like a child. Dolf is not forthcoming, which makes her all the readier to oblige and this time there is no fear, no anxiety, there is only relief and joy when he finally holds out his hand which she does not push aside. This is exactly what he had in mind for that bottleman, to be cuckolded in his own house, while he is at home but hasn't got the time to come up the stairs, with his thriving business which brings in all of three herrings a day. He puts his arm round her waist and whispers that she should come to his room, where he keeps the money.

Thys does not creep noiselessly up the stairs to see what the hell she is up to. He does not even become suspicious when he finds the kitchen and bedroom empty. Rage floods him only when the door to Uncle Dolf's room closes just as he puts his hand on the doorknob. He doesn't ask them to open up, nor does he shout and rage as deceived husbands are said to do in books. He braces himself in the narrow corridor with his back against the wall and his feet placed squarely in the middle of the lower door panel. Of those three, Thys, the wall and the panel, it is only Thys who cannot yield, for his strength has no bounds. The panel gives with the brief cracking of dry old wood. Pointlessly, Uncle Dolf threatens the huge bulldog that leaps at him through the opening, that he will shoot him down. For this he would need enough time to take his revolver from the bedside table drawer. With this bedside table and a chair balanced on top of it, he pushes Thys so hard into the corner, against the metal wash stand, that all the objects standing on it become part of the general shambles.

He feels he is being seized by the throat and he knows that two Uncle Dolfs would be as powerless as one. This is the end of him, his hand finds nothing better than the glass from the wash stand. He breaks it on his son's forehead and he goes on hitting with the piece that is left in his hand. How does a tiger roar when a fragment of glass pierces his eye? There is nothing human in the howling of this man who tears around in circles, blind and crazy, crashing into the walls, the mantelpiece. The two hands on the eye become filled with blood.

Lett steals cautiously towards the revolver in the drawer, but Uncle Dolf is lying with one arm across the table and when he becomes aware of her soft sobbing he realizes what she is after. He takes the revolver himself and she does not stop him, he may go.

But he gets no further than the corridor. There he bursts out sobbing, he turns to Thys with outstretched arms: 'Thys, what has happened, what have I done?'

Thys reaches out with his left hand, groping for him, and when he has touched his sleeve he knows where to find the neck. He grabs that neck with both hands but the blood makes their grip slippery and this is what will make of Uncle Dolf a tired, absent-minded man: the sight of his son with the bleeding eye, clenching his teeth, trying to throttle him. Now he can go. Down in the street he rings the hospital and then Uncle Dolf vanishes, the man who brought destruction.

TWENTY-ONE

While Thys was having his wounded eye removed and was being nursed as if he, just he, having seen that man is evil, no longer needed two eyes, Lett looked after his children, waiting for his return.

He returned. Prepared for more, and harder beatings than she had ever received in her life, ready to drop dead at his feet if he in his wisdom should wish it so, she bent her head and back in anticipation, but could not stop herself from glancing up askance to see if his wound had healed properly. His eye looked sternly into the kitchen. He kissed the three children one by one, finally fixed his eye on Lett, pointed towards the door and said: out.

He had thought much about this punishment. Beat her he could not do, that would be cowardly. In the past she had so often been beaten, for every little triviality, sometimes for no reason at all. He wanted to find a punishment for her which would make her see that this was worse than anything in the world. He had finally decided on this curt order: out. He knew that she had nowhere else to go, that she had been frightened of going to Tieleghem and hated Ridge Farm. So she would wander around the town until evening and then she would come back and knock at the garage door. He will open, she will throw her arms round his neck, he will remain severe. But at last he will allow her to spend one more night in his house, in the morning he will make her wash the children, she will then find it even harder to leave, and then he will tell her that she may stay for the sake of the children. He will have to keep this up, for a month perhaps. He will reject any attempt at reconciliation, reminding her that she is there only for the sake of the children. Then he will listen to her explanation, because he is convinced that she was either taken by surprise or tricked, it certainly could not have been ordinary unfaithfulness. All the same, she must be made to feel how dreadfully she has sinned. His eye does not leave her: out.

This is worse than anything she could have imagined, this is worse than death. Softly, fearfully she asks if she must go outside and Thys repeats his order with that same, single word. Where must she go, Thys? He doesn't care. To this she replies: 'All right Thys, I'll go.' She gets up and her life has come to an end: he was her life. There hangs her hat, there hangs her coat. And in the cupboard under the ironing blanket is the money. She puts it on the mantelpiece and says with her back towards him that this money is for a leather coat. She waits. If this doesn't help she knows of nothing better to soften his mood before it is too late. Perhaps it is a good sign that he says nothing. More softly she repeats: 'Thys, this is the money I saved up for a leather coat.' How happy he used to be with any savings, but now he remains stubbornly silent. Her poor heart loses its last hope. She asks who will look after the children, but Thys only repeats his order. As if from now on it is none of her business what will happen to the children.

By the stairs she turns round once more. Thys, when may I come back? He cannot send her away with a promise to let her come back. He certainly must not say: oh, tonight, of course. Just for this once she must suffer the agony of a final separation. For the third time Thys repeats: out.

At the top of the stairs she says good-bye, sweetly and meekly, to Nic, Leo, Dolf and Thys. Her wanderings are soon over, sooner than those of the man with the grey beard. Not because of a premeditated plan, it is only an impulse. Indecisively she stares around the garage, sees the bottles of acid. She puts one to her mouth and drinks. When Thys warned her against the poison he did not exaggerate. He knows everything. You squirm briefly.

You, the educated, are interested in many people you have never even met, but who are important to you because of what they think, write, discover, do. Often you do not even know whether they are married or single, alive or already dead. But we in the countryside only know one another and the things that are important in our lives are the basic things of life itself: birth, marriage, death. No matter how far we may drift apart, we keep track of these elementary things about each other. Two from our village went to America to seek their fortune, two brothers. The younger one was killed in the docks, we learnt of it at once. The older one got further. He married a teacher who gave him lessons in English because he wanted to get a job in an office. Now he is teaching her lessons instead, because she wasn't an easy

one to get on with; and they have taken over her father's
drugstore. Of course, it's much easier to keep up with people
who have only gone as far as Brussels. That Lett, who married that fellow Thys a few years back, had died, we knew by
the morning. And he himself has lost an eye. Didn't we
always say it, that his chickens would come home to roost
one day; well, here you are!

She died without being ill. We heard it from Jan the
Poulterer. He met Thys in town that morning and naturally,
they both slow down and exchange a few words. 'What's the
matter with your eye,' and so on. 'But at home all is well?'
'Yes, at home all is well.' And in the afternoon Lett is dead.
Ah well, these things differ from one family to another. It
happens here occasionally that someone is found dead in his
bed, but how often do you hear of that? People who die in
the afternoon were usually already pretty sick in the morning, and then you don't exactly say that all is well at home,
do you? Karel from Ridge Farm now, he died without being
ill, too, and Thys said nothing. He'll say even less now. He
won't tell anyone what has happened to his eye. Jan the
Poulterer says, in an explosion, but Lett is silent the way
Karel was silent. And did you know that Rosa went down
there in a tearing hurry? She'd put the grey mare to the gig
again. She is no longer the same as she used to be. Who? The
grey mare? Yes, she's on her last legs too, but I mean
Rosa.

Rosa forgets all about Lett when she sees Thys standing
before her with a rigid, burning eye. Only one thought
flashes through her mind, that once again they have
wronged him, they have done him an injustice. Of course, he
pretends it was nothing, as usual, a small explosion, well,
there had been several more before, but this time a glass
splinter from a bottle had hit him in the eye. You've got to
understand, these are dangerous poisons he works with, she
can tell from his hands, can't she? The first time a bottle
exploded was at night, when no one was around, all by
itself.

Nothing seems more plausible than his explanation, and why shouldn't his voice sound weary and dull, now that Lett lies there, and why should he today make an accident sound bigger than it really was, as he usually does? And yet she cannot shake off her disquiet. How could Lett have drunk poison by accident?

'Thys,' she says, 'what happened? Tell me, Thys. It's not right always to hush up one's grief.'

The burning eye becomes restless the hands, eaten by acid and spirits, hide their trembling behind his back, but the mouth, which has to confess that he has killed Lett, closes. He must not confess, not even to the only woman who would understand. It is enough that he has taken Lett's life, he will not take her honour as well. If he is to unburden his conscience by confessing his own guilt, all he will achieve is the exposure of her even greater guilt.

It would have to be Rosa urging him to speak. With pain he remembers the fool who dragged her before the judges, as if there could be found the justice he always searched for with such passion.

Let him now go to the judge himself, let him confess that he has driven his wife to her death and that if there is anything on earth or in heaven by which his soul can be freed from that horror, it must be brought to bear. What will the judge do with a man who accuses himself and has to be defended by a lawyer who will prove that it was Lett who was at fault, a man who will have to be acquitted because the law does not recognize any guilt in him. His guilt lies concealed behind tightly shut lips; suppose he suddenly spoke, suppose he took all the blame upon himself and said to Rosa: I have driven Lett, poor innocent Lett, to her death. How would she stare at him: you dragged me before the court, not even on a suspicion, only because of a possibility. Now you yourself have committed a murder, this is a certainty, and you are silent. He can bring the judgment of man on himself by lying, by allowing himself to be convicted of something he has not done, undergo a punishment which will not unburden his soul because it bears no relation to his guilt; and meanwhile inflict a greater injustice on his children: undeserved stigma and neglect.

'Thys,' she says, 'what is it, I can understand everything, I am even more wretched myself.' Deep in her heart she hopes that he has murdered her. That he will say: Rosa, I held her mouth open by force, I pushed a broomstick between her teeth like a bit and then I poured poison down her throat. She would throw herself upon him. Thys, I am damned too, I shot him in the neck on purpose, with pleasure. I wanted to do penance and purify myself, to be worthy of you, but now that we are both of us damned, why should we worry about anything? Throw me on the floor somewhere among the tables and chairs and take me by force, we'll laugh at everything.

This lasts no more than a second. Immediately she is ashamed of thinking this of him. She will not kiss Thys in passion while Lett is still above the earth. The Lord sees her, she thinks, the Lord to whom she repeats all the details of her crime day after day, whispering in the darkness of the bedroom, committing to him every morning the suffering of the unconfessed. He knows that she drinks from this mouth, like a mother from a poisoned wound, before the poison of silence kills the soul with never-ceasing torment.

What are you doing now? asks Thys. He opens the door to the room where Lett lies. Sobbing, she throws herself on the pillows and prays to the simple, good woman. They both loved Thys. She must help her in heaven and save Thys. What are you doing now? asks Thys again; for those who are utterly defeated often repeat the same words as they cannot form new sentences. She does nothing except pack the clothes of the three children. The eye looks on in resignation. Listlessly he watches her go out into the street with two big parcels and three children. She hurries, fearing he will come to his senses and take the loot away from her.

That same day Dina and Lieneke arrive. They have been sent by Pol. They do not weep for Lett, they cover their faces at the sight of Thys's eye, but even Dina's concern does not last long. Chiefly, they are proud of Pol who has told them at once to go and fetch the three children. He will look after those children, he will take on an extra servant for the purpose.

When they hear who has just left with the little ones, they are in an even greater hurry to leave than was Rosa. They have never forgiven Thys for allowing that woman from Ridge Farm to come to the house again, but this is the last straw. Lieneke says: 'then there is nothing more for us to do here.' Mother says: 'you'd better settle everything with that one from Ridge Farm then; it's no concern of ours.'

Thys keeps watch by the body alone. Tongues will wag in the village about the fact that he and Rosa are the only relatives to walk behind the hearse. He no longer worries about such things. The Lord will see her. They returned from the grave and it was she who reminded him that life goes on, whereas he thought it had ended at the grave. What was he going to do now?

The eye stares rigidly. He will work for his children.

The kettle boils, she pours water on the coffee and asks him if he wouldn't like to come back to the farm. Looking askance at him she sees him startling slightly. Still pouring water on the coffee, she says she knows that there will be gossip in the village and among the relatives. But those things, Thys, don't bother her any more. What would people say if they heard her talk like this. But Lett hears her, from heaven, Lett who loved him as much as she loves him, and Lett understands her. He is silent. She sits down opposite him. They do not touch the coffee. She hangs her head, resting it in her hands, so that he cannot see her eyes. She says that he thinks she does not know him. 'You've always lived for others, haven't you?'

Her longing for him is making her ill, it puts foolish ideas into her head. Now it suddenly makes her cry. She sobs: 'You're too good, too good.'

He makes a weary gesture, as if to say: I know better than

that. She doesn't see it, but hangs her head still lower and says that for once he should think only of himself, leave all his belongings in the garage for the next tenant and come to the station with her, come and live with your children on the farm, we'll bring them up together. For the first time Thys doesn't brag and lie, for the first time he doesn't act big. He is silent. Then he puts a hand on her shoulder: 'Go home now, dear.' She stands up under his hand and asks him if he wouldn't let her stay here with him, she could fetch the children back. He merely smiles. 'You're a good girl.'

He stays alone amongst his bottles, in the garage where he found Lett dead, the kitchen without children, the room where he fought with Uncle Dolf and the other room in which he will never be happy again.

He goes out collecting bottles, from morning till night, fills his garage with them, fills Uncle Dolf's room with odd specimens of which he slowly bulids up a collection; patiently he searches for reliable, regular customers and this part of Thys's history is quickly written. It is the tale of those tough, steady plodders that periodically turn up from the Brabant countryside and who will not leave the city until it has bestowed on them a share of the riches which lured them. The share they demand is a large one.

He allows himself neither rest nor amusement. His only pleasure is his work, to which he gives importance, his business which thrives at last and is fast expanding. After a time he becomes in his turn a buyer of small lots which have been collected by others, by men who pick up what they can when they can, from old rags to old iron.

After a few years he buys the garage, has it pulled down and builds a house, albeit not with four, yet at least with three floors; a warehouse downstairs and a rinsing room in the basement. He lives on the first floor, the two floors above he lets. While his bottles are collected and delivered by horse and cart he is at the pressure pumps, and helps with the rinsing and sorting. And he buys and sells.

Four times a year, always on exactly the same Sundays, as

befits an orderly, businesslike man, always on the same train, at 7.35 in the morning and always alert to the slight oscillation of one to five minutes which necessitates revisions of the railway timetable, Thys travels to Ridge Farm with a heavy suitcase full of toys and goodies for the children, presents for Rosa, for father, mother and Lieneke.

Rosa is always frightened that he will take the children away. They fill her life, numb her remorse, deflect her longing for Thys. It is not the Lord's will that she should be his wife and the Lord is right. She is already content if she is allowed to mother over his children. Thys takes no notice of the gruffness that greets him at home, where they cannot forgive him that his children are with Rosa. To them he is the queer fish, the son of Dolf. Dina's eyes sometimes brighten proudly at the sight of this elegant visitor with his quiet self-composure and his ever-serious concern for others, but it is in spite of herself and she looks at once at Lieneke. Magnanimously Thys hands out presents to everyone, beautifully wrapped up and with the gold-paper seal of a quality shop, and he won't allow them to hide their joy by putting the present away and not mentioning it again.

For Do he invariably brings two big litre bottles of liqueur. Of these at least he has satisfaction. The drawn, ageing face screws up unrecognizably, like an old purse when the strings are drawn, as if it is suffering dreadful agonies. When it opens up again the eyes are filled with tears and Do always makes the same comment: that you never find such good stuff hereabouts, you've got to be in the city for that. Lieneke loses no time telling Pol that father loves liqueur and Pol is not to be out-trumped by Thys. But he may bring the same brand, the same bottle: Do insists that liqueur from Brussels is better. 'You can tell me what you like,' says Do, 'I can taste the difference.'

How glad Thys would be to see his mother thaw into her former warmth, but she sees through no other eyes but those of her sour daughter. Between those two no wedge can be driven. He tries to soften them by a display of his growing wealth. They can compare him with Pol now, if they like; he has done better than Pol, but it is no good. In order to get Lieneke to talk, he asks interestedly after Pol, dropping subtle hints that he is doing far better still, but the slightest word in that direction is enough to make Lieneke shut up like a clam.

In moving his children to Brussels after their first communion to give them a thorough grounding in French and commerce at a boarding school, first Nic, then Leo, then little Dolf, he robs Rosa of everything. In loneliness she longs for him again, but now with a quieter, humbler longing. She has brought up his children for him, is there nothing more she can do for him now, is there nothing she can be for him?

When she visits the children she tries to make him give his housekeeper the day off, as she says, to let the woman have a chance to enjoy her Sunday too, but she is a quiet, elderly spinster who has been in service all her life. She has nowhere to go except to her elder brother who works for a countess, but he plays cards on Sundays with the two maids, spinsters as old as himself, one of whom has received a medal for thirty-five years of loyal service. 'But I don't play cards, Ma'am,' says the housekeeper. So Rosa cannot even show Thys what it would be like if they lived here together. Sitting quietly in his chair he talks about the village. He is a man who has proved his worth, he feels mighty. He talks of the roads in the village, how bad they still are, about the excellent specialist doctors available in the city, about the lack of hygiene in the country, the lack of organization and co-operation. She listens, smiling: this is still the same Thys as ever, fond of big, important talk, the Thys to whom all the village ought to come for advice. It is enough for her just to sit near him and to see him contented. She does not realize that unwittingly he still stirs up a hankering which will bring him to her one day.

For when we have wrested our due from the city and when our work is slowly beginning to allow us more rest and leisure, we awaken in ourselves the memories of our village. The distance of many years gilds them and they become nostalgia. We want to return to the place we left as poor boys. Mon ami went back, when his wife died, when Paul had become a big industrialist, Maurice a doctor, when Irène had married a famous musician and when, last of all, Corinne had gone to Argentina with an unknown Argentinian. He had a villa built for himself, of his own design, on the crest of a Brabant hill, rustic, he thought, because it had farmhouse window shutters, and of course, he couldn't forgo the red-painted beams in the front gable. He moved mainly his books, had a large garden laid out and forgot the past; at first he endured reluctantly the visits from his three children but gradually began to enjoy them when they started bringing little ones along. He was an old man, reconciled to life. And Thys will return too.

When his children have learnt enough French and commerce they come home to put it all into practice. His business runs by itself and is growing as fast as he could wish, but they find all sorts of things wrong with it. It's not modern. The transport should be better organized, both the collections and the deliveries, and they prove to Thys that with his method of bookkeeping one never knows exactly where one is, even though Thys knows it to the last centime and no scholar will ever persuade him that with one column of outgoings and one column of incomings a man is unable to know exactly where he is. By eight o'clock in the evening they have all gone out to their various commitments in clubs, societies and organizations Thys has never heard of. On Saturday afternoons they are out as well and on Sundays they can hardly be seen at all. They never talk about the business and yet they have complete control of it, for whatever action Thys decides to take, they have already anticipated. They'll do it presently, this way or that, or they have already done it. They sit at the table with him, three black, brilliantined curly-heads of which they are proud. They resemble neither him nor Lett, but they speak as quietly as

Lett and are always active like him. He wants to know whether this or that has been done. Yes. If he goes on asking they say gently and firmly: dad, stop fretting. His softness towards a workman whose wife is ill and another whose child is coming up for his first communion, they do not understand. The workmen are well paid, for the sick there is the sick fund, the business is not a charitable institution. Thys has to satisfy his heart's impulses on the sly, talking quietly to those concerned, stealthily pressing something into their hands.

Only the youngest, who feels he is being dominated by the inseparable older two, remains his child. He loves listening to Thys talking of his childhood and he needs comfort and contact. 'At Aunt Rosa's, sitting by the fire in the evening,' he says, 'I used to love it there.' And his eyes become large and dreamy. He says odd things, for instance, he will sit down by Thys and say: 'if I had learnt Latin I might have become a missionary. Or a doctor. Healing people.'

Discussions about politics he follows in silence, reflecting that money and ideologies are the cause of all troubles, and he remarks that people think too much of money and too little of the positive sciences. The two brothers protest that they are talking politics, but he replies: 'So am I.' One day he wonders aloud why man can only feed himself with living things: animals and plants, this, he says, is the root of the food problem. We should learn to replace it all by chemicals. 'Making bread out of earth!' he exclaims.

It seems to Thys as if he hears mon ami all over again. His mind wanders to what years of hard work have taught him to forget. When he puts down his paper he has that old feeling which used to oppress him so often in his childhood: a confused world, unable to find happiness for itself, a world misled and cheated. He listens intently to the discussions between his youngest son and the older brothers, but his simple, upright mind gets lost in the maze of arguments. Words, words. Mon ami, for all his wisdom and learning, was never happy either. His boys know everything better than he and yet when he goes downstairs among his work-men, they almost hug him and when they are in trouble they always secretly come to him. Thys can't keep up with the modern world and gradually the pull of his village grows stronger and stronger.

TWENTY-TWO

In the village there are still the same old bad brick-paved roads, disorder and poverty still reign. It seems to Thys that they need him there, while here in town he is well replaced. The money which he has plodded so hard to earn becomes valueless to him, it never was his ultimate goal.

When on Sunday morning he strolls from the station to Ridge Farm, the fields stretch wide and open all around, and in them lie the scattered houses and farms. A strange voice, known and familiar to him since his childhood, but always mysterious and inexplicable, speaks within Thys: come to me, all of you, and tell me your troubles. I am Thys, I want all things to be well with you. I have suffered enough to understand everything and if you want to see what I can achieve, go to Brussels and see. The blows I have suffered have not broken me, I come to you still at the height of my strength.

Tist Vranckaert, you still live there in your hovel, and how many children have you got? Where do they all sleep, and have you still got that mud floor, that can't stay like that. Jan the Planter, your cottage was burnt down wasn't it, and you've been living in the barn for a year, why aren't you building, man, what's the matter with you?

Thus Thys speaks to each house, a mighty man, merciful to the many who have remained what they always were. And it is only the continuation of this inner monologue when he says to Rosa that the stable roof will collapse on top of the cows one day. One more bad season and the roof will be down. She doesn't know why it is that this time he touches on things she has been patiently waiting for. Oh yes, Thys, she knows that the place is becoming dilapidated, but to pull it down and build it up again, she hasn't got the energy, you need a man around the house for that. The maids are still about in the kitchen, the doors are open, this is not the time for confidentialities. And yet they both feel that her words have put something between them and they are silent. A thousand signs have told him that a woman cannot treat a man so unless she loves him dearly and patiently; this seemingly casual remark of hers, this answer given from by the cooking stove, sticks in his mind. He stands by the window, before him lie the vast possessions of Ridge Farm; there is so much that has to be rebuilt. A dream stirs in Thys. He does not speak. There is something that warns Rosa not to disturb the silence, lest her words are smothered by others while they are trying to take root.

After dinner the servant folk disappear. Thys is standing by the window again. Rosa clears the table herself. When she has finished she joins him. 'You're so quiet,' she says, 'what is there to see outside?' He is still preoccupied by those alterations, you see, pulling down the stable, that is all very well, but it isn't only the stable, can't she see how the whole shed on the other side is sagging? On both sides of the yard everything is bound to collapse one day soon.

She asks whereabouts the shed is sagging, she can't see it. He puts her close in front of himself and points over her shoulder, she must keep her eye on the left hand support of the gate, that is exactly vertical, and now look at the shed. It has a bulge, says Thys. She takes his right hand with which he was pointing, puts it on her shoulder and her own hand on top of it. He leaves it there. When he points with his left hand at a crack running diagonally from the roof half-way down to the ground, she takes that hand too and puts it on her other shoulder. She asks him more softly what he thinks ought to be done about it all. Thys uses the big word his sons are always using: modern. He would rebuild everything to modern standards.

A modern model milking parlour and a modern barn. Modern farming machines. Ploughing, sowing, harrowing, cutting, all of it to be done with modern machinery, as in America.

She leans a little with her back against his breast and asks: 'are you going to pull it all down in one go or first the stables and when they're ready, the barn?' He doesn't seem surprised that she assumes it to be his work. He says he will have to think about it carefully, what is the best way to go about it. She pulls his two hands gently round her neck, rests her head against his breast and whispers that whatever he decides will be all right. He bends over to her lips. The weariness of many years has stilled their kiss. Her mouth opens to make the confession. 'Thys,' she whispers, but remembers that in *True Devotion*, the old family book, it says on a page she has thumbed many times, that the terrible sinner who was contrite and wanted to repent was unable to confess his sin because a slimy toad came into his mouth each time he opened it, preventing him from speaking. Only sobs rise in her throat, she turns round in his arms and this is the old, impetuous Rosa again. She hangs on him, sobbing, kissing his breast, rests her head on it, holds his head. 'Thys, is all forgiven then?' 'Be quiet now,' says Thys, 'my little one.' He holds her against him with his big, calm hands, soothing her with little kisses on her forehead.

Very softly she whispers that there is something she must tell him.

He waits a long time. At last she asks: 'is God as good as you?' Thys laughs a little, with happiness. 'Am I good?' asks Thys, because she repeats her question. Close to his mouth she asks it. He sits down and takes her on his knee. Her head lies on his shoulder and at his ear she whispers whether he thinks she will go to hell. He smiles, pressing her closer, like a child that is still asking questions but needs no more answers, it will soon be asleep. Her body becomes warmer and softer, her head lies more heavily, their thoughts are floating peacefully over the long road they have both travelled.

Suddenly she startles: 'I nearly fell asleep.' And she cannot explain to herself the peace which has settled heavily and languidly in her blood, the first true peacefulness since Karel found eternal peace under her window. She says: 'I don't know what is the matter with me, I could sleep for a week.'

This year Thys has his annual photo taken a little earlier than usual, at his farewell party. He sits amongst his three sons in a Malines chair with lions' heads and the closed eye gives his face a strange severity. One can see that this is indeed the man who had it in him to create the firm of M. Glorieus et Fils out of nothing.

He is surrounded by twenty-one workmen, who look stolidly into the camera, conscious of their responsibility not to show how much they have already drunk.

Afterwards Thys wants two mementoes. He wants to have his photo taken together with his first two workmen. They must stand on either side of him, he puts his left foot forward in a bold stance, but lays his hands fraternally on their shoulders. His sons look on with an indulgent smile but before the second memento they leave the room. Thys fills the glasses of the twenty-one and poses smilingly with the bottle in his hand, while twenty-one glasses are raised to him.

Then he talks of a picture in which he would be pushing a handcart, wearing overalls, in memory of the early years, but Nic, Leo and Dolf exchange a quick look. Nic says he wouldn't know where to find a handcart, Leo thinks the photographer has already left and Dolf explains that father is making a mistake, wanting such a picture. In the days when father pushed a handcart he was twenty years younger. Anyone seeing him photographed with a handcart at his present age would ask: what's this, has monsieur Glorieus gone bankrupt?

So Rosa from Ridge Farm is getting married to that Thys Glorieus. It's disgraceful, but then so were those constant visits to the farm disgraceful, and if they want to be together, well, it's better they should do what decent folks would do and marry in church. They're not stinting themselves either: a late, expensive mass. Yes, there's no lack of money there, more money than decency, as usual.

Still, it's a long time ago now since she came out of prison and since he did his wife in. The young people around here don't remember any of it, there won't be any kettle-banging. Taking it all in all, you can't really say much against her, they were both free to go courting and we've heard it said that the workfolk at Ridge Farm have never had it so good as now with Rosa. People who live down that way won't hear a word against her. So why should we care? Us people that are getting on a bit, we have our own ideas, we keep our thoughts to ourselves and we say nothing. Let everyone mind his own business.

We can hardly see the people for the cars. Dina and Lieneke are not there, didn't we hear they are moving, they're going to live with their elder son, wasn't his name Pol? A fat fellow with his hair *en brosse*? Exactly, and wasn't he married to an old woman, it seems she's dead now. None of her brothers have come either, that one there is her brother-in-law, a vet or whatever, from Tieleghem. Those three youngsters we already know, smart young men they've grown to be.

But does anyone know that old general? Look at him, congratulating Thys with both hands.

'Sir,' stammers Thys. More he cannot say. Ah, mon ami, don't be so surprised, he's a loyal subscriber to *The True Brabanter*. No one in the region dies, no one is born, and no one marries but he knows it.

'I know,' he says, 'where there is a horse or a heifer, land or hay for sale. I know where there is a fair or a shooting competition or a bowling match. I know everything, mon ami.' So when he read that M. Glorieus, born in such and such a place, was getting married to . . .

'Madame,' he says, 'my sincere congratulations. M. Glorieus, M. Glorieus, but that can be none other than my good old Mathieu. Wait, I said, I'll give him a surprise, I want to be the first one to wish Thys happiness.' Look, mon ami, there's Monsieur Paul in the car, he's brought him here.

Mon ami is as grey as a dove and has a gouty leg which he drags a little. His laugh still booms as mightily as ever, but more jovially. He knows that Thys has done good business in Brussels and he has been very pleased to hear it, mon ami. And now he has done well to come back to his village, that's what he himself has done too, he lives quite near, we're almost neighbours. Less than an hour from here he's built himself a country villa. He'll be writing, mon ami, because he mustn't keep him talking any longer now, but you must come and see my chickens one day, no, no, out of the question, he's not coming to the wedding party, that's only for the intimates and anyway he's an old man, he's got to live soberly, because he wants to enjoy his life as long as he can, ha ha! Same as you, I daresay, ha ha! Write to him at his villa 'Mon Repos'.

When Thys sits in the carriage he forgets his married bliss. His one eye weeps a little, he leans his head back and whispers: that really made me feel happy. Softly Rosa says that the captain must have remembered his name for twenty years, how many orderlies has he forgotten in that time? But she has waited for him for twenty years, doesn't that make him feel happy too? Still overwhelmed by the surprise, Thys muses on: 'people are good, really.' He has been robbed of an eye which had seen the wickedness of man, but his heart has been spared, his heart which would, for the sake of one just man, forgive and reprieve all others and which has to believe in a better world.

But the heart next to him contracts in anguish at the thought that tonight it will have to confess its wickedness.

She gives a gasp, with the back of her hand she closes her mouth which wants to scream that people are not good, that she herself is wicked, that he alone is good, that he is once again paying the penalty for his good faith, by getting married to a murderess. He laughs at her for still being so formal with him, kissing his hands, what use is that! Come here, nobody can see us here, this is how you kiss!

God sees her that night when she goes to bed for the first time with the man she has always loved, him alone. For him she has committed the murder of which her soul has not yet been absolved. She has gone back to him to make amends at least to him for the wrong she has tried to expiate by prayers, good works and the torments of her remorse. When he came to fetch his children from her, her longing became once more overpowering, but she desisted, conscious of her unworthiness. When he took her into his arms, Dear Lord, she was not strong enough to renounce. Now she will be his. Let her be doomed for all eternity for this one hour, this hour with him is worth the price of eternal fire. She no longer worries what he will do afterwards. He may kill her. And as he strangles her she will thank him, while she can still speak, for this hour. Dearest, kiss me while I die. Perhaps he will not want to survive this last mockery. Then they will die together, here in this bed, in each other's arms. The gun is still there, in the cupboard there is plenty of curtain cord, downstairs there is poison.

Dearest, choose, for an hour I have been with you, for an hour I have been happy. He sinks heavily into her arms, she groans: you are my god. Then she lies still in his arms and speaks in a soft, unwavering voice. Thys, she has been yours, this happiness must suffice her. Now she has to tell you something. Perhaps you will kick her out of the bed and chase her out into the night. Perhaps you will grab her by the throat and strangle her. Perhaps, no, come, no more of that. Listen, Thys, she murdered Karel knowingly, deliberately. On that Saturday evening she asked you to come on the Sunday and if you had come she would have told you so much about Karel, truth and lies all mixed up, that you would have gone to meet him and strike him dead. Yes, honestly, she really did think you would have done that, so little did she know you then, so blinded she was by her hatred for Karel, by her unbounded love for you, by her fear that you would marry Lett. She hadn't intended to kill Karel, but that shrimp man had come groping along the barn and the house and had gone into the stables. In despair she had taken the gun. She had experimented to see if she could shoot straight down from the window and she had waited in the bedroom with the gun in her hand.

When Karel came into the yard she recognized his step. It was rough and windy weather but she was quite sure it was Karel. She can say it quite plainly and frankly now: she was absolutely certain that it was him. The window was open, she held the barrel flush against the front of the window ledge and fired. Then she waited for someone to come who might have heard the shots. She would have called for help if anyone had come, but no one did. She looked out of the window and there was Karel, lying on his back. She called out his name, to see if there was any life in him still, but he did not move. Then she went to wake up Lett, she told her she had shot somebody and was afraid it was Karel, but Lett wouldn't wake up. She kept answering yes and all right. Then she went back to her own bedroom and towards morning the labour pains started. As if Karel's child did not want to stay within the murderess of its father. She had wept about that afterwards, very much. She loved that child only when she lost it. She would have loved it, even though it was his child.

Thys, you are so quiet, you don't even take your arm away from under her neck, you're still wondering, perhaps you have not yet made up your mind what you're going to do with her. Perhaps you want her to go and give herself up and confess everything; all right, she will, she will do whatever you say, Thys.

She hadn't expected you to tell the court what there had

been between you and her, but she has never been angry with you for it, on the contrary. It was through this that she really began to know you properly, it was only after this that she really fell in love with you, with a love, she can't tell you how, she loved you so, so boundlessly, boundlessly. Oh Thys! And it was because of this that she denied everything and mocked you. It was foolish, but she wanted to be saved.

What exactly she thought at the time, she can't remember very well, she must have been out of her senses, but she thought something like this: If I tell them the truth I will lose him forever; I must be acquitted, he's sure to forgive me one day. Afterwards you were nearly beaten to death, and how she suffered then, what anguish, remorse she felt, unable as she was to talk to anyone about you, never hearing your name mentioned. One morning she heard the bells tolling while she was having breakfast with Lett and the servantfolk. She fell into a faint and of course the servants thought that it was the memory of Karel.

Thys, thank you, dear boy, darling, dearest, dearest, dearest husband, she thanks you because you are allowing her to say all these things, but the worst is still to come. She is damned, for ever. She has never yet confessed her murder, she daren't, she can't. Once she tried, do you remember that first time she came to see you in the little shop? You told her then that we would never talk of it again. She was so happy then, everything seemed simple to her. If Thys is so good, she thought, God will surely be no worse. She went to the church of Finisterre but when the priest came she ran away. So she still lives with a murder on her conscience and with hundreds of blasphemous communions and she knows that she is hopelessly doomed. What her life has been like, hell cannot be as gruesome. There are no words for it. People like you, who have never done wrong, cannot possibly understand it, even if she were able to explain it. She has suffered, she has done penance, always trying to pacify her conscience, but deep down she always knew that she was only kidding herself.

Thys, nobody will ever know what she has been through. For once, she wanted to be completely happy, with you, as now. She has had this moment of happiness now, it is enough, she thanks you for it. She dare not touch you again, but look, she thanks you with folded hands, thank you. Kill her now, strangle her, shoot her in the heart with the same gun, or in the neck, like Karel, as long as she can speak she will say: thank you. Hell is awaiting her, she is no longer afraid; thank you. Hand her over to the police, send her into the street naked, tell her to go and drown herself, it's all right: thank you.

Thys knows that no human justice can restore our wrong-doings, that a sinner cannot escape his inner torment. What else can one do but say to such a sinner: come, and take him in one's arms and lift him out of his desolation. Come, says Thys, he takes her into his arms.

This naked woman is out of her mind, she kneels on the bed by the naked man, joins her hands like worshipping angels in a painting, and she says she knows he is not a man, but Christ, the son of God. I worship you . . .

Appalled, Thys sits up, he forces her to lie down, he orders her to go to sleep at once and not to say another word. She meekly lays her head on his arm and falls asleep automatically at his command.

He stays awake but she sleeps until the cocks crow.

She sees him lying beside her with a clear, open eye and closes her own, to remember the night. It seems to her as if she had fallen asleep too soon and missed the most import-ant thing of all. How strange it is that she is still lying by his side, how is it now between them? Gently his hands begin to caress her, words are superfluous, her happiness continues still. Thys opens the window. Sun and air pour into the room, in the yard the bustle of farm life is already in full swing.

'Well, Rosa, what do you think, aren't we getting up today?' She lies radiantly on the bed, her arms wide open, greedily breathing in the fresh morning air. No, she is not getting up, there are no more days. She will do no more work, she will no longer do anything, she will stay here forever, waiting for him. He sits down on the bed, and says she will have to get up some time, to go to confession.

'But I am damned, Thys.'

He does not make fun of feelings that are alien to him, but asks her earnestly if she thinks she would no longer be damned if she made her confession?

'Of course not.'

'Is she absolutely sure of it?

'Of course.'

'Get a move on then,' says Thys, 'and quick. We're going to Brussels, to confession.'

She resists, she cannot confess, it's too late now, she has resigned herself to her fate. Thys insists that this whole business has to be got over with once and for all; it's been going on long enough.

He travels to Brussels with her, takes her by the hand in the church of Finisterre, right up to the confessional. A few rows in front of them there is a priest, reading his breviary, and Thys does not do things by halves. He tells the priest that there is a penitent who has a difficult confession to make and is a bit frightened. Then he tells Rosa that the priest knows about it already.

She kneels in the confessional with her hands in front of her face, so as not to be recognized. Thys waits for her.

Long ago, in his boyhood, when he still went to confession, the priest used to wish him Proficiat after giving him absolution. 'Proficiat,' says Thys gravely when she emerges, with a dark red face. He sits down beside her at the back of the aisle. 'Now pray your penance,' says Thys, 'we've got all the time in the world.' She weeps softly, now and then he presses her hands in which the paternoster moves busily, and waits patiently till she gets up. They walk through the crowded shopping streets to North Station. There is a light in her eyes, she says nothing, in the train they sit in silence, hand in hand.

<h1 style="text-align:center">TWENTY-THREE</h1>

Then began the glorious years of Thys Glorieus, the unforgettable gentleman-farmer of Ridge Farm, a sensible, wise man. If you knew Ridge Farm in the time before he came, you'll know that it was a large, rambling old farm like so many in Brabant, a bit dilapidated, everything old-fashioned, still the same as in the days of our ancestors, centuries ago. The roofs slope as if rising out of the ground and their ridges follow the line of the land. But now! From far and wide farmers and gentlemen come to see it. Thys has torn down the old cattle sheds first, and rebuilt them more than double their old size. Now there are thirty cows, which are milked by electricity, six horses, and I don't know how many pigs. The air is as fresh as it is outside, you walk on a stone floor as clean as you could find in any house. After that, Thys pulled down the barn and rebuilt it three times as large, in brick, steel and concrete; fireproof. You could set fire to the immense stacks of hay and straw, it would burn inside the barn like osiers in a baker's oven, but without any damage to the building. All along the side facing the yard, which has no dung pit, the roof slopes down beyond the wall and rests on a row of concrete posts. Under this overhang stand the modern farming machines, each between their two posts, modern, four-furrow ploughs, machines for seeding, harrowing, mowing, binding, threshing.

Where now are those who laughed at the conceited fool who was never more than a cowherd in his youth and who now thinks he can teach farmers their job because he's grown rich in Brussels, selling dirty old bottles? On Sunday they came strolling up to the farm, old tenant-farmers, still with clay pipes, umbrella trousers and silk caps. They stood there talking and snickering, with stooping backs and crooked legs. That must be the chapel, they said, pointing their pipe stems at the new barn. Yes, and that's the dance floor; they pointed at the smoothly paved yard. And that's the new school, they pointed at the stables. Then they pointed at the old house which had remained what it always had been, crouching shabbily between the magnificent wings. So the people didn't live any better than they did themselves, ha ha. The cows have got electric light to read the evening paper by, but the masters still huddle by the old fire place with a block of sulphur sticks. The money has run out. So they'll have to work to pay the interest. Come on, they sniggered, we'd better get out of their way, they'll be starting those machines any minute and then we've had it. They stumped off, stiffened by work, and obstinate, to their card tables in the village cafés.

But Thys pulled down the old dwelling and rebuilt it with two floors, with spacious rooms downstairs and neat, comfortable bedrooms upstairs, for the maids and men as well. The most hardened mockers said it was no longer a farm but a priory, an abbey. However, they were soon hushed: so much wealth and power! They saw Rosa and Thys walking across the yard arm in arm, and respectfully stepped aside; she looked so smart, not at all a farmer's wife, and he such a gentleman. She called out a greeting to them; Thys came up to talk to them. Thys showed them round the stables, the barn, the house.

The most reluctant amongst them were silent and followed at a distance, whispering among themselves, but when at last they were all gathered in the huge kitchen and Rosa was pouring out as much beer as they could wish, their mood softened. They started boasting about their age, and where were the days gone when that little boy of Do Glorieus's used to push the sick mistress of Ridge Farm to church in a wicker wheelchair. In those far gone days one of them was already married, another was about to join the army, yet another was already the father of four children. The memories mellowed them still further.

Yes, they have remained poor peasants whereas look at this gentleman here!

Thys: we're all farming folk together, we should help one another.

They are silent and each one thinks of his own troubles: one of the rent which is too high, another of the sickness in his stable which is threatening his livelihood, a third of the piece of land he would like to buy. A fourth needs to do repairs, a fifth is dreaming of a horse, a sixth is having a hard time without his son who is in the army, a seventh worries about his right of way across a neighbour's field. They come back during the week, each one separately and in the dark, so as not to be seen. They chat at length about the weather and at last, when everyone has gone to sleep and they are alone with Thys, they cautiously come out with their problem. Thys's eye looks grave. He is happy because he is being asked for advice. He says: I'll call in one of these days. Or he asks them to bring the cow along to the farm, the vet is coming anyway so it's all in a day's work and it won't cost them anything. Or he'll send one of his men with the plough, he's got men and machines enough to plough and sow for the whole village. So they don't need to spend the money on a horse and the son in the army is no longer so sorely missed. Or he'll talk to the neighbour about that right of way and he doesn't think the neighbour will refuse him. He'll even lend them money and doesn't mention interest.

They have no illusions about any of it: they'll find out soon enough why he's doing it, nobody does anything for nothing, that would be unthinkable. He's got the finest farm in the land, most likely he wants to become mayor. Or senator. Perhaps one of his sons is in insurance, he'll probably be on the doorstep one of these days. Or maybe he wants them to go to church more often. Or not at all. Perhaps he's hoping to buy up their land so that they would all have to lease it from him. Whatever the reason, he wants to be in their good graces, well, they'll take advantage of it. If afterwards he comes to them to ask this and that, they'll make up their minds what to do when the time comes.

Before long they have become brave enough to come in broad daylight. They no longer hide their troubles from each other. It's no disgrace to be helped by Thys, he's there for all of them. His machines must not be left to stand idle under the eaves, he makes them work on everyone's fields, he ploughs, sows, harrows, flattens, mows, threshes for all. Fertilizer, seed, seedlings he buys in bulk for all of them together and he sells it without profit. He shares out the work over the whole village. The heavy labour of each man for himself, the solitary plodding and toiling, are replaced by more delicate cares: the fields produce more and better crops, the houses begin to look neater, with fresh paint and whitewash. The village has a friendlier face, the dahlias shoot up above the hedges in bright colours and on Sundays Thys and Rosa stroll along the paved roads and the sandy tracks. His eye roves this way and that, to see if everything is going well. People are waiting for him in the doorways. They ask him to come in and have a look at this and that. Rosa talks to the wife, every sentence begins with Thys and ends with Thys. Thys who cares for them all. They walk on and Thys makes a mental note of some improvement that needs to be made, and he won't forget.

This is what he has wanted all his life, with a vague but irresistible longing: a better world in which he gives himself to all; he, a wise and powerful man who creates order, peace, happiness. But he cannot give it a name, he has no method, he is a man of goodwill, of unfailing instinct.

When the captain comes he cannot even answer a simple question: what method does he use in doing all this? In a word: his system. System? Thys hasn't got one.

For hours the old soldier drags his stiff leg around the farm and the village. He has heard of this remarkable gentleman farmer who has transformed the area. It excites him, it stirs him, j'aime ça, mon ami. Everything whirls before Thys's eye when he drags into it civilization, which is still only in its infancy and does not consist in knowing whether it is Thor, Allah or St. Peter who sends rain and thunder. Civilization is science and technology. 'Don't you think that's prosaic, down to earth?' he asks and gives out a bellow of laughter. Thys tolerantly shrugs his shoulders and smiles. The captain points to the fields and says that this is Russia, Asia, pre-history. Poor Flanders, he says. He actually dares call it Flanders now, he used to say North Belgium. According to him, Thys is busy civilizing Flanders and before Thys has thought of a reply to this crazy notion he is standing in front of the farming machinery, arms akimbo, making double chins and declaring categorically that this is the first real bit of progress since the prehistoric peasant ploughed his field with two sticks. He turns round to point through the open gate to a brick kiln some distance away: that's how father Adam used to bake his bricks too.

Back in the house, exhausted, he asks Rosa if he may put his feet up on a chair, he lights a tall cigar and now, mon ami, he has seen your splendid work, splendid work, really splendid, now he wants to know *one* more thing: the system. There he is again with his philosophy, against which Thys always used to be so totally helpless. Thys lets him talk.

Rosa says to the captain that Thys is a good man, everyone should be like him, and that's all. Because Thys is much respected around here, the captain won't believe it perhaps, but they'd go through fire for Thys. But he deserves it too, she can assure the captain. What Thys does for the people here, there is nobody who knows all of it, even I don't know all of it.

The captain smiles affably as her eulogy rises higher and higher. Memories can no longer make him feel depressed, only grave. He says softly that a man who has such a wife . . . he inclines his head.

There is a pause. But look here, mon ami, all right, so you don't have a system, but there must be a system somewhere which has inspired him with certain ideas and plans. He mentions communism, socialism, other isms of which Thys has hardly heard, but Thys continues to shrug his shoulders and evades discussion with him, the useless talker. 'Just a bit of goodwill,' says Thys.

Mon ami ponders, he sets his face into double chins and looks severe. His cigar burns too fast, with a long stump of fire.

When he has found what he was trying to work out for himself, he clears his throat, leans his head back and abandons himself to his old delight: his useless theorizing. Mon ami, what he sees in you is our Flemish nation. In the world of ideas it doesn't count as yet, it is only just beginning to think, mon ami. The global struggle for new patterns of life hasn't touched it yet. But it has amazing energy and a strong, healthy constitution. These are trying to find their way. You are trying to find your way, mon ami. Isn't that your parents' house, over there? We both come from such a house; I have thought, you have worked. La cigale et la fourmi, what do we call them again in Flemish? The cricket and the ant. I am the cricket and you are the ant. Ha ha, look at the way he sits there peering at me, madame, all sorry and worried, that's just the way he used to look in the old days. He didn't like me talking philosophy and that was why I always asked him to come to my study. And he would sit there looking at me, madame, with a face of: poor captain, you're ill, there's nothing I can do for you. A good boy, madame, a heart of gold, I know him. Yes, I see in him a whole nation, madame. Don't forget, I can remember grandmother's days and I used to think that everything always remained the same around here. Now I see that even here things change. Life recreates itself of its own accord; the Flemish nation is being born, it seeks, he seeks, Ah, madame, how beautiful, madame, beautiful. Is there anything left in that bottle, I know it won't do my leg any good, but I want to drink to the Flemish nation with Thys. Cheers!

The thoughts whirl around in Thys's head when he has gone. He hasn't understood much of it, except that one is supposed to have a system and search for new patterns of life. The captain may keep his philosophy but what about a system, and what about those new patterns of life?

When the next morning a farmer comes to ask him if he will please send a machine a day later than he had promised because they are not ready for it, Thys advises him to work more systematically. 'I am looking into everything, writing things down,' says Thys, 'so that we can work more systematically. When we've learnt to work more systematically it will be easier and we'll earn more. You see,' says Thys, 'we're changing everything. It's no longer as it used to be in grandmother's days. New patterns of life, you see. That is something,' says Thys, 'which must grow all by itself, you can't force it, it creates itself. We shall get there,' says Thys, 'we are all of goodwill, I am confident.'

And the man of goodwill believed in a better world because it was growing around him, it was growing because of him. He saw the poor better dressed, he heard the timorous speak more boldly, he saw the young look gayer and more self-assured. They all knew him to be their guardian and protector, not asking anything in return, making them stronger by uniting them.

But we, who had been running the parish for years, we said to each other: of course he's hoping to become mayor. And why not? We could do with him as our mayor. Or perhaps he wants more, who knows, because Ridge Farm was becoming famous all over the region and he was as hospitable to strangers as to his own people. A far-sighted man. Such a man, we said to each other, should get into parliament, he would do something for the people. And we went to see him, the priest, the secretary, the brewer, a committee of five men in all. To be truthful, we couldn't do anything else, he had the entire village on his side and the brewer said: suppose he stands as an independent presently, how foolish we would look. So, we explained the situation to him and said he only needed to say one word and he would become our mayor next spring. He was as pleased as punch.

If we thought we needed him we could count on him, he was willing to take it on in addition to all the rest. We knew all about that. So we were as happy as could be, it had been asked and promised all in five minutes.

But when we got down to brass tacks we soon found out what a blunder we had made. He didn't know the first thing about politics. He was against a contest. Yes! He wanted to be elected by everybody without a party contest. You can imagine how we looked at each other, we who have been waging a battle of life and death for forty years against four other parties and remember that time when old Mr. Van Mander the notary got the shove, was that our doing or wasn't it? The Secretary gave us a wink, we couldn't contain our laughter and quickly took a swig to swallow down a giggle. All right, a good man, a thoroughly good man, very sensible too, when you hear him talk, and sincere down to the marrow in his bones. But not an atom of political sense. He was sitting there imperturbably, telling us at leisure that he wasn't this and he wasn't that, he was nothing, he hoped the priest wouldn't take it amiss. He was a simple man, he didn't concern himself with such things, everybody should mind his own business. From anyone else you would have resented it, but he was so honest and frank about it, I can't say I don't respect the man, you know where you are with him, that's for sure. And he's got a point, too, it's true that our political fights tend to smack of self-interest.

But there you are, that's life, we're no saints. Progress, he says, making life better for everyone, what was the word he used, he's got something in that head of his you know: new patterns of life. It was at this point that the priest interrupted cautiously, saying something about the old patterns of life, our good old Flemish Christian traditions and so on, and then, yes, I remember it now, Rosa started getting on her high horse. The way she talked, well, there was nobody like Thys, no Christian nor anyone. There was no stopping her.

Thys and the priest tried to calm her down but it was no

use. 'Struth, but in fact we rather enjoyed it secretly. When a woman gets on her high horse, and you know Rosa! Talking of Christians, she said, I do my best, every day of my life, but I'm not a Christian, and you do your best too, she said to the priest, but you're not a Christian either, but Thys, she said, I've known Thys since he was a little boy, and Thys, he's a Christian. The priest is a good chap, he laughed like the best of us, there was no ill feeling. 'Why should I become mayor,' said Thys, 'you can have Rosa on your list instead.' 'No,' said the priest, 'she has just told us she is not a Catholic.' So then we all had a good laugh again.

Now we only had one fear: that he would still decide to stand as an independent, then we really would have been in a spot. But he didn't and that was sensible of him. Now everybody knew that he had no axe to grind and his power grew and grew. It doesn't do us credit, but it has to be said: beside him we simply did not exist.

People worked hard and enjoyed themselves. There was greater prosperity, it was a good place to live. It was all his doing. The whole village was one huge farming community centred round Ridge Farm, and we sometimes said to each other: what would he have done if he had lived in an industrial village, for instance, how would he have managed things there? Or: if he cared only about himself he wouldn't make any less money, only the others would notice the difference, so it all stands and falls with his goodwill, it's not a system. But it worked all the same, and it was wonderful.

If only it could have lasted, we would have seen great things, because we heard somebody say, but we won't mention names, that he was really a socialist at heart, but didn't know it himself, didn't really know what he wanted, but in our opinion he did know, in our opinion he knew more than he said and it wasn't for nothing that he was always talking about 'new patterns of life'. We believe, but no, one man can never know another man well enough, and we shouldn't talk of the great things he might or might not have done, the man is dead, he died the way he lived: for others. On the night of the fair.

Poor man, and he had even provided an entertainment, he had brought twenty horses together that evening and put a musician on each one. They came riding into the village, with little balloons dangling above their heads. He was riding in front and led them all round the village. They played familiar tunes and dances, stopped here and there, and all the people danced round them, he liked that, he liked seeing people enjoying themselves. It had got late and he was about to ride home when all of a sudden there was a shout of fire. Thys Glorieus galloped towards that fire at top speed. 'The Dappled Ox' by the church was ablaze. He ties his horse to the pump in front of the church and you know what he's like, he first makes sure that the crowds that are getting in the way of the rescue workers are kept at bay, he sends young boys to fetch buckets, he orders this group to carry furniture out, that group to pour water, while he himself lifts and carries what he can.

'The Dappled Ox' is run by two fat sisters who have a handicapped brother and an aged mother to look after. The wind is unfavourable and blows the flames all over the roof. The water-pourers soon have to abandon the upstairs floor but downstairs everything has been cleared, when suddenly from the field the two sisters, who had fled as soon as the fire started, come running back, screaming 'Our ma, our ma.' A man shouts: she's downstairs. They shriek that she is upstairs. Thys Glorieus walks into the burning house. By the door two of his musicians grab him. If only they had been able to stop him, but all they do is make him lose time. You know how strong he was, he simply flings them aside. We see him on the upper floor walking past the burning window, he's holding his arms in front of his face as if he is warding off a blow. The crowds howl because they can't see him any more, but he reappears and yes, he has the old woman in his arms. He goes to the stairs but they are burning, he goes to the windows but they're burning too. Hot roof-tiles are falling all around him, everything creaks and groans. The roof is about to fall in, he sinks, suffocated we think, down on his knees, half the roof falls on him.

That is how he came to his end, pointlessly. If only those two men hadn't tried to stop him, he would have had time to get down again, it was a matter of half a minute. Perhaps it was meant to happen, we sobbed, the crowds wept, it was terrible.

We can still see him, burning in front of our eyes and still we cannot believe he is dead. How long ago is it now? A year. We often listen to his wife who can't meet anyone without stopping for a chat. From a distance you can't notice anything wrong, but from close by she is wizened, shrivelled like an apple in winter, there is no light left in those eyes. She wanders about the village, she walks into any house where she sees people and talks of Thys, softly, monotonously, but gently. When she has gone we become aware of a nostalgic longing for that strange man who truly believed in a better world. Is there anything more childish than that? And yet we could never laugh at him, we did seem to sense that he was a great man. His son is now on the farm, the youngest of the three, a small, quiet chap. We shall wait and see how he turns out.

Bestselling European Fiction in Panther Books

QUERELLE OF BREST	Jean Genet	60p	☐
OUR LADY OF THE FLOWERS	Jean Genet	50p	☐
FUNERAL RITES	Jean Genet	50p	☐
DEMIAN	Hermann Hesse	40p	☐
THE JOURNEY TO THE EAST	Hermann Hesse	40p	☐
LA BATARDE	Violette Leduc	60p	☐
RAVAGES	Violette Leduc	50p	☐
MAD IN PURSUIT	Violette Leduc	40p	☐
IN THE PRISON OF HER SKIN	Violette Leduc	35p	☐
THE TWO OF US	Alberto Moravia	50p	☐
THE LIE	Alberto Moravia	50p	☐
PARADISE	Alberto Moravia	35p	☐
COMMAND AND I WILL OBEY YOU	Alberto Moravia	30p	☐
LASSO ROUND THE MOON	Agnar Mykle	50p	☐
THE SONG OF THE RED RUBY	Agnar Mykle	40p	☐
THE HOTEL ROOM	Agnar Mykle	40p	☐
RUBICON	Agnar Mykle	50p	☐
THE DEFENCE	Vladimir Nabokov	40p	☐
THE GIFT	Vladimir Nabokov	50p	☐
THE EYE	Vladimir Nabokov	30p	☐
DESPAIR	Vladimir Nabokov	30p	☐
NABOKOV'S QUARTET	Vladimir Nabokov	30p	☐
A VIOLENT LIFE	Pier Paolo Pasolini	40p	☐
INTIMACY	Jean-Paul Sartre	40p	☐
THE AIR CAGE	Per Wästberg	60p	☐

All these books are available at your local bookshop or newsagent; or can be ordered direct from the publisher. Just tick the titles you want and fill in the form below.

Name____

Address____

____

Write to Panther Cash Sales, PO Box 11, Falmouth, Cornwall TR10 9EN
Please enclose remittance to the value of the cover price plus 15p postage and packing for one book plus 5p for each additional copy. Overseas customers please send 20p for first book and 10p for each additional book. *Granada Publishing reserve the right to show new retail prices on covers, which may differ from those previously advertised in the text or elsewhere.*